SHADOW SONG

Lorina Stephens

Published by Five Rivers

Published by Five Rivers Chapmanry, 704 Queen Street, P.O. Box 293, Neustadt, ON N0G 2M0, Canada www.5rivers.org

Shadow Song, Copyright © 2008 by Lorina Stephens

Cover Photograph, Copyright © 2008 by Gary Stephens
Cover Design, Copyright © 2008 by Lorina Stephens

All rights reserved. Without limiting the rights under copyright reserved above, no part of this publication may be reproduced, stored in or introduced into a retrieval system, or transmitted in any form or by any means (electronic, mechanical, photocopying, recording or otherwise), without the prior written permission of both the copyright owner and the publisher of the book.

Publisher's note: This book is a work of fiction. Names, characters, places and incidents either are the products of the author's imagination or are used fictitiously, and any resemblance to actual persons living or dead, events, or locales is entirely coincidental.

Manufactured in the United States of America
Published in Canada

Second Edition
First Edition: Lulu Publishing, 2007

Library & Archives Canada/Bibliothèque & Archives Canada Data Main entry under title:

Shadow Song
Stephens, Lorina

ISBN 978-0-9739-2781-8

1. Title

for Gary

I come
Trembling
Weak and unlearned
Teach me!

a *Midewewin* chant

PART 1
NANABUSH

Chapter 1

I remember the summer I met Shadow Song was so green it hurt my eyes. It was as if the world were carved from jade – something sacred and equally fragile. I, Danielle Michelle Fleming, was to become mesmerized by this world. This land, this Upper Canada, was a place where I would learn to breathe.

That had been the summer of 1832. What brought me across the ocean from England, ultimately, were dreams. The priests said these visions were devil's work. I was a child. How was I to know there were things the priests feared? How was I to know my visions were ambivalent? The irony of it is I never asked for this gift. I was content with a life revolving around a household of parents, governess and servants.

My journey began earlier than that green summer of 1832. It began with the July Revolution of 1830 in France. I will forever remember that day, young as I was, remember how my safe English universe unravelled around a slip of paper quivering in Papa's hand. Such moment can ensue from something as simple as words on paper.

I'd heard the bell ring at the front door, heard Mrs. Barton, our housekeeper, answer, the usual banter between her and the courier. As always, being curious – nosy my governess called it – I crept along the landing to watch. Papa would come to the foyer I knew. Mail was always important. It carried news of his business, news of the world, news of family. In this case it was to be news of all three. By the time I reached my favorite place, face pressed between the railings, Maman joined Papa in the foyer.

Sunlight gleamed on the white marble floor, like lace where it passed through the transom over the front door. There were lilies, white and frail, in a vase on the table against the paneling. The lilies' fragrance was pungent, like a drug to calm the nerves.

"Que est que c'est?" Maman asked, pointing to the letter in Papa's hand.

He paled. He shook his head slowly, as if the weight of what he thought were more than he could bear. He looked up from the paper and over to Maman where she stood in a halo of light. The expression on his face chilled me. A gentle man, Papa had never been wordless, never shown the slightest indication he was anything less than invincible in his steady, calm manner. Completely bewildered was how he looked. Bewilderment faded and was replaced with something I could only think of as fear. It was there in his voice when he said, "The French government has failed."

Maman, I was sure, was on the verge of shattering. She had always been delicate, like the lilies in the vase – intoxicating, enchanting, and tender to any misuse. Today she was dressed in russet silk, fashionably high-waisted with enormous gigot sleeves, her hair arranged like a dark, sleek ribbon on the crown of her head. For a moment Maman searched for words and when none sufficed she touched Papa's arm. Finally: "King Charles?"

"Has exiled himself here, England."

"And the indemnity?"

He shook his head.

"Nothing?"

Again he shook his head.

"But it had been made law. All émigrés who had their lands confiscated by that Republican nonsense were to receive an indemnity. The King guaranteed it."

He didn't even meet her look when he answered, "There is to be nothing."

Another moment of silence passed. I could hear the floor-clock down the hall ticking, ticking, ponderously ticking. Its sound thumped in my head like those ominous words, meaningless and yet full of portent. It echoed the thump of my heart. Then Maman asked, "Will Edgar foreclose on the loan?"

Edgar, the elder Fleming, my uncle. Just hearing his name gave me a shiver of apprehension. I drew into myself on the staircase. My uncle's name always connected to bitter words and hardship. I didn't know him. Uncle Edgar sailed away before I was born, taking the family fortune and his luck with him to the colonies of Upper Canada, yet somehow he always seemed present whenever bad news blew in. I had come to think of him as the maker of ill fortune, and came to know him as the engineer of my misery.

"Edgar has no security now," Papa answered. "Everything I borrowed from my brother was secured against your lands in France, and the indemnity guaranteed by the Bourbon government."

"But will your brother foreclose on the loan?"

"Yes."

Another moment. Maman asked another question. "Have they taken everything?"

"Yes."

Maman smiled, although it was plain her smile was one of those let's-be-brave smiles. "Ça va, my Lord Fleming. Now we are both titled and indigent. You the youngest son of an English nobleman, and I the exiled aristocrat of France."

"At least we have our heads."

Maman let out a small gasp, poor attempt at a laugh, and laid her head against Papa's chest.

The demise of the Fleming mercantile house of Gloucester came swiftly, although I understood little of what occurred, only that the loss of my home, and my belongings, were because of an uncle in some land over there, the colony beyond the ocean. The first few months staff disappeared from our household: the above-stairs maid, then the scullery maid.

The day my governess was paid off Maman arrived in the classroom, arranged herself on the chair beside where I waited at my desk. She was attired in sensible grey linen, a spotless apron of white tied at her waist, a cap of white linen on her head. Such a contrast to the brilliant silks and rich, printed cottons and wools I was accustomed to seeing her in.

She was pale in the morning light, the shadows of a sleepless night around her eyes. Her mouth, usually full-lipped and rosy, this morning was pale and thin.

"Are you not well, Maman?" I asked.

"Eh, bien. De rein."

"Where is Miss Abbott?"

Maman looked away out the windows of my study to the view of the kitchen gardens. I had climbed the window seat earlier and opened the casements to let in the air which was rich with the scents of the herbs that grew there. Two weeks ago there had been two gardeners who worked for us. One of them would have been there in the garden, harvesting the cook's needs for the day. Today it was the cook herself who harvested.

"Maman?" I said when she gave no response.

"S'excuse moi, ma cherie," she said, turning her attention back to me. "We have had to let Miss Abbott go."

"Did she do something wrong?"

"No, no. Nothing wrong."

"Then why did she have to go?"

"We have to make economies, Danielle."

"So I'm not to have a governess?"

"Your papa and I feel you are quite capable of governing yourself, and I will continue with your lessons." She managed a wan smile. "You will of course honour our trust in you?"

"Of course, Maman." I wanted to hug her, to make her laugh and see her face brighten, but I knew it was important I conduct myself in an adult fashion. They depended on me to be responsible. I swallowed the lump in my throat along with my wish to have at least been allowed a leave-taking with Miss Abbott. "What shall we study today?"

That seemed to settle Maman's concern. She smoothed her apron. "I believe Miss Abbott had you working on maths and ancient history."

"Yes, Maman. I completed the assignment she gave me yesterday." And handed her my work.

And so we passed the morning without speaking again of the new arrangement. I became accustomed to studying under Maman's guidance, and over the next weeks her time with me became less, usually brief instruction in the morning as to the path my study of the day was to take, assignments given, assignments collected.

While I was lonely, I didn't mind the solitary study I undertook. In fact I quite enjoyed the digressions while reading about one thing and discovering another. After awhile Maman allowed me free access to the library with the comment all knowledge was valuable.

Cook was paid off shortly after that. Along with her went Maman's lady's maid and Papa's valet.

Shortly after that furnishings and possessions went out the door with businessmen my father invited and saw to and from our home by himself, without the aid of Mrs. Barton who had left some weeks before, chewing on tears.

Maman took to cooking and cleaning, and I found myself in her wake, scrubbing floors and chopping vegetables along with her. The grand home with its grand grounds proved too much for we three, and so the final economy was made.

Within six months I found myself shuttered into two small rooms shared with Maman, Papa, and the rats scurrying through the tenement. None of Papa's former associates came to call, which to me was amazing. Our home had always been full of people, meetings in Papa's study, business discussed over elegant dinners, ladies in rustling gowns. Considering we no longer had the floor-clock, the silver, the study or the garden, I supposed my parents didn't wish to entertain in rooms as these. The reasoning of a child can be so facile, and sometimes so utterly clear.

The positions Papa found between then and the November of 1831 were many and varied, and never enough to keep us. He seemed distant, still as a pool of water before wind ripples its surface and obliterates its reflections. I learned what it was really like to be hungry, to have your belly churn in the dark so you couldn't sleep. We subsisted on barley, bread and cheese. I think Maman could have published a book of receipts on the uses of barley. We ate a pottage of barley with rationed bits of salted pork. Endlessly. She made a sort of savoury barley pudding augmented by whatever vegetable greens she could scrounge from the waste at the Gloucester market, and when greens weren't in season it was rotten onions and turnips she carefully pared down. I am sure she cried enough over these dishes to preclude the need for salt.

Papa tried very hard to keep our spirits bolstered when we would gather to table. Always there was some little anecdote of the day, some absurdity with which he would try to tease a smile, perhaps even a laugh from Maman and me. When anecdotes failed he'd resort to mimicry of some street-seller or market-person or character of note we knew.

It was upon one such moment of escape Maman slammed down her knife and fork, her hands fluttering to her eyes in an attempt to staunch another flow of tears. "I wish he were dead!" she cried. "That he should visit such suffering upon his own family! May there be a special place in hell for him!"

I turned to Papa, watching for his reaction. He raised his eyebrows, looked down to the table and then seemed to gather his resources. "Hell, my dear? Oh, I think even hell is too strong a punishment for my brother."

"How can you say that? He has shown nothing of human compassion whatever. Just look at what he's done to all those families of fallen soldiers! Thieved them of what little estate they had, left them penniless and he attempts to justify this by saying better invested as he would do than squandered."

"And just look at what ruin he has wrought upon his own!"

"Agreed. But neither has he done anything so heinous as to warrant eternal damnation. Forgive me, my dear, but I believe he will receive his punishment. I think the Almighty is too clever at dispensing justice to offer him mere purgatory. I do believe that instead of joining the congregation of angels and rewarded souls, he will be relegated to the menial tasks of heaven. Perhaps my brother will receive the position of Midden Master, shovelling human waste for all of eternity."

My mother removed her hands from her face and looked across the table at my father as though he had gone quite mad. And then she laughed, truly laughed. "Midden Master! Oh, I would like to see that!"

And from there they amused and comforted us all with speculation of just how Uncle's heavenly reward would unfold.

That evening Papa tucked me into bed and we continued telling the story we were creating. I found myself distracted, concerned for the welfare of my parents, and when it was my turn to add a bit more to the tale, I turned my face away, blinking away tears.

"What is it, Child?" Papa said, brushing my cheek. "Are you not well?"

I sat up and threw my arms around him, trying hard not to give way to the sobs that were there. Papa enfolded me, rocking back and forth.

"Why does Uncle hate us so?" I asked when I felt I could speak without giving way to histrionics.

"Oh, now, that is a tangled story. I'm not sure you would understand."

"Papa! I read a great deal of what was in our library. You know I can handle maths and sciences beyond what most girls – no, children – my age and even older can comprehend. Surely I can make sense of what lies behind Uncle." I looked up at him, watched the way the fading light of day softened his angular face.

"It's complicated, Danielle."

"Please!"

He sighed, ran his hand through his hair. "I think Edgar despises me because he thinks I received the attention and love that should have been his."

"What do you mean?"

"Your grandpapa, my father, was always hard on Edgar. Edgar was the oldest. The family fortune was to be settled on him and Papa felt, and rightly so, that Edgar should be responsible. But in doing so Papa indulged me where Edgar was given no latitude. And then to add insult to my brother's injury there is the question of your Maman."

"What about Maman?"

"It was my brother who knew her first, and my brother who loved her first. She didn't know. Neither did I. Edgar had learned to hide his feelings rather well, part of being the responsible heir. And so when your Maman and I finally met, and found ourselves in love, Edgar saw our happiness as just one more proof of his ill-treatment. We quarrelled. And then Papa and he quarrelled. Papa took a stroke and died. Edgar blamed me for that as well."

"But none of that is your fault."

"I know this. But sometimes the heart doesn't allow us to see clearly, Danielle." He gave me a hug and kissed the top of my head. "Now come, Child. I have said too much. And you must sleep."

Reluctantly I separated from his embrace and lay back on the straw mattress, feeling it scrunch under my head. "I love you, Papa. I think you're a good man."

He inhaled sharply, his face set with profound emotion. "As I love you, Child. Always. Forever." He bent and kissed me again, rose and pulled the curtain across my wee corner of the room.

It was shortly after that the dreams came, dreams that were like waking moments. It was like staring through a keyhole into a situation that was, or might be. My stomach would lurch and I'd lie there in bed half aware of the rats, half aware of the scene playing out before my eyes. I wondered if it was a demon in me, threatening to violate the temple of my body as the priests often warned. Maybe it was nothing at all but hunger.

For a while the daylight hours were safest. One didn't have dreams in the sunlight. One didn't fear demons. Soon even the sanctity of the day failed. I dreamed of Papa and his stillness. I dreamed of all his reflections shattering. I wished it not to be so. My wish was in vain. Papa withered as an apple kept too long in the sun, as if something important shrank away inside him. When once he would have dandled me on his knee, he now only allowed me to sit there, his blue eyes pale like the faded colours of the curtains.

It was in this quiet, still way he died, with me on his knee. We wandered early that morning down to the Gloucester docks. Such industry there. Everywhere were longshoremen, spectres in the river-mist, unloading and loading, transporting to and from warehouses. All sound was muffled, deadened by the heavy air. The grey spires of ships could be seen in the river. Shouts rippled through the air, the toll of a bell aboard ship for the change of watch. I wrinkled my nose to the smell, something despite familiarity I could never abide: the stench of refuse and urine, tar and tobacco, sulphur and in the distance salt.

Papa overturned a used nail cask that had its top head stove in, settled onto it and pulled me onto his knee. I could feel the frailty of his frame. His wrists were raw from flea bites, the cuffs of his coat stained and ragged. I lifted his palm to my cheek. He inhaled sharply.

"Once, child," he said. "Once …."

He didn't need to say the remainder. I knew. Once some of those ships were his, once the timber and corn and commodities of the dockyard were the currency of his life. Once, before that letter, and those that had come subsequently on its heels. Uncle, through the arm of his lawyer, pursued Papa for payment, which had been settled with the sale of our home and chattels. But existing after that proved a hazard. Papa found other positions, means of supporting us, only to have Uncle reach again to destroy yet another hope, close another door.

This morning Papa had been told the firm of Bosworth and Boone could no longer employ him as a junior clerk. Seemed one of their new investors was

Edgar Fleming, and one of the conditions was to refuse employment to his recalcitrant brother, my father, whose only sin it was to believe in the sanctity of family.

"Once," he said again, and said no more.

I knew he was dead. That stillness growing in him simply pooled out over his limbs so that, finally, after all these months, he rested. I leaned to his cheek and brushed my lips against him, missing the small nuzzle he would give. I thought I might never be able to breathe again there was such a cramp inside my chest.

"S'excuse moi, Papa," was all I could say. Perhaps he might hear me wherever he had gone and forgive me for dreaming of his death. I knew God would never forgive me. It was my fault he died. Dreams, you see, did come true. Whether you wanted them to or not.

It was late in the afternoon when Maman found us and said nothing, dried eyed as I. Funeral arrangements were made, paid for with bitterness and harsh words. A pauper's grave for Papa. The loss of our two rooms for Maman and me.

I celebrated Christmas in the streets. Maman tried to find employment, but it seemed a lady, especially an aristocratic lady, was suited to no occupation, and it is amazing how quickly friends and associates forget you when you are indigent. She tried to find work using her skill with the needle. Neither milliner nor glover would consider her. She attempted to teach, but her lack of references and fall from financial grace barred all roads. Remarriage was as unattainable as our lost paradise. In the end she plied the only trade that ignored social status or lack thereof. The men who called were from our former class of people, men who salved their conscience with fripperies and coin.

I took to lurking in Gloucester's cathedral. It was dry. When the sun shone I'd dare to sit in a lake of colour cast upon the stone floor from the stained glass, and I'd turn my hands this way and that, watching the ripples of blue, red and yellow, and sometimes, when I felt alone and in need of benediction, I'd turn my face up to the lofty windows and let the blessing of colour shine full upon my face. I was sure if I sat still enough, was good enough, I would dissolve into colour and become this liquid light.

It never happened. But, as I said, it was dry. Periodically someone would throw me a coin with which I would return to the streets and haggle for bread, sometimes the luxury of cheese. The night dreams became worse so that they haunted me constantly, leaving me confused. Like Papa, Maman retreated farther and farther, shrinking, withering. Maman died coughing blood on the dawn of a brilliant day.

It had been a mistake that day to retreat to Gloucester cathedral, for my situation was discovered by a well-meaning priest, and it wouldn't do to have an orphan lurking around the grand edifice. Bad enough I begged on her steps.

All I could do was press myself against the stone wall of the cathedral, mumbling apologies. Of this, also, I had dreamed. All of it was my fault, a fact made painfully clear when I was hauled off to an orphanage.

In all fairness the orphanage was better than the streets, and at least afforded a box with straw for my bedding, although I shared the straw with lice. I didn't mind. The lice crunched satisfactorily when I pinched them from my skin, and it was a familiar task by now.

We received a thin gruel of either oat or barley once a day, and lessons on God's justice throughout. We hired out as servants and sweeps, runners and labourers, our earnings going to the orphanage to assist in our keep.

Throughout my brief stay dreams dogged my days. I was thrown out of an embroidery shop where I worked as a monkey shoving needles back up through the massive frames for the deft hands of the workers who stitched. For me the blue ground of silk dissolved into water, the threads and needles ripples stirred by paddles. The master of the shop took me for a useless idler, hinting I was touched in the head.

My keepers then placed me in a laundry where my job was to scrape soap flakes into the vats of steaming water, except the soap flakes became a white blizzard of snow through which I trudged on strange wood and sinew shoes. I nearly drowned that time. A hazard to the laundry, I was deemed. My punishment, back at the orphanage, was to be denied my rations for two days and beaten to rid me of the evil of my dreams.

Even a child learns to be stoic about these things after time. It's called survival. And I was becoming good at it.

By then Nanabush – the one the Ojibwa call the Trickster – had begun his vigil, though I realized this much later. Edgar Fleming, my uncle, was notified that his niece was in need of her next of kin, had been placed in an orphanage and could no longer be kept in light of the fact she had living kin. It is to be noted I had also become a liability to the orphanage, as I was unemployable.

On Monday, June 11, 1832, I boarded the *Baltic* out of Yarmouth, a brig of 400 tons and carrying 152 passengers, and I, for my part, with ice in my heart and dread for my future, ploughing through heavy seas toward a rendezvous. I spoke little, although I was certainly a curiosity to the others who shared the foul-smelling hold. There were mostly men, a few nervous-looking women going to an uncertain life in a wild land, and among them children, although few of us. While I shared uncertainty with them, I was sure I shared little else. None of them dreamed like me. None of them killed off their families.

As for my passage, it would seem my uncle was not a man to spend money freely; I slept in the hold with the other poor passengers as there had been no provision for a cabin. It was like living in debtor's prison, I imagined. The hold stank, a vile, gut-wrenching mix of faeces, urine, vomit and bodies. For all of us there were only 11 beds, and those made up with thin straw mattresses that quickly soiled. The rest of us slept on the rough planks below decks, which was in itself a misery that left many of us with cuts and splinters that quickly infected. Many were sick, or became so. Babies cried. Women moaned. Men quarrelled. I found a dark space and made myself small. Cold, hungry, I wasn't optimistic that my lot in life would improve greatly when finally I met Uncle Edgar. The only thing for which I could be grateful was that it seemed I was well-suited for naval life, as the pitch and roll of the ship bothered me only slightly at the outset.

What was a plague were the dreams. There was a man who became a hawk and flew to England. He knew Papa. He knew Uncle Edgar. Sometimes the dreams showed the man with a woman. He spoke the name of Katherine. There were books that became swords, and swords that became walls. And the walls dissolved into water through which the man swam, and from which he emerged into a world dense with forest and dark with ancient spirits.

Sometimes, when my turn would come to climb onto the deck and take some air, I found it difficult to navigate, unsure if I walked through dreams or reality. At such times I would curl into the hollow of a flaked line and hang on to whatever shred of sanity remained while the passengers took their wobbly way across the decks.

We had, apparently, sighted the coastline and made contact with a mail packet out of Halifax the day Captain Earbage summoned me to his cabin. It caused quite a stir among the passengers. They hissed secrets behind their hands, thinking I was too young to understand. For a girl of ten years I was sure I knew more than they suspected.

The first mate escorted me and an older girl appointed as chaperone; he paid me no more mind than he would a mop. He opened the door onto an oaken cabin, closed it firmly behind me. My chaperone stood discreetly at my back. I stepped away from her. The captain's cabin was small but orderly, gleaming from polish no doubt he didn't sweat over. There was a repeater clock ticking loudly on a table behind his desk, mahogany and brass, carved, expensive. Standing there all I could absorb was the ticking of the clock. Tick. Tick. The way another clock had measured off the minutes, like a woman measuring fabric, cutting. So much for this. So much for that. Only so much time for each of life's courses.

Captain gestured to a silver plate of sweets on his desk, a rare commodity on land let alone aboard ship.

"No, thank you," I replied, watching his weathered face, his sharp blue eyes, the way a bald patch on his head shone. My mouth watered for want of one of those rare and almost forgotten delicacies.

"Not hungry?"

"No, Sir."

"Every girl your age is hungry for a sweet."

"I'm not every girl."

He arched a brow at that. Clearly he thought me impertinent, but I'd earned that right. Impertinent, was I? Had he had his whole life taken from him? Had he suffered from dreams that all too often bloomed into terrible reality?

"Indeed I can see that," he replied, now studying me as if I were some specimen. I became aware of my unkempt frock of faded calico, the way the collar hung askew because of a seamstress too harried to bother to correct it. My shoes pinched. I balled my hands to hide the dirt. "Sit yourself down, child."

By now my heart thudded in time with the clock. The ship groaned around me. Carefully I settled myself into the hard ladder-back chair across from him, watching him over the desk.

"Do you know why you're here, girl?"

What a thundering stupid question, I thought. My parents dead. My only living relation in the backwoods of this colony. "Yes, Sir."

He affected a smile and leaned back into his leather chair, his fingers tented before him. "How about you tell me so I can be sure?"

"I'm being shipped to my Uncle Edgar in Upper Canada."

"Shipped?"

"Sent, Sir."

"Aye. Baggage is shipped. Young ladies are sent."

"Yes, Sir." Which, I wondered, was I?

"A letter from your uncle arrived in the mail packet." He extended the much abused envelope to me. I stared at it a moment, hesitating, remembering all the hardship that descended with the opening of a letter. When I still had not accepted the letter he gestured, withdrawing the letter slightly.

"Of course, if you are not lettered, I would be pleased to read this to you."

"I can read."

"Ah." His hand moved forward again, and this time I accepted the letter.

"I see from my passenger list that you're to disembark at Quebec."

I glanced up at him. "I thought I was to go to Montreal?"

"That may be, but the *Baltic* only goes as far as Quebec after having stopped at Prince Edward Island." He gestured to the letter. "Perhaps there is further instruction?"

I nodded and broke it open. It was from Uncle Edgar through his lawyer in York, instructing me once in Quebec to inquire aboard the *Preston*, or at the counting house of Messrs Isaac Preston & Son regarding passage from Quebec to Montreal, and then with the stage proprietors of Messrs. Norton & Co to catch the Sunday noon stage from Montreal to Prescott. Once at Prescott I was to take the steamer, the *Queenston*, to York, and from there to travel by series of stages to Orangeville. This journey was to be aided through a guide, a Monsieur Paul Rogette, whom I was to meet in Quebec.

"Is it as I thought?" Captain Earbage asked.

I nodded. "Although I barely know how to undertake all this."

"May I be of assistance?"

I glanced up at him, unsure. How to know who to trust? But he was a captain, and although that status was no guarantee of a gentleman, at some point I would have to hazard the risk. I offered him the letter, which he accepted. After a moment he looked over to me.

"I know this Rogette," he said. "He's a fair guide." He frowned as he watched me and added, "And a fair man. You'll be in good hands."

"Thank you, Sir."

He stood then and I stood also, sure my interview was over. With a wave of his hand he motioned me to be still, came around the desk and bent down before me so that we were at eye-level. "I knew your father."

I made no reply. None seemed to be required.

"Well, I suppose you could say I knew of him. I often ran goods for his company." I watched his blue eyes, the weathered seams of his face. He seemed puzzled. "Be you afraid, girl?"

Oh that was so close, so clever. I shook my head in denial.

"You know, there isn't a sailor aboard my ship who isn't afraid from time to time."

I tried to look as brave as possible, stared him right in the eye and answered, "I'm not afraid."

He touched my cheek with his fingertips. Why was he doing this? What did he want? He stood and now I was truly afraid for he was a tall man and his height only added to the authority I knew he wielded. Anything he wanted aboard this ship would be his. He was the law here.

"How'd you feel about sharing the captain's quarters?"

I stiffened, my heart lurching. "No thank you, Sir."

He cocked his head. For a moment I thought him angry and then watched his features soften so that it was more sorrow. "God in heaven what's become of you, girl? You're only a child."

What was I to reply to that?

He turned away from me and then wheeled back around. "Look, I meant nothing other than offering you a safe and warm place to sleep, a separate cot and a screen for privacy." He nodded to my chaperone. "And of course she accompanies you. I'd do the same for my own daughter."

"You have a daughter, Sir?" I asked.

"Aye. About your age."

"If you were so concerned about me why didn't you do something before?"

"Because I can be a fool at times. Do you accept?"

I nodded. His offer seemed safe enough, and almost anything would be better than shivering below deck for the next few days. It was. For the first time in a long while I was relatively warm, I felt safe, and my future was something that didn't preoccupy my every thought. Just to hear the captain snore was a comfort. It was also a sorrow for there was another man snoring I remembered and mourned silently in the night.

I was allowed to sleep and stroll the decks as I wished, ever shadowed by the girl appointed to be my companion. She was afraid of me, rarely spoke. I never even learned her name. Conversation with her proved futile. I was given the luxury of warm water in order to take a sponge bath, for which I was grateful. I spent my waking hours either huddling in blankets in the captain's quarters, or above-decks watching the industry of the sailors. Below-decks I'd indulge in a much-missed past-time of reading. Captain had a modest but excellent collection of works. I found myself drawn to Milton's *Paradise Lost*, and although the vocabulary was difficult, I soon found the tale compelling. Above decks I learned the names and properties of all the sails, spars, and rigging when I'd eavesdrop on the midshipmen's lessons.

Quebec came, as surely as the next hour and the next. Dawn was dreary, damp when we sailed into the roads, and yet despite the gloom of the day the forest rose magnificently above this grey settlement town. As to the city, all I saw was as dull as the slate skies – building upon building of pine board and stone, like skeletons rising from the mud. Everywhere the rain fell in a curtain so thick you could barely see. I shivered in my thin coat.

This couldn't be Quebec. An established settlement had to be better than this, but I knew my incredulity for falsehood even before the captain stood beside me. Rain dripped from the black brim of his cap, sheeting off his oilcloth.

The boom of cannon fire rolled across the harbour, puffs of smoke like ghosts.

"Drop anchor," the captain shouted, and in answer orders echoed across the decks. "Return the salute."

I could hear two of the four nine-inch cannon below decks squealing back on their trucks, felt the impact of sound in my chest when they fired. Shouts fell from the tops as men fisted the canvas into submission. An exclamation went up from one of the other passengers on deck. The first lieutenant drew abreast of Captain Earbage, saluting with British Naval efficiency, evidence of former employment.

"Sir."

"Mr. Aldritch."

"The quarantine flag is up, Sir."

"So I see."

"As do our passengers by now."

I glanced over to where the exclamation had come from the passengers on deck, watched their fear, their despair.

"Aye," Captain Earbage answered. "Much good that will do. Still, we'll have to wait for the city's doctor to arrive and do his inspection. It had been my understanding when we picked up mail the cholera had passed."

"Perhaps it's a precaution, Sir."

"Perhaps." He looked back out across the harbour to the city and the island between. "It's likely we'll have to disembark them at Grosse Isle, sail back downstream. It seems to have been made a quarantine station. Be so good as to have our ship's Surgeon meet me in my quarters. And then our Navigator." At that he turned and left. I remained at the rail, wondering what was to happen now with the threat of cholera or some other plague upon us.

In the end what happened was the city's doctor had us sail back downstream as Captain Earbage had suspected, and disembarked at Grosse Isle, which was a world of suffering if ever there were one. So many Irish who had fled the famine found their graves here, or as I learned while we were interred there, buried at sea. We were summarily inspected and marched back aboard a cleaned and fumigated *Baltic*, and held there while eight of our number were admitted to what they blithely termed the hospital.

Privy as I was to Captain Earbage's dealings because of my accommodations, I overhead an outraged report from the ship's chandler regarding provisioning the passengers.

"And to add insult to injury," the chandler said, "the commandant has dutifully informed me he can accommodate us with straw when he next receives a shipment!"

"So I am expected to bear the cost and responsibility of our passengers entirely myself?" Captain asked.

"It would appear to be the case, Sir."

"Outrageous!"

"Indeed, Sir."

"And I'll wager my next profit there will be straw and provisions aplenty, of inferior quality and superior prices if I were to inquire after purchase."

"Very likely, Sir."

"Well, I cannot leave them to further suffering, can I?"

"No, Sir."

I could hear Captain thump his desk. "Then be about it, man. And bring me the bill."

"Ah, Sir – I was informed any purchases would have to paid in cash."

"Cash!" I could hear him sputter. "Then see the purser. But be sure every farthing is accounted!"

"Yes, Sir."

I heard the cabin door close, and then Captain mutter, "Blackguards, the lot of them. Damn their eyes!"

So it was over the next fortnight we were fed and made a little more comfortable at the grace of Captain Earbage, and finally given a clean bill of health and able to continue on. For the passengers that meant being able to disembark at Quebec proper and there make our way to whatever holdings, or work, we had arranged. For me it meant making my way toward the man who had written my suffering.

The morning I was to leave a sailor dumped my one small valise near me where I waited at the rail. The girl appointed as my chaperone had already left without so much as a farewell. I stared at the valise, wondering how my life had been reduced to this small, tentative parcel. I used to have three dresses for every day, petticoats and underslips, stays and stockings, drawers and chemises, and shoes so varied there were a pair for every need and occasion of my life. Now there were only the clothes upon my back and the one good frock in that sad, battered valise. Some priests said it was because of my family's greed that we'd fallen from financial grace. Some said it was my dreams. Whatever the reason I was convinced I was damned by God. Perhaps I was one of his fallen angels, like those of Milton's epic poem.

Resolutely I walked to the valise and clutched the unlikely handle into my hand.

"I'll accompany you," I heard Captain Earbage say.

I jumped at that, unaware he stood near me. "You don't need to take me." I raised my gaze to him, forcing myself to look at him steadily. "It's not that I'm ungrateful, just that I already owe you more than I am able to repay." That sounded adult, responsible. It was important I sounded responsible. I was sure my well-being was my own burden.

"Lady Fleming, you owe me nothing."

Lady Fleming – a blow to the order of my thoughts, that. The title set me off balance. It had not occurred to me I was titled, should have been privy to all of England's opportunity. I smiled although it felt like a disguise. "Then if you would please tell me where to find my guide, I'll take my leave."

"It would give me pleasure to escort you."

A gentleman, this captain. I'd seen enough of men to know one. Maman, I was sure, would approve. I nodded my acceptance and allowed the sailors to truss me into the bosun's chair, held my breath as they swung me out over the side and down into the boat. Captain followed down the ladder and settled beside me, nodding an order to the men. Without thought I slipped my hand into his. He closed his fingers tightly around mine, and I felt safe if even only for a little while.

Once onto the streets of Quebec it became clear walking meant a sloppy journey whether on cobbled streets or those not yet paved. A carriage awaited us. I climbed in, settled across from the Captain and set to observing this world through the windows. At an intersection just beyond our route a wagon had become mired to the axles. Everywhere there were soldiers, odd spots of bright red against all that grey. There were men in slops, women lifting their skirts to an unthinkable height against the sea of mud and filth. Trees loomed beyond the streets, a forest so tall and seemingly endless it was almost a threat. Never had I seen such trees. To me the threat was lost. Beyond this settlement, so recently crippled by cholera, was a wild freedom that whispered freedom from all the guilt with which Church, priests and events burdened me.

My attention came back to our journey when the carriage came to a halt, and Captain Earbage led me out before the Nelson Hotel, ushered me in and ordered himself a room, a bath and food. Furnishings, décor, all were sparse.

"I'm expecting a Monsieur Paul Rogette to call," he told the desk clerk.

"I'll send him right up," the clerk replied, making a note.

We climbed the stairs to the second floor and walked down a bare board floor to one of a series of doors and entered our room. It was larger than those to which I'd become accustomed, but certainly not as spacious as those in my lost home. There was a tester-bed placed between two windows, covered in gaily-coloured counterpanes and pillows. Shutters were folded back from the window. A bed-stand with a rush-light stood to the right of the bed, a dressing table with a mirror and a plain wooden screen against another wall and a writing desk and chair against the third. Two battered ladder-back chairs were arranged beside the fireplace.

There was a knock upon the door. The captain bid whomever it was to enter. An older woman – the innkeeper's wife I assumed – with two lads and another girl bustled in, she with a tea cart filled with covered dishes, the lads with a copper tub.

"Maggie here will attend upon you," the woman said.

We dined before a fire that was laid with all haste, while the boys came to and fro with buckets steaming with water. A cot was arranged for me at the foot of the bed.

"And the bath is for you," Captain Earbage said.

A bath! What a delicious thought. I was aware I was filthy, likely stank. "Thank you," was all I could say and that inadequate enough. Dabbing at my mouth with the linen, I excused myself and stripped out of my clothes behind the screen and eased myself into the lavender scented water, first to my waist, then to my chin, and then immersed myself completely to wash out the infestation of my body. Maggie gingerly plucked up my clothes and ordered one of the boys to have them laundered immediately. I scrubbed and I scrubbed until my skin and scalp tingled and then, sure I was at last clean, slid back down to my chin and closed my eyes to lap at this luxury. I would not think. I would only feel. In that sensual state I must have fallen asleep for I became aware of a change of sensations.

Yellow lamplight now painted the room. I watched reflections from the fire dancing off the rose-stencilled walls. I lay in the large bed, nestled among those soft counterpanes and clean linen sheets, a veritable mountain of pillows under my head.

Voices rose and fell from before the fire, one louder than the other.

"The child's asleep, damn you," Captain Earbage said to a dark man in the other chair. "Lower your voice."

"But the governess – "

"There isn't one."

The man in the other chair was only partially visible to me, but his profile was sharp and clear. His hair was dark, tied at the nape with a leather thong, rather out of fashion. He was large, as though built for carrying terrible weight, his face swarthy where it wasn't covered by a bush of a beard. His clothes were all of deerskin, a fringed shirt and breeches, long boots upon his feet. Hanging off the back of his chair was a fur cap with the tail of some animal dangling near his arm.

At the moment the man shovelled the remains of our luncheon into his mouth.

"So, there is no governess," said the man with a noticeable French accent. I assumed he was my guide, this Paul Rogette.

The captain shook his head in reply to Rogette's statement.

"I doubt Monsieur Merde de Fleming will find his pockets deep enough to hire one," Rogette said. "They're rare enough out here."

"To what am I sending this girl?"

Rogette shot the captain a look. "An uncle."

"Aye, an uncle, but what sort of man?"

Rogette shrugged. "A man."

"For God's sake – is he decent?"

"No." Earbage arched a brow that prompted Rogette to add, "He's the one who bankrupted the girl's father. His own brother." He nodded in my direction and I shuttered my lids so as not to be discovered eavesdropping. "The poupee's papa," Rogette finished.

"Sporting of him."

"And the maman?" Rogette asked. "Do you know what happened to her?"

"I've learned the mother and child were turned out to the streets after Fleming died. For a Christmas present her maman died. Retribution, some have called it."

"Mon Dieu!"

"Even some of the passengers said the child is cursed." He glanced over to me. "What could be cursed about such a child?"

"I make no judgment on the church."

"Lest they judge you, eh?" Earbage replied, looking back at Rogette.

"It is wisest not to interfere, especially not out here."

"So. We send her to the only living relative."

"Oui. Le seulement."

"And he's in – "

"Hornings Mills. It's a new settlement in the Queen's Bush started by this Horning from St. Catharines. He's too old by all accounts to be undertaking such an enterprise, but he and this Lewis are going to try to make a go of it. There nothing else around them. Nearest settlement is days away. Fools, if you ask me."

Earbage shook his head. "Out to the Queen's Bush." As if it was some kind of death sentence.

Paul nodded. "By foot. Fleming allowed for no ox, no horse, no wagon, no canoe in which to transport the child once past Orangeville. Not that there's much past Orangeville but a blazed trail, and then not much of one."

"She's not able."

"That, mon ami, I can see too plainly." He braced his hands against his thighs. "So, Monsieur Merde de Fleming will have to wait – won't he? And you can be sure I will be recompensed for the expenses of this journey." He grinned, all teeth. "I'm not a slaver, and I'm not a murderer. If it takes us longer, and with a little more cost than Fleming would like, well, so be it. We'll have fine weather for many weeks to come – one thing for which I'm thankful."

Earbage smiled, lifted a mug as did Rogette, and drank. Rogette rose all in one motion, paused at the foot of my bed and then swept from the room. When left the captain stood with his back to the door, watching me. I wondered if he knew I was awake for he studied me a long while before saying, "So, my little woman. You're off for the backwoods."

Chapter 2

It was two weeks before Paul Rogette felt we were adequately supplied for our journey. By adequately I mean that he had provisioned himself with sufficient powder and balls, that we had hard tack and pemmican, blankets and waterskins. With part of the meagre allowance my uncle had given him he purchased me boots, breeches, coat and a sturdy shirt all meant for a boy larger than I. Our passage aboard the *Preston* was secured at the cost of seven shillings, six pence, mine at half that cost, which altogether I thought astoundingly expensive given we were dispensed the freedom of the deck and little else for our overnight journey upriver. We set off before dawn, having said our goodbyes to Captain Earbage the week previous. He had, to my astonishment, given me his copy of *Paradise Lost,* a gift I greatly cherished. Our only other companion was Paul's motley dog known as Chien, of questionable lineage and obvious loyalty.

The decks were crowded, mostly Irish immigrants, some English, some I recognized from my passage aboard the *Baltic*. Generally people tended to remain in familiar groups, sharing out their meagre provisions among themselves.

Paul kept me close to his side, entertaining me with a running commentary on the history of Lower and Upper Canada, the war that settled the conflict but not the political unrest between the French and English, and then the Americans and English, the settlements through which we were to pass, the properties of this mighty river called the St. Lawrence and the majesty of the freshwater inland seas into which we were to pass. As he chuntered on in his sing-song voice I turned my attention away from my fellow passengers to the scenery around me, and as dawn grew I held my breath for the very wonder of what grew before me.

Blue and green, colours so clear and sharp they infused a person with emotion. Mist eddied on the banks, pines, maples, oaks, ash, birch and beech dripping with dew so heavy it was like rain. Where the forest broke farmland stretched out like long, verdant fingers from the shore, cattle, sheep and goats grazed. In the distance I could sometimes make out the buildings of the farmsteads, watch smoke rise like a pale ribbon from a chimney.

The food Paul handed me was foreign, but I was hungry and had put far worse things in my mouth. At least the jerky satisfied the need to chew, and I cannot say it was altogether unpleasant. What did prove a challenge was the pemmican, a smelly mass of lard, jerky, dried berries and nuts. He assured me it was excellent fuel. I looked him up and down and took some comfort that he had not died from this food, at least not yet. And the hardtack, well, that could keep a person chewing all day, if one didn't loose one's teeth in the process. Still, I was grateful for the nourishment. I found myself forever hungry, yet unable to eat in quantity without being sick.

The following noon we made landing at Montreal. There was a great deal of agitation at that point, most especially from Paul, as we were to catch the Sunday noon stage from Montreal to Prescott, operated by Messrs Norton & Co. I was, quite frankly, shocked at what a benevolent bully Paul Rogette could be, amazed at the way he blithely shoved our way through crowds, hailed the stage operator, secured us seats under cover. His booming laughter and voice rolled over the crowds and left people laughing where others might have left only anger. I was breathless with excitement by the time he stuffed me into the stage and settled himself with a thump beside me. Chien tucked himself up under Paul's feet, periodically rumbling out a low growl. It was enough to quell any conversation anyone might have attempted.

There were five of us to a seat, packed like herring in a barrel and stinking quite as close. Passengers clung to the footman's perch at the back, scrambled atop. Bad enough there was no suspension on the coach, but with the added weight and the state of what the Provincials called roads, I soon wished for the pitch and yaw of shipboard life over this bone-cracking, jouncing journey we undertook.

A very short break was allowed us at Cornwall, where the more elevated of our passengers took a meal inside the inn, with the remainder of us making use of the outhouse and the small garden attached for our ease. Thank goodness for the fine weather, I thought, and was grateful for even the ground upon which to sit and ease the bruises I incurred from our journey. Mosquitoes, however, proved an almost insurmountable problem.

"Ça va bien?" Paul asked of me, his brow wrinkled with concern.

"Oui, pas mal."

When again we embarked Paul unbundled his capote and shaped it into a cushion for me, waving off my objections. He stared down the look of disdain one of the more lofty of our passengers gave him, and, as always, carried on his insouciant way. Somehow I did manage to sleep that afternoon, joggled along with my head on Paul's chest, quite accustomed by now to the rank stench of his leathers.

It was full dark by the time we made Prescott, and it was here we learned the *Queenston* had sailed and was not due back for four days. Because of Paul's earlier thrift, it seemed we had funds for bed and board, and he even allowed me the luxury of a bath and the services of one of the inn's servants to assist me. He, I noted, availed himself of a sponge bath at a reduced cost, but did go so far as to have my clothes laundered.

Bed was shared with five people, crammed into a stead that would have been magnificent were it not for the crowded quarters. The linens, however, were clean and smelling of soap and sunshine, and notices were posted in the rooms to warn patrons to bathe and keep themselves, their cohabitants and the proprietor's goods free of infestation.

Over those next few days he allowed me to sleep, and when I awoke sat me to board to fresh meat and whatever else the inn had to offer. I was ill after my first attempt at such fare, and after that Paul cautioned me to eat a little, frequently, and thereby accustom my body to proper nourishment once again.

"It isn't much time to put some flesh on those bones," he said, wiping his chin. "But we shall do the best we can, eh?"

I smiled wanly at him and sipped at the glass of milk. His rough charity of spirit was something I'd not experienced for some time, and although I was grateful for it, and drawn to it like a bird to shelter in winter storm, I was also afraid I would lose it soon enough and once again be set adrift. Almost better not to have had his charity at all, I thought at times. The lack of it might have been kinder than to kindle hope where I was sure there was no hope to be had.

Still, he continued to foster my well-being; at times we strolled the town, seeing what there was to see, although I suspected our perambulations had more to do with Paul's restlessness and his desire to have me fit.

By the time we boarded the *Queenston* I was beginning to feel much recovered, at least more rested than I had been. Our passage took fifteen shillings from our purse, ten for Paul, five for me. What he had spent on board previously at the inn I had no idea, and despite my age I was concerned for our financial well-being, a question I put to him once we were established on deck.

"I have made economies in other areas," he assured me. "And besides you are too young to worry about such things."

"I worried about them at home," I fired back, anger rising.

His eyes narrowed when he looked down on me. "Oui. Je sais."

My anger died. I looked down and away, ashamed I had returned his kindness with such a petty outburst. "I … I apologize."

"De rein," he answered, and patted me on the head. "Ç'est bien."

Chien whined and chucked me under the chin with his nose. That brought a laugh to my lips and my hand to his head.

"You see?" Paul said. "Even he does not want you to be upset."

I threw my arms around the beast and hugged him tightly, accepting that I was, at least for awhile, to be cared for.

Those next few days aboard the *Queenston* were spent in a pleasant idyll, despite sleeping and living on-deck. Paul rationed out meals to me more to accommodate my recovering body than to spare my uncle's purse, and daily exercise was something he undertook with me on brisk turns about the deck. The weather remained fair, pleasant zephyrs and brilliant skies.

By the time we reached York Paul opened Uncle's purse once more to afford us a room at one of the many inns, a bath, and a decent meal. He dabbed at my mosquito bites with foul-smelling ointments he said came from the natives. I was willing put up with the smell for the relief the ointment gave. To my surprise Paul didn't hurry us to continue. If I slept he was content, and were I honest with myself his patience was an unexpected gift.

Soon, however, he took up our journey again. We made our way by stages as far as Orangeville, and from there northward, sometimes walking, sometimes jouncing along in some borrowed ride. I learned to keep a balsam twitch in my hand as a fan to help to keep the mosquitoes and black flies at bay, and Paul kept me slathered in that noxious but efficacious ointment he carried.

The roads – little more than blazed trails – were most often bordered by a forest of endless green. Despite the hardships, for me it was something wondrous, a place more alive than anything I'd known. I had the impression of being in Gloucester cathedral, the way the trunks towered into vaults where light was rare and sparkled in brilliant flashes. Yet the great grey cathedral couldn't compare to the treasure here. Everywhere there were flowers of white, pink, yellow and violet. Ferns grew like something from my imagination. Moss clung freely, left to grow rampant where in England it would have been raked, scraped and eradicated.

And the smell. Oh, it was rich, wild. I felt as though here there could be no demons. Here only paradise could flourish.

As would I. Although Paul kept us to a rigorous walk each day, I found myself better able to keep up as time passed, so that our pauses for rest, and his need to carry me, became less. Hunger no longer plagued me. Paul was liberal in his rationing of food, and often he took time from the day to hunt for some of the abundant small game, which was a relief to the greasy mash of pemmican. If luck held, evening would find us dining on roasted rabbit or grouse, very often fish. Of course, Paul's disregard of table etiquette pleased me no end and I took enormous delight in casting the bones of my meal into the fire.

Our second day into this new area Paul paused around noon, watching the trees with interest, almost sniffing the air.

"Aujourd'hui we camp here," he announced all of a sudden.

"But it's not evening," I protested, sure he thought I was tired.

His moustache twitched. "I feel like feasting tonight." A feast! I thought. "Peut-etre lapin. Oui?" Rabbit! Roasted over the fire! I could feel my mouth water with memory of our first camp, the stories with which he'd teased me, the fare on which we'd dined. He laughed now. "Or fish?" That, also seemed a tempting thought, for the fish ran so thickly in the rivers and streams you could pull one from the water with your hands.

"Yes," was all I could whisper.

"Well, which?"

"Any of them. All of them. May I help?"

He laughed and again it struck me odd how sound carried in the forest, like an echo swallowed. "Not today, little woman. You're to bathe in the river while I catch our dinner." At that I wilted a little. "But I'll leave Chien with you." It was bribery he used, but I accepted.

He led me by the hand to a likely spot, cautioned me to remain close to the bank as he didn't want me drowned. I watched as he left and again I noted how the trees affected everything. Just like sound, sight was tricky in the forest; one moment I could see him, the next I could not.

Alone with Chien, I stripped, careful to set my togs on a rock out of harm's way. Chien watched intently, cocking his head one way, then another. Mosquitoes droned around me, biting rapaciously. In a moment I stepped to the river, cautiously testing the temperature with one toe. Sunbeams smacked the water. Dazzling. Like stars caught there. They were mesmerizing in their brilliance, overcoming the torment of the insects. I could feel my heart beating, eyes widening, eager to absorb the sparkle at my feet.

The sparkle shifted, now to amber, russet. Something inside me tilted so that my perspective altered. Nothing was where it should have been. What was this? Was I going to faint? I watched the russet light swell. I could feel the river rushing round my knees. I could not see it. I felt my heart thud, once, twice. And then I knew. I could do nothing to stop it. Mist gathered round me. Still there was that brilliance, changing, coalescing into a thing I'd come to know and fear. There had always been these waking dreams. A thing to hide. A thing to keep from the ears of my elders. I wanted to cry out. Could not. Another part of me knew it was useless to cry out. This thing, this vision, would etch itself on my eyes. It would demand my attention. It always did.

There was a blaze now where the stream had been, stars in a dome of black where there had been blue sky and forest. Wood smoke. I could smell it. I inhaled deeply. There were other smells – pine, water, sweat.

Yes, there was sweat. Of that I was sure. The vision tilted again. Now a woman in white stood before me, her dark hair streaming out in an arc on the wind. The song she chanted wove itself through the snapping of the fire. I strained to catch the melody. There was none I could follow, only a nasal whine that brought goose flesh onto my arms.

Another voice caught me now – a voice from across the flames. I squinted. A man danced there, a man as I had never seen before, burnished, red-hued, his face hidden by hair blown in the wind. What was plain was an arrow he held aloft, clenched in the fist of his hand. White it was, like bone burned clean.

The vision left as abruptly as it came. I swallowed from a mouth like sand. I felt as though something older and larger than me watched from a secret place.

It was sinful to have seen what I'd seen. The devil's work, priests told me. I sat on the fallen birch behind me. What did this vision mean? I was frightened. I had never known a time when my dreams brought any good.

The scream of a hawk filled the forest. It was the cry of the hawk that brought me to my belly in the wet leaves and moss. Chien tensed beside me. The hawk's cry was as real as the sudden stillness of the forest. Everything seemed to hold its breath; I held mine. Despite every caution I railed at myself, I peered over the edge of the feathered bark.

Chien whined. Was it fear? Was I right to be afraid? I brought my attention to the bank. And prayed.

He seemed all one creature with the forest – brightness and darkness, listening to things I couldn't hear. The leather of his loincloth was pale, soft-looking, on his hip a pouch with symbols I was sure I knew. His black hair hung past his shoulders and was bound in a headband with a design like frayed black diamonds. Three hawk feathers hung from the right side of his headband and cascaded into his hair.

I wondered why he wore hawk feathers.

He was motionless. It seemed as if he neither breathed, nor blinked, nor did anything any human might. For a moment I wondered if he was real. When I studied his face I knew he was all too real. He watched me. There was something about him that breached time and reached through time, as if he knew things no mere man could ever comprehend. His skin was like mahogany, glistening as though polished. As hard as I tried, I could find no soft edge to his face. Angles and planes. Rock and ice. He was all of these. I was afraid of him and yet horribly drawn.

Again the hawk screamed.

He disappeared into his world of jade before I could see him go. Fear galvanized my actions. I shoved my way into my trousers, running as I continued to dress, toward our camp, reciting every prayer I knew. Chien bounded on my heels, barking. Within moments the forest trembled with the flutter of wings as birds took flight, shrieking.

Paul was upon me before I knew it, scooping me into his broad arms. I could feel myself shivering. His look was enough to loosen my tongue.

"At the river. An Indian!"

"Did you do anything to dishonour him?"

"I don't know."

"What was he like?"

I described for him that powerful figure, my muddied hands punctuating as I went.

"Ça va," he said after a moment. "That was *Wahtanuhgumoowin*, Shadow Song. I know this Indian." He set toward the river with me in his arms. I felt safer there and I was glad of the ride.

"Is that good?" I asked, "that you know him?"

"Perhaps. You have met with the biggest *midewenini* in the Ojibwa nation – a *midewenini*, a medicine man, a shaman of the highest order."

"What would happen if I'd dishonoured him?"

"He'd send you some powerful bad medicine."

"Nonsense," I muttered, frightened still and relying on the seeming surety of the church.

"So you may think. I've seen what their superstition can do."

"Like?"

"Like killing off people without even being there."

"Nonsense," I said again, louder this time, trying hard to keep the doubt from my voice.

"Is it?" Paul frowned and I could feel something disturbed him deeply. "One winter I camped with a family near Georgian Bay, a place known as Cranberry Lake. The girl had been cured earlier that year by Shadow Song, the *midewenini*. As payment, I was told, he claimed her, which was his right. The debt was never paid. Shadow Song found another way to collect. That winter, despite my friend's excellent hunting, his family died off one by one, we never knew of what, exactly, until only he and his daughter remained. Myself, I came to several near misses.

"Only a few days after the last relative died, Shadow Song snow-shoed right up to the wigwam. The girl went with him. It was very strange. He didn't say a word. He just stood there. The girl got up, packed together her things and left with him."

There was a pause after that, tension. I felt it in every sigh of wind. I found the courage to ask: "Why would the girl go with him, knowing what she knew?"

"To give him back his honour."

"But why?"

"Things, they are different here. The sooner you understand that, the better off you'll be. This whole land lives, every tree, every stone, the winds, the moon, the sun. Even one of their islands is called Manitoulin, spirit place, a place where the hair-covered spirits called the *maymayquayshiwok* live. I have spent long enough with the Ojibwa to understand they *manitou kazo* just as we walk." He looked over at me. "They *manitou kazo* – speak with the supernatural world around them. That power gives them silence in the woods, the food they eat, the comforts they find. Not to honour one who is adept at such things is to dishonour the world that gives them life."

That all sounded like witchcraft and fairy tales, the very thing the priests had said I was part of. I shivered, remembering the power I'd felt from Shadow Song, that eerie sensation he listened to things of which I had no knowledge. That feeling was confirmed in Paul's story. It whispered to me through the limbs of the trees, from the rock grinning like giant's teeth through the earth. This world was unknown, full of things I felt would one day be familiar. There would be changes yet in my life, I knew.

Paul deposited me on the ground by the river, this time surveying the area as I stripped behind shrubs and scrubbed in the shallows. Cleanliness would not wait. I was dried and dressed when a figure slipped into the clearing. Paul's attention slid to me and then back to the Indian. Paul turned his hands palm up. The Indian stepped forward. I couldn't ever remember seeing a man move like him, all fluid and silence.

He looked right at me and I shuddered. It was a warm feeling, which was even more unsettling. He asked, "*Waenaesh k'dodaem?*"

"Fleming totem," Paul answered. "She belongs to the Fleming totem."

Shadow Song never stopped looking at me. "*Waenaesh keen?*"

"From the people across the Atlantic," Paul answered.

Now Shadow Song's attention turned to Paul. "So she's English."

I felt shock at this, that he spoke English, clearly and concisely as if he'd attended Oxford.

"In part," Paul answered. "Her maman was French."

Shadow Song grinned and flicked a look back to me. "Bienvenue."

I felt my cheeks blaze, looked quickly down to my feet. "I'm Danielle Michele Fleming."

"You shouldn't speak your name. It will stunt your growth." I looked back up at him but his attention was now on Paul. "Don't you teach her anything?"

"I'm only her guide."

"That's broad enough. There are guides and there are guides. To what are you guiding her?"

"Hornings Mills."

A hawk screamed. "Then we are bound the same way," he said. He smirked. "It may be of interest what that dog does with this *wahboosoons*."

"What's a *wahboosoons*?" I asked.

He crossed to me, reached out and touched one side of my hair, letting his palm slide from the top of my head to my cheek. It was such a warm touch, such a tender one. I thought of Papa. "A young rabbit," he said.

"I'm not a young rabbit!" I replied, angered this stranger should make me think of family I could never see again.

"Aren't you? Aren't you afraid? Fascinated? All at the same time? Do you not tremble inside?" How did he know? "Then you are *wahboosoons*." His hand left my cheek; his attention returned to Paul. "I've some trout up a tree."

Paul laughed. "Then I guess I better build a fire."

Shadow Song inclined his head, turned and disappeared into the forest as if he'd never been there.

"Is he joining us for dinner?" I asked.

"For the rest of the journey."

I squirmed with excitement, with fear, clutching Paul's hand and dragging him back through the forest to the clearing we'd chosen as camp. Shadow Song was already there, bent to his heels, watching the fish he'd speared over a fire. Paul attended to the packs and other food preparations some distance from where Shadow Song sat.

Quietly, afraid to disturb this red man, I lowered myself cross-legged across the fire from him, watching him covertly. He did nothing to indicate he knew I watched, and so I felt myself safe. Such a curiosity he was.

"You should guard how you watch me," he said suddenly. I felt heat shoot through my chest, alarm prick my skin. "The children of the village would not dare such boldness."

Would not dare such boldness? How haughty he was. How sure. "And why ever not?"

He looked up at me, slowly, everything about him intense and alert. I wondered if this man ever rested. "Because I am *midewenini*, a shaman, a sorcerer."

And a man to be feared I added to myself. "You are the devil's demon."

One side of his mouth twisted into something like a smile. "You know that to be false."

"It's what the Fathers have told me."

"And did they tell you your dreams are evil, that you, for dreaming them, are evil?"

That closed my mouth and my smart retorts. This man knew too much! I only stared into the fire, feeling the heat on my cheeks that was more than warmth from the flames. To my relief, Shadow Song said nothing further and only turned the fish. We ate shortly, I in silence, Shadow Song and Paul with snatches of conversation. Soon the excitement and exertion of the day overcame me. I lay down before the fire and slept while the men's murmurs rose and fell like waves on a shore.

It was the sound of my uncle's name, not the evening chill, that woke me. I caught a look pass between the two men. I shivered and accepted the blanket Paul draped around my shoulders.

"Sleep well?" he asked.

I nodded briefly, unsure and more than a little nervous. We three sat there in uneasy silence, listening to the snap of the flames, to the evening requiem of the birds. Finally I found the courage to ask, "Why don't you ever speak of my uncle in front of me?"

There was a long pause and then Paul answered, "There isn't much of which to speak."

I considered the import of that statement, and then: "Why didn't Uncle fetch me himself?"

Paul had been stirring Oswego tea, his massive body bent to the task. His stirring paused, briefly, and then continued slowly as if he were stirring some sense into his answer. "Why, Monsieur Edgar Fleming is ploughing I expect."

The way Paul said ploughing set off alarms in my head, as if he had indicated the deed were loathsome. It occurred to me perhaps it was the person, not the deed, who was loathsome. "Is there some reason I shouldn't speak about Uncle Edgar?"

This time Paul looked at me and I felt very small. "Perhaps not. You could say your uncle is a good Christian man." His attention returned to the pot. Although he hadn't answered my question, I knew there would be no further discussion of the matter.

Suddenly the taste of the evening sat heavily upon me and I curled into a ball near the fire, eventually drowsing. Vaguely, I was aware of Uncle's name crossing their conversation. It was of Uncle I dreamed that night. It was a familiar dream that woke me with screams. I wouldn't speak of it when Paul cocooned me in his arms. He wouldn't understand. From the safety of his arms I saw Shadow Song watching, his face full of intelligence, and I knew my secret was not safe from him. He knew my dreams were more than dreams. He knew I stood helplessly while dreams congealed around me, that it had been that way the morning Papa died, that I had foreseen his dry, thin lips, his hair askew, his skin like something out of a wax museum. I had seen it all before. When Papa had died it had been like watching something I'd already seen, endlessly, as if I watched reality from a distance.

By morning my dreams of Uncle were spent, the terror set aside, but still there lingered with me a sense of foreboding, as if all the joy I would ever know had been spent in my first ten years. This weight remained with me throughout the remainder of our journey so that I paid little attention to the forest, to Paul or even to Shadow Song. What I did notice were the things not quite real, the way it appeared there was a hawk following us, the way Shadow Song sometimes hummed a nasal sort of tune, the texture of the air. There was nothing definite for me to mark as odd. But all of it felt odd.

Not until the night before we were to arrive at Hornings Mills did I make any further inquiries, this time not of my uncle. "Why has a hawk followed us?" I asked Shadow Song, this time looking him squarely in the face.

His mouth curled at one edge as I had seen it often do when he was amused with something. He watched the fire, not me. "Has one?"

"I'm not stupid!"

"I am aware. Who can say why a hawk chooses to follow someone?" I cocked my head to the side, unsure if that was more of an answer than I'd grasped. "Or a turtle," he added. I looked at the pouch he carried from his waist, at the symbols that very much resembled both the hawk and the turtle. He turned to me then and touched my hair the way he had the first day we'd met. "But listen for the hawk, watch for the turtle. You'll know I'm there." He rose over me – all polished planes and hard lines – turned and slipped into the darkness between the trees.

Gone. He was gone just as mysteriously as he'd come. I didn't bother to ask Paul about it. One didn't question power such as this.

The next morning Paul and I made an early start strung with silence, I in my one decent frock of sparkling white. Even Chien seemed subdued by the brilliant day. Our silence became acute not long into our journey, as if Paul guarded his conversation to spare me. Whatever the reason for his silence, we came upon a valley, revealing patches of pasture. Where the village began I couldn't see. However, near to us, perched amid a circle of immature maples, was a one and a half-story cabin of wood, unpainted, austere, as if anything living acknowledged the perimeter kept by the trees. To my dismay Paul guided us toward that house.

"Chez Edgar Fleming," was all he said. This time the contempt in his voice lay nakedly, there for anyone to hear. And I heard. Surely no one could be worthy of that kind of contempt.

Paul rapped upon the door, waited a moment, opened it and then closed it. He scanned the horizon. There seemed to be no one here. For a moment I wondered if Uncle Edgar would greet us at all, but then how would he know we were here?

A man walked from around the corner of the cabin. I forced myself to smile. That my uncle was dressed in trousers filthy to the thighs did not suppress my course of action. I knew it better to stand with my fears before me, and so I walked stoutly to him and embraced him, Paul's admonition in my wake.

When I clung to Uncle's bony frame there was no warmth to greet me. Only thin flesh over thin bones. Cold. His palm pressed my head back until I had to retreat from my embrace and look up into his eyes. I tried to swallow, but the angle at which he kept my head made it difficult, and instead the sound was more of a gulp. Which probably it was. When I met Uncle's eyes I could see only my own reflection – a dark-haired girl in pigtails, absurd in a fine frock.

His hand dropped away. My head fell forward as much in hiding as relief. At that moment all I wanted was Papa; Papa to jiggle me on his knee; Papa to insulate me in the protection of his arms, Papa to explain what I had done to receive Uncle Edgar's disdain. I retreated a step, another, one more, peering up at this tall, unsmiling man.

He was very much the way Papa had looked, a bony face, dark hair gone to grey, a nose that tended to make him look predatory, a mouth so thin it was more a slash. Altogether it was a very English face. In Uncle there was nothing of that inner fire Papa had. Nothing softened that austere shape. It was the face Uncle always wore in my dreams.

He nodded curtly to Paul. He spoke. The sound of his voice was something I was sure I'd forever remember. "There's a packet in the kitchen." Then nodded to me. "There's no bread for supper. I'll be in for dinner."

That was it. That was all. He turned and stalked back to the fields.

"Monsieur Fleming," Paul called out. Uncle Edgar stopped, his back to the guide. "There's no governess."

"I know."

"I'd be glad to make inquiries about – "

"Don't bother."

"But the child, she – "

"Will do well enough on her own. Good-bye, Mr. Rogette." He disappeared around the corner of the barn.

I whirled toward Paul. "But – "

"Hush!"

"But, Paul!"

"Ecoutez-moi!"

So it was to be like this. My protest subsided. I quivered with anger, with fear, my jaw clenching to prevent tears. There was no arguing with Paul. It was something I knew.

Dismally, I allowed him to lead me into the cabin. It stank. Sunlight fell in two shafts, one from a tiny paper window, another more substantial from the open door. To one corner was a wooden bunk, filthy, unmade, over which sprawled a pair of trousers. My uncle's bed.

In the centre of one wall was a fireplace of rough stone where a baking oven had been made. Neither had seen a woman's hand for some time, I could tell. Before this was a harvest table of pine, littered with an assortment of treen, all of which would need to be boiled before use. I didn't even want to guess what some of those dishes had contained.

Two chairs, a work-table on which lay a Bible, took up another corner and most walls were lined with shelves upon which sat various domestic items.

Paul nodded to the ladder. I ascended, Paul behind me while Chien whined pitifully below. It was clear the loft was to be my room. A new wooden bunk had been built into a knee-wall; a wardrobe and a mirror at the gable end also seemed to be new additions. To the other side of the loft was a jumble of trunks and valises, and much to my surprise I had my own shaft of sunlight from a lite of real glass. I pressed my face to it, blinking against the brilliance. Perhaps this wouldn't be so bad.

When I turned back to Paul I shuddered. He studied the open hatch, a look of concern on his face. I followed to where he watched. There was a lock on the hatch, of iron, out of which thrust a key. Paul bent, took out the key, lifted the hatch, inspected the other side for a lock and then let the door slam back to the floor. When the dust settled he slid the key back into the hole. The hatch locked only from below.

He looked up at me. Alarm? Was that alarm? He smiled. It wasn't happy. It did everything to fill me with sadness. "So this is your new home, Lady Fleming."

I swallowed hard, nodded.

"I'd stay, but – "

"I'm grateful for all you've done for me, Monsieur Rogette. There's no need for you to stay. I'll be fine."

He bent roughly to me, crushing me in his embrace. Helpless, I could do nothing to dam the flow of tears, tears for Papa, tears for Maman, tears for him. There had been so many good-byes.

"I'll miss you," I whispered, relishing the feel of his beard against my cheek.

"I'm always coming through Hornings Mills. We'll see each other often."

I nodded.

"And I'll speak to Mrs. Horning on my way through the village. She'll check on you."

Again I nodded, unwilling to move from the harbour of his arms. He lifted me and carried me down the ladder and back into the sunshine, Chien on his heels. When he put me on my feet he pulled a bottle of lavender water from his pocket, pressing it into my hand.

"For when we meet again, non?"

I dipped my head, sniffing. He turned and left. He was yet another person who was to pass through my life. Nothing I could do would stop him. He had no place in this future I was to forge in Hornings Mills.

Chapter 3

"If you're to stay here you'll earn your keep."

That had been the first thing Uncle Edgar said when he came from the fields that evening. I was to cook, clean, do all the things a woman would, and how I was to learn or cope was none of his concern.

Under the weight of his presence my appetite shrank. Numbly, I bit into the hard biscuit he tossed at me, sure if I didn't at least go through the motions I would set off something in him. That one bite almost gagged me. Specks I had thought were grains proved instead to be weevils, the same kind of specks that peppered the surface of my porridge. I could only think of the fare I'd had when journeying with Paul and suddenly there was not only hunger knotting my stomach but sorrow.

With a promise I would begin work in the morning, I ascended the stairs to the loft and stripped to my chemise. The mattress on the bunk was stuffed with straw. Grateful for at least this small comfort I pulled my one wool blanket up to my chin and lay back without a pillow. Moonlight shone through my glass, casting eerie shadows across the room. I fell asleep, shivering from dampness and fear despite the warmth of the night.

Uncle Edgar had already gone when I woke in the morning, in desperate need of a commode. In the half-light I looked under the bed. The cool of the forest had been more bearable; this was the cold of a grave and not the freshness of a July morning. There was nothing under the bed but dust-balls. Hurriedly, I shoved myself into clothes and descended the ladder, hunger adding to the discomfort of my bladder.

I moved cautiously through the cabin and outside, squinting at my surroundings with the hope of finding an outhouse. At last I located it and relieved myself, gasping from the fumes arising from that dark hole beneath my bottom.

Nature appeased, I returned to the wholesome air outside. By now strands of mist were evident in the fields beyond the cabin compound, like lavender silk in the early sunlight. The faint twitters of birds now grew to a swelling sound and I watched for a moment as blackbirds took flight from the hedgerows.

I felt the need to wash and knew I had to draw water, so I turned my attention to find the well which was situated not far to the right of the cabin door. Getting water from the pump was another thing. The pump was rusty, in need of repair. When I cranked upon its long handle the water that eventually spewed forth was foul-smelling and I quickly found foul-tasting. But it was clear, and as this was what Uncle used I assumed it safe enough. I drank as much as my palate would allow, scrubbed my face under its icy flow and plaited my hair to keep it out of my way. I found a pail inside the cabin and hauled it out without much hope of it being of use. It had been allowed to sit dry for some time. The staves rattled in the hoops. I was concerned the whole apparatus would fall apart before I was able to start it back toward soaking and swelling, maybe even eventually holding water. I remembered watching the way the lower maids of our household used to season the oak washtub on wash days, the way they'd let water run and run until the oak had swollen and the staves were tight. Employing that memory, I checked, as best I was able, that the staves were seated properly upon the head, used a rock as a hammer and a faggot of wood as a driver to bash the hoops down and so draw the staves in, and then began the slow process of pumping water into the pail until it stopped gushing and settled down to a slow seep.

By that time morning was well established, and my hunger inescapable. The thought of the hard, weevil-infested biscuits did little to attract my interest, and so I depended upon the experience the streets had afforded. This was a farm. Surely there were peas in the garden. It was July, after all. My circuit of the buildings brought me to what appeared to be a kitchen garden. Unlike the gardens of England, however, this garden was little but a few shoots of rhubarb and asparagus gone to flower. There were beans trailing along the ground, and to my good fortune bore a few slugy fruits. That didn't matter. It was food, and when I broke away the rotten sections, the beans were sweet. It appeared it was too early for carrots, and anything else I found was equally immature.

That avenue thwarted, I turned to the livestock, hoping to find the chicken coop, easily enough done if a person just listened to the clucking and scratching going on. After a few escapades with testy hens, I managed to collect a dozen eggs into a basket I'd found, some of which were malformed and strange looking. I washed them all, candled them, and tucked nine carefully into a basket in the corner of the cabin. One of them I confiscated for myself, cracked and swallowed whole. The others I returned to the hens as it appeared the eggs had chicks.

All of my immediate needs seen to I returned to the dismal cabin, looking at what I was to call home. I felt my brief sense of ease wither. This home was little more than a hovel. To bring it to order would have daunted Maman and her staff, I was sure. I was only a girl of ten, I told myself, although that age had often been suitably old enough for my purposes. What, I realized, did I know of keeping a home? Of caring for a man? Especially one it was plain would never care for me? Indeed I remembered watching servants in the kitchen, plucking fowl, kneading bread. I remembered the soft padding of a maid as she removed herself from cleaning the drawing room. And more recently I remembered my mother's own struggles with the labours of a household she had not been bred to attend directly.

Standing there, thinking these things, the more monumental my task appeared. This cabin was a cell and my life a sentence to be passed within its confines. This was no home. There would never again be Papa nor Maman nor any living kin who would claim me as their loving own.

I backed away from the center of the room, feeling myself shrinking, back until my shoulders touched a corner of the room. I slid down the wall, unable to stop my trembling, unable to stop the tears, and let the full weight of my situation crush me.

How long I sat there curled into the corner, crying, I don't know. It was the sound of footsteps that alerted me. I listened. This was not the sound of a man approaching. This person was lighter of step, accompanied by two others also light of foot.

Pride overcame me and I rose, rubbing at my cheeks to erase my tears. At that moment a robust female figure stepped into the light of the open doorway. Her face was obscured to me.

"Hello?" she called out, plainly as much disadvantaged by the light as I. "Is anyone home?" I stepped out of the shadowy corner toward her. "You must be Miss Danielle Michele Fleming," she said, somewhat breathlessly. "Mr. Rogette asked me to look in on you. I'm Mrs. Horning." She gestured behind her where two girls now entered at her back. "These are my neighbour's daughters, Misses Jane and Susan Vanmear."

By now she had stepped completely into the cabin, allowing me to see she was a sturdy type, plainly beyond her child-bearing years. The two girls with her were somewhere around fourteen to seventeen I guessed. I caught a look cross Mrs. Horning's face – worry, anger. She looked over to the girls. I dragged the back of my hand across my eyes to be sure there were no tears left.

"I'm sorry," I said, my voice catching despite my determination. "I – "

"Have more than enough for four women," she finished, looking around. She touched my shoulder gently, woman to woman, and then gestured to Jane and Susan to deposit their baskets and bundles. Everything just seemed to happen after that. Not a word. Not a complaint. We four set about putting a polish to the cabin without mention of my tearful state.

I was shooed out to the well, and found my attempt to season the pail had succeeded. I felt relieved for the company. And for the assistance. So relieved was I that I minded not at all that the pail was heavy and unwieldy when I hauled it back into the cabin. By the time I returned Susan Vanmear had already set her hand to the hearth.

"Leave it!" Jane snapped. "She'll have to learn herself."

"But she's only a – "

I set my pail upon the floor, grinding my teeth against the pain of this overheard conversation. "I'm the mistress of this household," I said as firmly as possible, hoping some of Maman's sternness put an edge to my voice. "I'll have to learn these things."

Susan frowned. Both Mrs. Horning and Jane smiled a little when I took my place by the hearth. Their faith in me, however, I felt was ill-placed; I knew nothing about lighting a fire, a task that took me nigh unto an hour and almost smoked us out before I had a cheery blaze. Sooty, but pleased, I heated water according to Mrs. Horning's instructions; it wasn't long before we had sufficient to begin our task.

Armed with lye-soap, an unused scrub brush and a rag I drafted for a washing cloth, I slowly, methodically, disinfected my new home, listening to Maman's words ring in Mrs. Horning's: *Remember the corners, Danielle. Filth breeds in corners. Don't swipe at it, child! Scrub! Cleanliness is next to Godliness.* If cleanliness was next to Godliness I would scrub and scrub and maybe then the dreams would wash away just like the dirt. Beside me the other three ladies laboured, amicably, purposefully and I felt the loneliness lessen just a little.

Often I strained in the attempt to move some of the heavy wooden furniture, adamant I would do it without any help. In anticipation Mrs. Horning and Jane often shoved a piece out of the way before I could reach it, sharing smiles they thought were secret. I worked fiendishly, my skin crawling with memory of bugs and rats. I wanted none of that here. When a nest of wood lice scurried out of the logs I shrieked, bashing them again and again until there was nothing left but pulp. The women laughed uproariously.

"I don't like bugs," I said, looking up at them sheepishly.

"A healthy dislike," Mrs. Horning said, her mouth twitching. So we continued again.

Susan had set upon the eating utensils like a woman gone mad. First she set them to boiling in water. This, however, was not good enough for the fastidious Jane. She then soaked them in soapy water, her nose curling with distaste.

Watching her I said, "Why not put them in the sun to dry? Maman always said the sun purified."

"Excellent idea," Mrs. Horning said, and soon Jane was out of doors with her soapy work, rinsing and laying the dishes out to dry.

By mid-afternoon we had the lower section of the cabin clean enough to cook in, sweet-smelling enough to live in. There was even a jar filled with wild flowers brightening the table.

Mortified I had nothing better to thank these women with than raw eggs, I brought out the basket nonetheless and offered them. Another look passed between the trio. "I don't know how to cook them," I said quietly, "but they're good enough raw."

Mrs. Horning arched a brow to that. "What did you eat for breakfast, child?"

I gestured to the eggs. "And some beans from the garden."

Oh. I could see the exclamation form on Jane's lips. Somewhere outside a red-winged blackbird shrilled, flies buzzed on the heated logs.

It was at that moment the mysterious baskets and bundles they'd brought were opened. For me it was like a long forgotten Christmas.

"We've brought you some things," Jane said.

Which was an understatement if ever I'd heard one. Someone set the kettle to a boil, all while a bounty flowed over the table. There was a small wheel of new cheese, a fresh loaf of bread, salted pork, a supply of dried beans, a crock of soup, sugar, jam and most welcome of all, a jar of sourdough. Cookies, a cake, a pie. There was a lovely tin – black with red roses – with tea. Tea. Out here. Oh, how civilized!

"I don't know how to thank you," I mumbled when the table was arrayed, clutching the tea tin to my breast.

"Just remember to do the same when your time comes," Mrs. Horning said. She leaned over the table to me, patting my hand. "And let's just keep this quiet. No need for your uncle to know who, exactly, brought these things. Besides, they're for you." She straightened again, instructing me on the etiquette of tea-making.

We ate biscuits and dried apples for lunch and drank no less than two pots of tea. After lunch we continued to work. There was wood to be stored in the bin, kindling in its place. One of the girls was to tackle the loft while Mrs. Horning and I were to begin culinary lessons.

When my guests left that evening I had started my first sponge for bread in the morning, baked a cake and cookies – all from flour supplied by Mrs. Horning. The women knew almost everything on the Fleming farm failed. Susan had mumbled something about the curse. The comment had been silenced by Mrs. Horning with a sharp glance.

Before Mrs. Horning left she inquired if I was able to read and write. I confirmed that I could. Quite well. She handed me several pieces of paper, some of which contained recipes, one with directions to the Horning and Vanmear homes. With a peck to my cheek and a promise she would check in tomorrow, she bustled off as she'd come, the two girls in her wake.

I turned back to the cabin. I could hardly recognize it. The hearth nearly shone as did the table. The bed-linens had been boiled and dried in the warm air, and as a gift Susan had spread dried rose petals between my sheets with a warning to remove them before sleeping else they would stain the linen.

Bread and cheese and cake and cookies ringed the vase of flowers upon the table while soup simmered at the edge of the fire. Surely Uncle would be pleased with all of this.

He stepped into the door at that moment. I rushed to fetch warm water from the fire and poured it into the wash basin I'd placed next to the door. He watched me, cold, unreadable. He washed without comment and then sat to table. Throughout the meal he remained silent, although he never stopped looking all about him; after he finished, he retrieved the Bible and read aloud by candlelight.

Not a word of welcome. Not a word of praise. I was to receive nothing but the austere word of God.

I rose to clear the table, my heart dead.

"Sit," he said.

I slumped back to the chair. Tears threatened to overwhelm me but somehow I held them, blinking furiously while he read from Jeremiah: *"Behold, my anger and my wrath will be poured out on this place, upon man and beast, upon the trees of the field and the fruit of the ground; it will burn and not be quenched."*

I wondered if he cursed me with this reading, or if he read it as a reminder of a curse upon himself. "Have I done something wrong?" I ventured.

"Little pigs are seen and not heard," he answered and again read aloud.

I little heard what he read; his tone and his mood were things I recognized. It had been like this during my short stay at the orphanage. I was baggage, a thorn. Now, as then, I bore it is silence, tired, heartsick, until he finished and then I struggled to clear the table, my eyes threatening to close for want of sleep. He made no objection when I banked the fire for the night and carried a pail of warm water up the ladder to the loft. I was very nearly asleep when I finished my sponge bath and slid into my bed.

What woke me that night I was unsure. Had it been the cry of a hawk? Did they fly at night? Whatever it was, I felt compelled to pull on my woollen socks, throw the blanket around my shoulders and tread cautiously to my small window.

It was one of those nights when the moon shone so brightly that the world seemed a place of ebony and silver. Mists drifted in the valleys beyond. Everywhere was the chirp of frogs. Were it not for Uncle downstairs I would have crept out to share the night with the moon.

My attention shifted to the ring of maples. I felt my heart still, my breath catch in my throat. I didn't know whether to shout for joy or fear. He was there. Shadow Song. I knew the outline of his figure too well to mistake him even in the mischievous light of the moon. He watched me. But how could I know that? Yet I knew for certain that he did watch me, silently, secretly, as if he were keeping vigil.

Listen for the hawk, watch for the turtle. You'll know I'm there.

Had he appointed himself my guardian? The thought was comforting. I turned and crept back between the sheets. Sleep that night filled with dreams of Shadow Song, pleasant dreams as I'd never known before.

When the dawn chorus swelled, I slipped into my clothes and descended the ladder, pail in hand. Even in the dim light I could make out Uncle's bulk bundled face to the wall. I looked to the hearth. There were coals yet. With them and a little kindling I soon had a blaze alight, went out the door into the half-light, rinsed the pail, drew more water and poured that into the kettle to set it to heating. Yesterday Mrs. Horning had shown me a clever substitute for coffee, which I now prepared from ground, roasted dandelion roots. Breakfast was rounded with bread left from yesterday and cheese. Easy enough. Little could go wrong with a meal like this. There would be time later for a proper breakfast, but this would do well enough until Uncle came back from the fields.

Pleased with my preparations, I nudged his thin shoulder. He turned all of a sudden, grey eyes sharp. Firelight caught the crags of his face, shadows eroding them deeper. Had he been awake all this time? I stepped back a pace. Was this the way he woke? All at once. From sleep to alertness with nothing in between. He stared at me.

"Breakfast's ready, Uncle," I said, afraid my words would receive his disdain.

He replied only by rising, pulling on his trousers over his drawers and dumping himself at the table. When I poured his coffee he sniffed at it suspiciously, his eyes upon me over the rim of the cup. "From where'd you get coffee?"

"I made it."

"From what?"

"Dandelion roots."

He sipped noisily, set the cup on the table. "You've had help."

"Paul showed me," I lied, hoping God would forgive me this one small transgression, "during our journey here." The falsehood was sharp enough. Paul would have knowledge of these kinds of things.

He said nothing else until he rose from the table, although it was clear he speculated from where the sudden bounty had come. "I'll take a lunch with me."

Hastily, and careful to avoid contact with him, I bundled together what I could find for his lunch and tied it into a clean cloth, pushing it across the table to him.

"I can return to England," I said, "if you don't wish me to stay."

He barked a laugh. "And how will you do that?"

"I could earn my passage."

"You're a fool!"

"It's plain you don't wish me to stay." How I wanted to cry, but I dare not.

"And what would give you that impression?"

I swallowed, hoping to bolster my waning bravado. "We've hardly spoken at all since I arrived. I thought you might want to know how Papa and Maman died."

His face twisted then between bitterness and anger. "I know well enough how they died, and why. They, like you, are the instruments of my revenge, and God is taking his for my sin. Stay if you like. Go if you wish." He leaned close to me then and smiled, although there was no warmth in that smile. "But remember this, dear Niece: if you go I will find you. I will have my revenge."

"Revenge for what?"

He left without another word.

I wanted to smash something I was so angry and hurt. Or scream. Something! What good would any of that do? There was little enough by way of household equipment that were I to smash something it would mean more hardship for me, and likely a beating in the bargain. Screaming would signal my defeat to Uncle and possibly bring on that dreaded beating.

What was there to do?

But to succeed. To be a model child, servant, chattel. I'd learned that much in the orphanage, how to allay the bias of my elders. So the rest of the day was mine. And I would make the most of it, and see what knowledge I could gain along the way.

Cuffing away my tears I set to my toilet and then assessed my work for the day.

Bread had to be the first order, and I'd already tarried too long. I drew another bucket of water and took it into the cabin and set it on the table out of harm's way, then turned to the hearth to stir some life into the fire that had died down. My attempts today were better than yesterday, and after carefully feeding in kindling and then larger fagots, I succeeded in a steady blaze, dumped water into the kettle and set it on the hook to heat. It was too dark yet in the cabin to work with any ease, so I dared to light the nub of a candle and from there set to mixing my sourdough sponge from which I'd make my bread. As there were only two of us, I opted to halve the recipe Mrs. Horning gave me, and hoped whatever saint watched over bakers that he'd watch over me.

That done I tidied, cleaned, boiled his soiled clothes only because I knew if I didn't there would be his disdain to receive – perhaps worse – and no one to take care of me if I didn't take care of myself. By early afternoon the sponge formed a satisfactory froth, and so I divided it into portions, returning part to my mother, adding flour, salt and water to the remainder. It was a sticky, glutinous mass that I feared would use all the flour I had but soon it formed a ball and it grew warm and elastic under my hands, just as Mrs. Horning said it would.

I put the dough into a bowl I greased with a small bit of the butter Mrs. Horning had brought, covered it with a towel that was the cleanest I could find and set it close to the hearth to rise.

Mrs. Horning checked in on me shortly after that. Her stay was brief, however she did come with a few more recipes to try. That pleased me well enough. I felt as though I were gathering all the defences I could. Anything to protect me from my uncle. I wanted to ask her about him, but thought wiser of the matter, unsure of how much she might know, and how true a friend she might be.

By mid-afternoon I was exhausted and took a reprieve after shaping my risen dough into loaves and stoking the fire box of the oven.

Drawn by the warmth of the sunshine and verdant earth I took myself out of the cabin and lay in the long grass amid flowers and birdsong. I watched high, thin clouds, sighed for this stolen moment of pleasure. How long had I been in this new world? By my calculations it was July 30. My birthday. Eleven years old. I closed my eyes. It was better not to think of birthdays, of celebrations that might have been, of laughter long since past. It was better to sleep. To sleep and forget.

Something cold and damp on my arm startled me. I opened my eyes all at once, jerked away from the thing, then laughed. It was only a painted turtle. A passing gift far from his home. I laughed again and ran my finger over the turtle's deep green back, laughed once more when his legs and head popped into his shell.

At that moment a hawk screamed overhead.

Listen for the hawk, watch for the turtle. You'll know I'm there.

I looked up. Sure enough Shadow Song was there, standing before me, a string of fish dangling from his hand, his rifle at his back. If I should have felt any fear I was too lonely to acknowledge it. All I knew was that Shadow Song watched me, guarded me, and now had come to visit.

"Are you thirsty?" I asked.

He nodded, a smile twitching at his lips.

"Tea or water?"

"Water."

I was on my feet in a moment, dashing for the cabin and a cup. When I turned back for the pump I collided with Shadow Song in the door. We both laughed at this and it felt good. It had been so long since I'd felt this kind of joy.

He was wet from his head to his shoulders, water dripping off his nose.

"I guess you didn't need a cup," I said.

He had a quizzical look to his face, his earth-brown eyes sparkling as he shook his head. It occurred to me he spoke very little, just as Uncle, and yet with Shadow Song the silence was different, as if words were insufficient to express the mood of the moment. With Uncle Edgar silence was punishment, a way to assure his power.

He gestured with his hand, the fish bobbing.

"For me?"

He nodded.

What a meal they would make!

"But I don't know what to do with them."

"If you were a girl of our village you'd simply spear them over a fire."

"But I'm not, and I don't think Uncle would like fish innards."

A haughty look crossed his face. "No, I'm sure he wouldn't. Then we'll need two buckets, one with water."

I set off to fetch the pail and a large bowl, and when I had done so he slipped a knife from his loincloth, made one swipe at scaling and then handed the blade to me. I held the thing awkwardly, glancing first at him, then the fish. "Like this?" and raked the blade against the shimmering skin.

"Pas mal," he answered, touched my wrist and guided my hand. "Comme ça."

I nodded and continued. The lesson went much the same way when it came to cleaning and filleting so that within the hour I had more than sufficient fish for our meal that evening. This despite the fact there was more flesh on the bones than in the fillets. Shadow Song told me not to worry. Time and patience would sharpen my skills.

It was then I remembered my bread, scraped the oven clean and slid my loaves home. After that we returned to the open air, my senses partly on Shadow Song, partly on my bread.

"You should boil the bones," he said after a moment.

"Why?"

"You'll have need of needles, combs. Our women use them often still. And the broth will be good, and the rest for Mother Earth."

I frowned.

"Fertilizer. Does wonderful with roses, I understand."

Roses. As if I'd ever have roses. I found it difficult to think of a future that would have anything so gay and frivolous.

My attention strayed to him, the way his hair glistened, the headband and hawk feathers, the scar that rippled between his brows, the other on his well-muscled shoulder. Without thinking I reached out and traced the one on his brow, realized what I did when he smiled and I snatched back my hand, alarmed.

"I'm sorry – "

"You were curious. I received that one searching for a dream."

My eyes widened, horror filling me. His laughter subsided when he looked at me, concern on his face, his palm touching the part of my hair. "Oh, *wahboosoons*, they've taught you dreams are devil's work."

"But they are!"

He cupped my cheek and let his hand fall away. "Not so. With my people dreams are things by which we guide our lives."

"Then you all must be devils!"

"Would a devil do the things I've done for you?"

"If he wanted to lure me."

"To what could I lure you? You know pain enough to last your lifetime. Ask yourself, would a devil do things as your uncle has done?"

My gaze dropped. I couldn't answer that, wondering how he knew. "I dream and the dreams come true," I said softly, afraid of my confession, afraid that demons would come dancing out from beneath the trees and drag me back to the nether world.

But Shadow Song's response was one of hope. "Then that is a powerful gift we must make grow."

"But isn't it evil?"

"Only if you make it so." He titled my head until I looked at him. "My people, the Anishnabeg, have walked here for far beyond white man's reckoning and I assure you we are no evil. What is evil is the way the men deafen themselves to Mother Earth, the way they take the trees from the land so that the rivers fall, the way they kill the animals without having hunger. This is evil. Dreamers are not."

"How can you be so sure?"

"I've lived in your world, *wahboosoons*. I dressed as they dress. I learned as they learn. I spoke as they spoke. When they told me the things I'd dreamed were evil, when they told me the spirits of the land could not speak with me, when they told me things of Mother Earth were for taking – then I knew that the evil was of their world, not mine. I have dreamed dreams by which I lead my life and guide my people's. I have spoken with the spirits of the land when I sought council and they have answered. I have always lived to take care of Mother Earth and she has taken care of me. I am not wrong, *wahboosoons*. These things I know are real."

"And so you left?"

He nodded.

"But it's not like that in England."

"Isn't it? I found it so."

I could only stare.

He smiled. "To Cambridge," he said, as if answering my incredulity. "I can read. I can write. I was well accepted in that august college when I spoke English and French." He looked away, his gaze searching the hills. "I learned all they had to teach me, and when I tried to teach them they found nothing of worth."

Silence again. I let it settle between us for a while until I had to say, "Paul told me you were someone important."

That brought his attention back to me. "I am only a child of Mother Earth. Nothing more." He frowned. "Are you well, *wahboosoons*?"

It was my turn to frown.

"Does he treat you well?"

"He's done nothing to hurt me."

"But he's done nothing to make you happy."

That aching thing inside returned. It was too much to have to meet his eyes and so I dropped my gaze, shaking my head for fear if I spoke my words might break and I would cry.

"Happiness isn't something someone gives you. Learn to find it for yourself." He touched my hair. "It sounds harsh, I know, but most lessons worth knowing are harsh." He rose then, drawing me to my feet. "Tell him nothing of my visit."

"Will I see you again?"

He smiled and turned away to the forest. Somehow I knew that was more answer than I needed. He would come, he would go, silently, constantly, just as his world would demand.

In the end the bread was perfect.

Chapter 4

There was nothing I could do to stop it. It was as if the wooden bowl in my hands elongated, tunnelling. Desperately I tried to keep myself in the kitchen, surrounded by the yeasty smell of baking bread, but all the colours of the kitchen shifted into autumn golds. The bowl stretched out into a road that bent off to my left, sliding round a hill of leaf-spattered rocks, trees threading the sky with their show of colour.

Everywhere was the sickly-sweet odour of rain-rotted leaves, the air cool against my cheek. Not even the doe-skin skirt and sturdy moccasins were enough to prevent me from shivering. I wondered if I shivered from cold or from sorrow. And wondered also how I came to be wearing such garments.

The next moment exploded with a crash. The bowl tottered at my feet, although I was only barely aware of it. I looked up at the open door, a furtive glance to be sure Uncle hadn't caught me at this sin. Only the brilliant day filled that space. For the moment I was safe.

I bent, trembling as I clutched the bowl into my hands, trembling as I set it upon the table. I turned and fled to my loft and the comfort of my bed. Why now, when there was some measure of peace in my life did these waking dreams persist? Despite Shadow Song's support of my gift, I was sure Uncle would find my talent evil. What would happen to me then? It had been bad enough when I was orphaned in England, but at least there I knew the land, I knew the customs. Now I had been transported across the ocean, deep into the forest where no authority could grant me even the hope of rescue.

I scanned my room as if there might be some answer there. There was none. Only time to settle my pulse and straighten my thoughts. Sunlight drifted through my window, lighting motes of dust. A fly buzzed through that shaft, left it and struck out over the trunks and valises that shared the loft with me.

Listlessly, I rose from my bunk and crossed the floor to Uncle's cast-offs, wondering, vaguely, what he stored in them if anything at all. I couldn't imagine him keeping anything for memory. He seemed devoid of anything but the now and his all-consuming revenge.

A film of dust coated their surfaces. I wiped it away from the nearest trunk, only to reveal a brass plate engraved with the initials KJO. Who was KJO?

I tried the latch and found it unlocked, pushed back the lid and gazed into mystery. A doll lay at the top, porcelain, pale and fragile and exquisitely beautiful so that I caught my breath in wonder, reaching eagerly to lift it into my arms. She had an emerald green coat of velvet, taffeta dress, curls of gold cascading round a face that reminded me of a doll long since lost in a life almost fairy tale in its joy. This doll was not mine. I set it on the sill of the lid.

Curious, I dug farther through the layers of petticoats and an assortment of dresses both for fancy and work-a-day and found a tiny portrait. It was skilful, that much I could tell, of a girl somewhere between childhood and womanhood, dark hair, dark eyes, skin as frail as the trilliums I'd seen on my journey here.

Who was this girl? I set the portrait next to the doll, wondering if this was the KJO of the trunk.

What I found next was treasure indeed – a bolt of fine shot silk, blue and green. Despite myself I cried out for pleasure, draping a length around my dungareed form. This was the stuff of princesses, of legends. Oh with this around me would my knight come riding, riding and sweep me away from misery? I twirled and fancied myself the Lady of Astolat in her tower. He would come, surely. Surely this kind of dream could come true as well.

I froze where I was, facing the hatch of the loft. Uncle stood there, cold, menacing. My heart beat wildly, echoing in my throbbing hands, my drumming ears. "I was only playing," I stammered, peeling myself out of the silk. "I didn't mean any harm."

In one stride he was beside me and snatched away the silk in his blackened hands, threw it into the trunk. The doll followed, its face catching on the edge. There was no mistaking the sound of cracked porcelain. I winced. The lid slammed shut. A key slid home. A lock snicked.

He said nothing and turned away, leaving me frozen in his wake. When he descended the ladder he pulled the hatch down over him and I heard the key turn. I could only stand there, stunned, not knowing what to feel, what to do, hardly realizing yet that I was now indeed a prisoner, the lady locked in her tower.

Uncle's lack of words wounded as harshly as blows. I blinked. What had I done that was so wrong? All I wanted was to know. My gaze shifted to the window and I crossed to it. Out there the world remained level, sane, robust. I could hear his footsteps recede beneath me, thump on the ground and fade into the distance.

What had I done to make him hate me so? Was my moment of play so terrible? Surely not. If only he'd told me what I'd done, explained to me the way things were to be. From the time I'd arrived he'd made no attempt to speak with me, to chatter in a way that would afford us both a better knowledge. If he didn't want me, why had he invited me to come and stay with him? He could have easily left me in the orphanage, an ocean away where he needn't concern himself. Surely he hadn't merely wanted a live-in servant, cheap and readymade. Surely he wasn't as cold as that.

I remembered the terror on Papa's face the day that letter had arrived. There had been something about a loan that belonged to Uncle, a thing that had caused both Papa and Maman to die and leave me in the streets.

I remembered Uncle speaking of his revenge.

Yes, Uncle could be as cold as that. There would be nothing for me here.

That realization sank deeper and deeper like a splinter in my heart until I felt myself only a thing to be used the way one would use a shovel or an axe. What could I possibly do about my situation? I was only eleven, a girl, without means or money or friends to assist. I had only these dreams that insisted on becoming reality and they helped me not at all.

By and by I heard the sound of skirts, of a basket dumping onto the table. Then a familiar female voice: "Danielle? Are you here?"

"Up here, Jane," I answered, turning sharply from the window. I tried not to hope for rescue. The ladder creaked. The hatch rattled.

"You're locked in?"

My heart beat wildly again, as if it would fly up and out of my mouth. "Yes."

"Well unlock it."

"It opens only from your side."

Jane's shock was evident in her silence. Finally she said, "Have you done something awful?"

"I suppose."

"Well?"

"I was playing with some silk."

There was no answer from Jane, and again that was eloquent. "There must be keys here somewhere," I could hear her mutter, the ladder creaking again. After much rustling and a few righteous invectives, the lock snicked and Jane appeared head and shoulders when the hatch banged open.

I stood there shaking, whether from my growing rage or fear or relief I had no idea. All I knew as that my body quivered as if it would shake apart.

Jane's eyes narrowed. "What else has he done to you?"

I shook my head to indicate nothing. Her mouth thinned, but she extended me a hand. It occurred to me at that moment the Vanmear girl looked like a Jane – sensible, sturdy, quietly efficient in a completely feminine way. The girl's face softened into a smile. I liked that smile. It filled her blue eyes with sparkle like ponds rippled by the wind. I smiled back as much in relief as with pleasure.

"Well, come on," she said and descended, her meadow-gold hair in a disarray of curls, a frock of blue swinging around her legs.

For a moment it seemed as if my world folded into another, an odd sensation that would come when I knew something was about to occur. Another scene overlay this one, a scene with this girl and unsaid good-byes. Death. Perhaps. This was a friendship I shouldn't pursue. Even then I knew it would end in heartache. But I was only a girl who knew she was lonely.

In the sunshine it seemed we wouldn't be touched by the oppression of the cabin. Out here things seemed safe, green and alive in a way our garden in Gloucester had never been alive. There everything had been verdant, yes, healthy, yes, but always tamed. Everything had been so tamed — the beds of flowers, the topiary trees, the hedges, the lawns, all so domesticated and tamed. Here, wildness was always present, pure, untrammelled. I was sure Eden had been in the west for surely one could find paradise in a place such as this. Yet even Eden had its demon.

We walked without apparent direction and found ourselves in the dimness of the barn. A broody hen clucked about, what should have been a warm, comforting sound until I saw her and realized it was the one-legged bird. That wasn't quite right. She had two limbs, but one was more like a flipper and flopped uselessly about as she lumbered along. She was a testy hen even when not brooding and so I avoided her as much out of fear of her pecking as her deformity. It seemed no matter where I went there were signs of Uncle's malice. He should have long ago put the hen down, but didn't as he said it was a reminder of all he had lost.

"Has he done this to you before?" Jane asked when we were settled onto the grass beneath the maples, again safe in the cool of the shade. I shook my head to say no and in that moment Jane grasped my hands, her face full of worry. "Listen to me. You must be careful with him."

"I know."

"No you don't! He's dangerous!"

She was so agitated that I couldn't help asking her what Uncle had done to make her so afraid.

"Nothing we can prove," she said. "We only know there was a girl he brought from Ancaster — a half-breed — who ran from him the day they were to be married. Mr. Silk, the shopkeeper, says she often came in with bruises." I frowned, not understanding the significance of this. "He beat her," Jane said.

Oh. I could feel myself mouthing that exclamation but unable to give it voice. Yet none of this surprised me and that was more chilling than Jane's revelation. There were those dreams, you see, those dreams where Uncle Edgar had beaten me.

"Ever since she ran off, his land's been cursed," Jane continued. "People say it was Shadow Song who cursed him."

I looked up at her suddenly, shocked she should know of this elusive man.

Jane took my look to be one of non-comprehension because she launched into an explanation of him. "Haven't you met him?" she asked in the end.

"No," I lied, unsure of why I did so but sure I was right. Suddenly it was imperative I get rid of Jane and I made some rather lame excuses although Jane acquiesced. After she left I baked the bread I'd started earlier, more for my own survival than out of any sense of obligation, all the while concerned with how I would lock myself back into the loft. When the bread was done, near to perfect, I'd still come up with no solution to my predicament. Frustrated, I took my loaves up to the loft, descended once more and slumped into a chair, fully prepared to meet the full might of Uncle's wrath.

It was late in the afternoon when my rescue arrived. A turtle ambled into the cabin. I felt the hairs rise on my neck. I looked up to the door but Shadow Song was nowhere to be seen. The turtle continued its slow, methodical walk into my alien world. At that moment a hawk screamed. I could only stare wide-eyed when the bird swept in to join the turtle, perching upon the table. It watched me with bright glittering eyes, its head turning from side to side. In another moment it looked at the keys that lay near my fingers. It lunged. I nearly shrieked with fright when its razor-sharp beak missed my hand and grasped the keys.

I will never know why I did what I did. The world had entered a mystical place that I only half-understood, and in that state I ascended the ladder, turned as if in a dream and closed the hatch. It thudded into place, echoing through my mind. I could hear the rustle of wings, of a key sliding into the lock, metal scraping on metal, keys falling with a clink to the floor and then only the warble of a meadow lark filled the silence.

I crossed the loft and sat on my bunk, wrapping my loaves of bread into a clean cloth made for easy transport. Not long afterward I heard Uncle approaching, his boots thumping heavily upon the ground and then the cabin floor. My heart was beating rapidly now. I could hear him say, "What the – " And then felt the air become unnaturally still. I could feel something building around me, some strange sort of power that was thick and real. It became difficult to breath and I was desperate to make myself as unnoticeable as possible.

I heard wings flutter, fold. Silence. Flutter again, this time in flight and then a shriek, another, this time a man's. Such triumph in the bird. Such horror in the man. I clamped my palm over my mouth to stop myself from shouting.

"Damn your heathen soul!" Edgar screamed. I knew he screamed at Shadow Song wherever he might be. The sound of Uncle's voice chilled me, ice between my shoulders. Such hatred in his voice!

There was the sound of feathers brushing the air once more, farther, farther away. Gone. Now there was only the sound of Uncle rummaging and a periodic curse. I felt my tension slowly unwind, became acutely aware of the coarse woollen blanket beneath my hands, of the sweat trickling down my neck. For how long I sat there in that hyper-aware state I don't know. I do know it must have been for some time because the sun had left my window when I heard the key grate in the lock and Uncle's movements back down the ladder.

I frowned at this. He had unlocked my cell but was not going to open the hatch. What did this mean? Did it mean I was a prisoner of my own fear? Did it mean I was at liberty to come out when I chose?

From somewhere I gathered the courage to rise from the bunk, cross the floor and haul open the hatch. Trembling the whole while, I stepped down the ladder, carefully, rung after rung until at last I stood upon the floor. Uncle sat before me at the table, staring at me, his shirt torn, bloody, a darkened bandage wrapping one side of his head and covering one eye. It didn't take a lot to figure out the hawk had attacked him. Another part of me wondered if he'd lost the eye; I felt glee at the thought.

I said nothing to him, keeping my attention upon my domestic duties of preparing a modest meal out of eggs and biscuits. I burnt everything. We ate it anyway, in silence. I found the courage to say, "We need some supplies."

He looked up from his plate sharply. Such fury was there. To my surprise he looked away from me, back down to his plate and said, "Tell Silk I'll pay him in trade." With that he rose and retreated from the cabin.

I watched him go, watched his heavy movements and rigid gait. Long after he'd gone I sat there, numb, unsure of what the next hours or even days would bring.

When darkness filled the cabin I rose and closed the door, banked the fire and crawled into my bed. I lay there for a very long time staring into the darkness. A howl broke over the night. I shuddered, for this was no bay of a beast. This was a man who howled from somewhere in the direction of the barn. His cry had been long and twisted and tortured as if he were crying from hell itself. Again he howled and this time I wrapped myself in a blanket and crept to my window of glass.

There was nothing to see out there; the night was moonless and close. Even so, I knew that from somewhere out there Shadow Song watched, even listened, while Uncle spent the night in madness.

Shadow Song

Chapter 5

It rained in the night, a violent, quaking storm that shook the earth and rattled the cabin. Alarmed I might be swept out of the relative security of my home, I crept down the ladder, sure at every step something would leap out of the darkness. At last I found the locking post and set it into place on the door, a feat performed with difficulty as the wind played havoc with my struggles. Just when I finally managed to succeed, a howl rose over that of the storm. And then the scream of a hawk. I felt the hairs rise on my nape, goose-flesh swell. That howl lingered long in my mind, far more chilling than the thunder and the wind. It had been my uncle, I knew. Tortured was the only way I could think of that sound. Tortured, as if Uncle fought his own private hell in this mad night.

Light-headed with fear, I ascended the ladder once more, and huddled under the thin wool blanket. I would not cry. That was something babies did. I was no baby. I could cook. I could bake bread. I could trek through the wilderness and survive the streets of Gloucester. I did not intend to let this night rob me of that.

Still, I watched the sudden shadows thrown into my room when lightning flared, listened for the smaller sounds under the roar of thunder, and somehow, finally, slept.

I woke to bird song and a golden dawn. From out of my window I could see rain dripping from the eves. It was damp, chill in the cabin. Rubbing sleep from my eyes I rose and dressed, descended the ladder and started a fire for tea although I wasn't pleased the heat would further add to the intense heat of the day. That done, I faced my fear of opening the door. Who knew what lurked on the other side of that bulwark? Uncle could be waiting there, knife in hand, ready to slay me in his madness. There could still be demons from the night, waiting to take me to the hell the priests said was my birthright.

It was a glittering world that greeted me when at last I had the courage to open the door. The sky was unmarred, brilliant blue. Unlike the cabin, the air of the morning was clear and welcoming. Sunlight refracted on the wet grass. High in one of the maples perched a hawk, by the door a painted turtle. It was all like a gift, a promise.

I clutched the handle of the pail by the door, dumped the rain water as it was now quite thick with flies, and made my way to the pump. As I filled the bucket, I watched the yard for some sign of Uncle. There was none. I returned to the cabin and set water to boiling, ate a small breakfast and set about my chores with determination.

It was mid-morning by the time I was done and still there had been no sign of Uncle. Unsure of what to do, I resolved finally to wrap his meal in a cloth and leave it on the table, as I had supplies to purchase in the village and could wait no longer. For a moment I debated whether I should dress a little better than my overalls and sturdy shoes, but memory of last night's storm quickly made me rule in favour of the latter as the paths would likely be sloppy.

Basket, list and directions in hand, I set off, unsure of how long my journey would take. I set my pace moderately, enjoying the morning light as it played through the leaves. By the time I reached the village I was soaked through, shoes heavy with mud. I was mortified at my appearance and used a fallen stick to remove as much of the grey mud from my shoes as possible, resigned to the remainder.

Hornings Mills was an odd collection of buildings sprawled among the trees. The river formed the link for all. A grist mill had been established near the Pine River, and from what I understood from Jane, a saw mill was further downstream. Not far from the grist mill was a rude wooden building that belched prodigious amounts of sooty smoke. This could only be Mr. Vanmear's smithy. On the river itself I could see natives paddling canoes, some half dozen of them, probably come to Horning's mill to have their grain ground or to trade furs at Silk's general store. I watched them with interest, curious that they should seem all one spirit with the river and yet so out of place when they left the canoes and entered the village. Some were almost clownish in their attire – top hats adorned in feathers, cut away coats over bare chests, jet hair shining and long against their ruddy skin. Some of the men had painted faces, brass wire wound round their ears from which dangled an assortment of baubles.

The women who followed them were equally odd to me; some wore simple dresses of print, some of leather so soft it rippled like waves around their legs. Those who wore leather sported lavish beadwork. I was sure it burdened them with its weight. Round the adults dashed children who were like wild, woodland creatures, watching from shadows, alert, crafty.

With difficulty, I tore my attention from them and made my way to Will Silk's general store, a building of rough hewn logs with a large covered porch on which was arranged a number of barrels and crates and two chairs.

When I stepped across the threshold an odd mélange of smells was my first sensation – coffee, textiles, pickles and candy. It was pleasantly dim in here, although not dark as it was in the cabin. Here there were two modest windows of paned glass letting in the morning light. Along all three windowless walls ran shelves to the ceiling, and before these, counters, some lined with jars filled with that candy I could smell. It was all rather dreamlike and it was a lure I could not resist. I almost forgot why I had come when I stared longingly at the peppermint sticks.

Voices from the far end of the counter filtered through my wishes. "Up and died," a man said in a marked French accent.

I felt my heart lurch. I knew that voice. I turned sharply, eyeing the man who leaned against the counter, his leather fringed vest, leggings, listening to the way his voice rose and fell. My mouth was dry and I walked, hardly believing Paul Rogette was here, down the length of the counter and stood beside him, grinning. He pivoted, his dark beard glistening. He stank, it was true, but still I was glad to see him. The man behind the counter stopped in mid-reply. Paul laughed then, saying, "You've stolen a visit from me."

I grinned. "I have?"

"I was on my way to see you when I was done here."

"Well I'm here now."

He placed his large hand upon my shoulder, assessing me. "Is your new life treating you well?"

I nodded, at a loss as to how to answer. Certainly my life had improved greatly from the streets of Gloucester, but to say I was happy would have been an untruth. How could I tell him I was miserable, that it had been a mistake to leave England, a mistake to depend upon my Uncle's kindness? It had become my belief the happiness we were accorded was meagre and barely enough to last from trial to trial. I couldn't tell him this. It seemed too dark a thing to voice, safer hidden in that small part of me I kept shrouded and silent. All I could think to do was divert Paul's interest and so I asked, "Who up and died?"

"Edgar Fleming's fiancée," he answered. It seemed no matter what I did Uncle's curse followed me.

"When was that?" the man behind the counter asked. I assumed him to be the proprietor, Will Silk.

"Spring, two years ago" Paul said. "It's a common thing for the family of a shaman to suffer."

Suffering. Indeed I had seen and known enough of it for his pronouncement to chill me and add to my conviction. I could still hear the sound of Uncle's howls, those long, twisted cries of a man in anguish beyond his ability to bear.

Now Paul spoke of suffering that shaman endured. Was Shadow Song not a shaman? Would he suffer as well? "Why do shaman suffer?" I asked.

"It is as I told you before. When bad medicine is sent out, it eventually comes back to the sender."

"All your talk of bad medicine," Will said. "I've lived with them and never seen sign of it."

"That's because they are on your ground, not their own."

"Rubbish. Why, Shadow Song's up to good medicine, as you'd call it, at the moment. Horning asked him to see if he'd take a look at his missus."

"And?"

"He's been out gathering slippery elm bark, says it's a simple remedy."

"It will work," Paul agreed, scratching after a louse in his beard. "I've used it myself." Paul's eyes narrowed. "But I wonder what Horning will have to pay for this service?"

"Whatever it is, let's hope he pays and is done."

"Ah yes. We all know what happened to Fleming."

"What happened to Uncle?" I asked, my sense of dread growing. I could feel things larger than I at work here, things I suspected Shadow Song heard and followed. A look passed between Will and Paul.

"Now that was smart," Will said.

"She has a right to know," Paul said, measuring the caution Will passed him. "I should have told her before." So he knew more than he'd let on, bringing me through that endless forest with some dark secret hidden in his head. All his talk of missing me, of coming back to see me, and all this time he had information that very likely would have made a substantial difference to my situation.

His attention came back to me. "Edgar Fleming got his land from the Indians without paying for it, before the surveyors were out and the treaties were signed. He now suffers with a curse and his farm will not prosper. Shadow Song saw to that, just as he saw to Fleming's fiancée running off."

My sense of dread reached a peak. Jane had alluded to something similar yesterday. All I could think was: Was it true? Had Shadow Song that much power? I thought of the contaminated flour supply, the way eggs showed up oddly-formed from time to time. There was a cow that should have been in calf a month ago, and yet she showed no sign of fever, of disease, of anything wrong with the pregnancy. Still the calf didn't come. Another calf had been born with two heads and died within the hour.

Was all of this Shadow Song's doing?

"I'm sure there's a simple explanation for it all," Will said, reaching for my list, plainly uncomfortable with the direction the conversation had taken. "Did your Uncle say anything about paying?"

"He told me to tell you he'd pay in trade."

Will snorted and shook his head. "In trade. As if he's ever paid me anything of worth in trade. And where's all that money he has from his estates in England?" He looked over at me. "But for you, I'll do it. I'll not see you starve."

To my relief, the next hour passed in filling my order. There was even a stick of candy thrown into the bargain, which made me pleased despite the fact it also made me feel like a child. Will promised he'd have one of the Horning lads deliver the goods in Silk's wagon. That done, Paul offered me a turn in his canoe.

"But I've chores to do," I answered, sure if I remained too long there would be punishment.

"You have to play sometime," Will said. "Just because you're the woman of your household doesn't mean you can't enjoy yourself."

Paul nodded, smiling. What could I do but accept? Uneasy with my decision, I stepped out into the sunshine with Paul. No longer did the sunshine feel warming, welcoming. I felt exposed out here, felt the harshness of the heat. A sense of urgency welled; I should return home, right now, this moment.

I flinched when I saw Shadow Song. He hovered near the mill, that look to his mouth somewhere between mockery and flattery, his long rifle slung over his shoulder. As hard as I tried I couldn't keep my eyes from him. It seemed at that moment as if all the world froze. There was no sound, no motion, only his eyes keen and glittering as he watched me across the dust of that hot summer day. Was that power there? Was it evil? Was he evil?

In the next heartbeat I dropped my gaze. Such an effort that had been. I reached for Paul's hand. A trickle of sweat slid down my back. I murmured a prayer that Paul wouldn't see the shaman. He didn't. The moment passed but my sense of urgency didn't.

We passed into the shade of the trees. Paul tweaked my chin, bringing my attention up to him. I favoured him with one of my best smiles, although I felt none of it. Every nerve of me reached for the cabin, testing what, exactly, about the conversation at Silk's had shrouded this fine day.

I followed Paul silently to the river, indifferent to his musical banter. But who could resist Paul's charm for long? His last remark squeezed a giggle from me.

"So you know how to laugh."

I looked up at him, comforted by his size, his burliness, his rough way of barging through life. If it was scary, yell at it. If it was threatening, bark at it. Never back down. Never show your fear. How I longed for a little of that bravado.

My attention moved from him to the trees overhanging the river. Cicadas sang a scratchy chorus to the day. The river gurgled softly, green as the forest. Three canoes were beached here, like pale pods of birch against the grass.

I settled into Paul's with his assistance, nervous of the precarious balance of the craft and glad I had no petticoats with which to fuss. Petticoats, or not, I sat rod straight in the bottom of the craft, clutching my breath, my knuckles white on the gunwales. Even to look around caused a sway and roll. This was nothing like the *Baltic*. To keep my attention anchored on the bottom of the canoe seemed the prudent course.

"It's all right to move," Paul said, paddling us away from the bank.

I looked up at him carefully, mortified to find him grinning broadly. Pride as much as anything forced me to relax. The canoe wobbled. I stiffened again, sure that even to breathe would end in disaster. In the next moment my pride shattered. Jane appeared at the bank, all prettiness in calico, begging Paul to let her join us, her blue eyes flashing winks in my direction.

"With her like a board in my boat?" he replied, gesturing to me.

Jane's blue eyes widened. Oh she did know how to use them. "I won't be afraid. Honest. I go canoeing with the Indians all the time."

I watched Paul's resistance melt under the warmth of her feminine guile. With a gesture he invited her on board. I could have died right there from mortification because of Jane's ease with the canoe, mortification that increased when she took up a paddle at the bow, her skirts arrayed just so around her as if she were about to have tea in important company. I felt suddenly awkward in my overalls, ungainly. In short, I felt I was everything Jane was not.

Flustered, I turned my attention to the river and let its calm greenness soothe me. Once past the bustle of town all I could hear were the screeching cicadas and the hissing of the paddles. This was part of that world I wanted to discover, to taste, to touch with every fibre of my being. I could almost feel the pulse of the land around me, like a friend I wanted to greet and didn't know how.

"Your uncle doesn't know we're together, does he?" Jane asked suddenly, the paddle thudding on the gunwales.

I fell from dreams and back to that foreboding. "No."

"That's good," Paul said.

I wished I dared look at him, to read on his face exactly what he'd meant by that. I asked instead.

It was Jane who answered. "Because my daddy tolerates Indians. That makes him a heathen in your uncle's eyes."

"Are they so bad?"

"They are God's creatures. Your uncle doesn't see it that way."

"Then we shouldn't be friends." It seemed as simple as that. What other choice was there?

Jane laughed. "And who's to stop us?"

My uncle, I thought but wouldn't say. I had no doubt he'd do anything to have his own way. The dreams told me he would. My dreams never lied. That was one truth I could depend upon. The taste of my journey soured, a taste that became bitter when Paul took us ashore.

"Aren't you coming?" I asked when I was safely on land. He remained in the canoe, avoiding my gaze.

"I have to be going," he said roughly.

Going. Of course. What else? The people in my life were always going somewhere, and it seemed somewhere I couldn't follow. "Where to this time?" I asked, more out of courtesy than curiosity.

"North. Always north." He dipped his head to me. "Adieu, Danielle Michele. Be well till I come back next spring."

I mouthed my good-byes. By now it was familiar and caused me little pain, something I could do by rote. Good-bye to Papa. Good-bye to Maman. Good-bye to England. What was one more good-bye to Paul Rogette?

Chapter 6

I watched from the bridge as Paul rounded the bend of the Pine River, letting my gaze fall to the rolling green water when he had disappeared. Jane remained at my side, quietly, perhaps sensing my mood. Idly, I watched the natives there, listening to their soft manner of speech – all lisps and breaths. I couldn't help thinking of wind. When they, also, passed from sight, I was still watching the reflections of the birches. They were like white arms on the water, creatures that might succeed in luring me down to those watery depths and dreamless oblivion.

Jane tugged on my sleeve, all feminine pretensions gone. "Come on! Oh for goodness sakes! Stop mooning around!"

Reluctantly I turned away from the river, towed in Jane's wake to the mill where we met with the other Vanmear children – Susan and Oliver, both Jane's juniors – and young Lewis Horning, as I was told while we approached.

"Hey, Jane," Lewis said. "Dad's cow's gone missing."

"The one in calf?" she asked.

"The very one." His face had a conspiratorial look to it, rough, brutish. "He's told his man he'd pay him a quid to go search for her. A quid!"

Immediately I could tell what the boy was thinking. It was a veritable fortune to a young person.

"Imagine!" Susan breathed.

"We could earn that ourselves."

There it was. I watched the remainder of them, feeling that earlier dread loom. They all were suddenly eager, like cats on the hunt.

"What makes you think we could?" Jane asked, clearly the authority here and clearly interested.

"Don't be dense!" Lewis said. "Figure it out. My folks are all busy raising a barn with the relatives from Ancaster. Father will be gone from the mill soon. We can go off before his man, find the cow and collect our reward."

"Which way did the cow go?" I ventured, sure already of the answer.

All attention shifted to me, as if I had suddenly sprouted from the ground like some toadstool, ugly and unwanted. My cheeks felt hot.

"Who's that?" Lewis asked.

"Don't be rude," Jane warned. "This is Miss Danielle Michele Fleming."

"The girl Mama and we've been visiting," Susan added.

Lewis made a face. "I'm not splitting five ways."

"It's okay," I mumbled. "I can't go anyway. I've got to be getting back." I inched away, desperate to be gone from their scrutiny and this growing dread.

Jane rounded on Lewis, her face flushed with anger. "You apologize right now, you – "

"Aw let her go – "

"That's no way for a – "

I lost the rest. I slipped into the shadowy interior of the mill, stood there in the dimness, letting my nose tell me what my eyes couldn't. My pulse settled. My wounded pride healed. There was warmth in here, dryness, a yeasty smell. It was the fragrance of life, something basic. I inhaled deeply, letting the health of that smell overwhelm me. Dust clung to my arms like a shower of talcum that pinched my nose and parched my throat. I could feel the way the hair on my arms stood away from my skin.

It wasn't the dryness and the dimness and the delicious scent of the air that most overwhelmed me. It was the sound. Stone grinding against stone, of gears and wheels meshing, un-meshing, of axles moaning under weight, of water rushing like a dark fiend caught in a purgatory of pushing a wheel that had no part of its wet world. Sound filled this arena of activity. It throbbed through my body.

At that moment I realized I stood exposed in my rash retreat. Even so, I found myself incapable of discovering this turning world from secret niches. I wanted to see it all, closely, to experience it with every sense available.

It was that endless throb that drew me up the stairs, past adults bent to their tasks or standing in conversation. One conversation had been heated, between one of Horning's hands and two natives.

"No. Earn your food," the hand said. "We've had enough of your begging here."

"But you have driven the game from our lands," one of the Indians said. "What are we to do?"

"Work."

The hired man stalked away. The two natives glanced at one another, turned and left.

I walked by them all as if I were a ghost, unnoticed, until finally I stood by those massive disks of stone, orbiting each other like twin constellations. Mesmerized, I watched their rotation, listened to their speech of power.

Some moments passed when I realized there was another voice in the wheels, a voice that moved like music – deep, melodic, something that could lull me into dreams. Step by step I rounded the wheels, drawn by that rich male voice. A hawk screeched outside the mill window. I froze with tears in my eyes.

He stood there beyond my reach, a man of mahogany skin and a pale loincloth, ebony hair adorned with a headband and three hawk feathers, a long rifle over his shoulder, listening to things I couldn't hear. The miller, Lewis Horning, seemed ineffective beside this Indian, and yet Horning was broader, taller, burlier. There was something about this man, this shaman, that made me believe Paul Rogette's stories of him. Shadow Song was powerful. It was something that was a part of him, like hands, or legs, as real as he. A *midewenini*, as Paul had said, a medicine man, shaman, healer. He was like a pagan god to me. Why had I not seen this before?

At that moment he spoke – the voice I'd heard within the wheels: "You can offer me nothing."

Horning bristled. "I have everything to offer you as payment. You know you only have to ask."

"*You* know I only have to ask."

The look on Horning's face spoke clearly of his understanding. I knew from that look Shadow Song could demand anything of him and receive payment.

"What do you ask?"

"I ask for nothing."

"You can't just leave her to die!"

"If it is the will of the *manitous* then she will die. Even my medicine is ruled by that."

Horning scrubbed his hand over his face. "Guns?"

Shadow Song smirked, the beautiful long rifle at his back evidence he needed no other gun.

"Food?"

Again he smirked as if that gun brought him all the game he could ever need.

"Whiskey."

The Indian's face expressed disgust. "You have nothing I require."

"But I must give you something!"

"Why?"

"I can't just let her die!"

I felt somehow Horning was more afraid of a curse than of his wife dying, that he had somehow insulted this native.

Shadow Song's attention remained upon Horning. "Then we will find another way to pay the debt."

That didn't seem to be the answer for which Horning was looking. He pivoted, roughly, stalking away as if what this Indian would take as payment was more than he could or would afford. Only Shadow Song remained, a part of that moving, mysterious world.

He looked at me, his sienna eyes bright as a wild creature's. Everything about him seemed hawk-like at that moment, the way his nose fitted to his face, the way his eyes stared, unflinchingly, beauty and power and deadliness all there in his body. If I stayed somehow I knew the momentous things around him would catch me. He rode the winds of storm. Change echoed through him. For me there had been enough change. I'd have no more of it, fascinated as I was with him.

My heart lurched, mouth dry. I could do nothing else but flee, down the stairs, through the press of bodies, out into the sunshine and to where I'd never been. Toward Melancthon Swamp.

What drew me I didn't know. All I knew was that I had to go this way. I had to see what was here. It was like walking through my dreams. And knowing that filled me even more with dread.

It wasn't long before I found footprints in the soft earth, four sets, definitely not adult. I followed them, as I had in my dream. Shortly after that the footprints divided, one set to the west, one to the east. I chose the path that led to the west, just as I had another time. I heard voices, real ones that interfered with my memories, calling.

Jane? Was that Jane? Had she gone after the cow?

I stumbled in my uneasy state of mind, unsure of what was real and what was memory. I caught myself upon a swamp alder, paused. Another set of footprints now joined these, uneven, large. Like a man's. My panic rose. I remembered the dream fully now, remembered Uncle Edgar, remembered his hands. Bile stung my throat. I swallowed, and now ran.

What made me check my pace I had no idea, other than the other sense my dreams gave me. I walked now, stealthily. Jane's calling had stopped and now only faintly could I hear the boys off in the distance, somewhere to the east of here.

A shadow in the trees caught my attention. Nothing. Only trees. I glanced back to the ground, nearly stepped on a turtle. The hairs on the nape of my neck bristled. Carefully I stepped over the creature, scrambled over a log and sank to my ankles in mud. I pulled myself free with a sucking sound from the ground and continued, following the footprints. For a moment I thought the boys' voices were nearer. Now there was nothing. No calling. No movement. Only red-winged blackbirds shrilled loudly through the swamp.

Whether it was a trick of the sunlight, or a moment when dreams and reality meshed I will never know, but I glanced off to my left. Froze. My hand covered my mouth involuntarily and then I retched into the rushes. Susan lay beyond me, thrown like a broken doll across the fallen cedars, her face smashed, her throat slit. Gore still gouted.

I thought my trembling would take my legs. A moan like a plea ran through the scrub. From somewhere I found the courage to walk past the corpse. Not far along I heard a struggle. Using a bush for a screen, I watched a nightmare come true. Uncle Edgar was there, plainly in a drunken rage, his fingers like grips around Jane's shoulders. I could see how far they sank into her flesh. In the next moment the back of his hand detonated on her face. Her head swung toward me, her eyes glazed in pain so that I was sure she saw nothing. With one great tug he shredded the bodice of her gown, exposing her stays. She didn't even flinch. He groaned, and fell to the ground with her under him. Like a coward I hid my face in my hands, biting sobs, trying not to hear the way my uncle grunted, the slap of flesh against flesh, the way Jane whimpered, once, and was still.

A hand, hard, demanding, closed over my mouth, a whisper in my ear before I could gather enough wits to cry out: "Quiet. We'll get you and the boys to safety."

I didn't see my captor until he carried me like silence itself from that scene, but I knew who he was just from his voice. I wasn't sure whether to be relieved or terrified.

The two Indians whom I'd seen begging for food were waiting for us when we arrived in a dry clearing, Lewis Horning and Oliver Vanmear with them. Oliver's eyes were wide with terror, his lips moving around soundless words. I was set upon my feet, face to face with Shadow Song. He laid his fingers over my lips.

"Quiet now, *wahboosoons*. We must be quiet."

Why did I trust him? Wasn't he a sorcerer?

He looked to the other natives. Sounds passed between them, soft, lisping sounds like wind. They turned in a moment, took the boys with them and headed for the deeps of Melancthon Swamp.

"What are you doing?" I whispered.

His attention came back to me. "We're taking the boys to a safe place where we can heal them. They saw everything you saw."

I shuddered. "And me?"

"You're to go back to the cabin."

"But he'll – "

"He doesn't know you were here. He knows the boys were. You'll be safe. Just clean the mud from your clothes."

"But the boys – "

"He followed them. When he's finished with the girl, he'll try to kill the others."

I couldn't help it. Tears brimmed and spilled. "He killed – "

"I know. He is *ohnemoosh* – a dog." He turned me to the east. "Follow the trail. It leads to your cabin. Listen for the hawk, *wahboosoons*. Watch for the turtle. I'll be there."

I ran, my insides cold, my skin tingling with horror. When I reached the cabin I set into a burst of frenetic activity, putting the large kettle to a boil, stripping off my clothes, telling myself I had to be fastidious, I had to be careful, I had to be sure I removed all evidence I'd been at the swamp. My shoes were scraped of mud with a stick and then cleaned and polished. I put away the supplies that had been left inside the cabin, washed and hung clothes, cleaned up my mess, cooked and prayed fervently that everything would be all right.

Everything seemed to be in order when Uncle finally staggered into the cabin, the bandage on his head spattered with both gore and muck. I had waited supper for him. There was no conversation as usual. He simply sat to table and waited for me to serve him. To my surprise he spoke.

"You were to town?"

My insides felt utterly still. "Yes."

"Silk approved the terms of payment?"

"Yes."

"And delivered?"

"Yes."

"You're amazingly clean for a girl who's been to town." He crushed a louse from the back of his neck between thumb and finger.

I set the pot of soup back on its hook over the fire, keeping my back to him so I could hide my fear. "I don't like filth. I washed when I came back."

His chair scraped across the floor. Still I kept my back to him. What was he doing? I heard him go to the door, come back. His fingers gripped my shoulder. Despite myself I gasped. My attention was forced to bear upon him now. He held a stick in his hand, a stick covered in black mud, the stick I'd used to clean off my shoes. How could I have been so stupid? I'd cleared away all other evidence and never given a thought to a stick, a commonplace thing in the backwoods, but a stick covered with mud that would condemn me. There was a greedy look to his face as if he'd waited for this moment since I'd come to live with him. I took a steady breath to ease the racing of my heart.

"For a girl who doesn't like filth," he said, "you certainly have walked through enough."

Somehow I continued to look him in the eye, to keep myself from running, to keep myself from crying. "It did rain last night."

He turned the stick in his hand. "Funny thing is, the soil around here's brown. This looks like swamp muck."

Caught! I ducked away from him. He lunged, blocking my way to the door. All in the same moment I hauled myself up the ladder to the loft, slammed the door and managed to haul a trunk onto the hatch before he came after me. My heart was racing so badly my head pounded. All of my efforts proved little use. He pushed at the hatch, cursing me. Dust rose in puffs around the seams of the door. Truly terrified now I dragged another trunk to the hatch. This time the hatch didn't move at all when he shoved.

I backed away, touching my lips to prevent myself from screaming as I wanted. Was I safe? What would he try next? In those trembling moments I wondered if he would fetch an axe next, hack his way in and then hack me. Anything was possible. I was so afraid, afraid as I'd never known I could be. I wanted someone to make it all go away, to make the fear stop, to hold me and still my shaking that had grown so intense I felt convulsive.

I heard the key snick in the lock. Outside a hawk screamed. I turned my back to the hatch, slumped down into the evening sunlight on the floor and wept for the sound of freedom in the hawk's cry. Out there, somewhere, Shadow Song walked through a forest of green while I, who had wanted no part of change and only something secure, sat in a puddle of fool's gold.

Chapter 7

Eleven days I spent in that garret. I felt as though I'd never be free again, never be rid of the sound of Uncle's voice, of Uncle's disdain, of Uncle's humourless world. His world was exemplified by this room – grey, silty, smelling of things caught between death and decay, and now made fetid for the heat of the summer. All of this I faced during those eleven days, evaluating the exact worth of an orphaned, indigent girl's life. In the scheme of things my life wasn't of much value, only enough that a few people had shown a passing interest. After all, I wasn't their problem. They could afford to be pleasant for a few days, a few hours. After that they could return to their own lives, feel better for their charity. And I, well, surely I would be all right, surely no one really ever suffered, not in this modern age.

I capitulated after two days to his demands to remove the trunks from the hatch. Hunger and thirst were excellent motivators. He knew this. As did I.

In return for food he took my shoes. It seemed an odd thing to do at first, but then I realized the insane reason of what he did. A girl running barefoot through the woods wouldn't get far. He was determined to keep me captive and keep my knowledge firmly hidden.

He brought me food when he came home from the fields in the evening – a rind of cheese, whatever fruit was available. That, also, seemed odd until in a cold flood of shock I realized he might very well use me as he had Jane. Why else keep me alive?

When he cleared away my commode I offered him neither thanks nor any word of apology, although I knew for my own sake I should have. It would have been wiser to submit. I could have stretched my freedoms just a little if I had, but my stubborn pride prevented me and so I remained caged, like a pet.

This morning, like every morning, I listened for the sound of his footfall as he receded out to the fields. He would likely limp in harness, hack at stumps, do everything he could to subdue the land as he subdued everything else in his life. For him, I realized, life was a war, and either you crushed your enemy, be that enemy a person, a forest, a cow, or you were crushed yourself.

In the ensuing silence I took comfort in the fact I was alone again, free of any immediate harm he might contemplate. No one would visit, I knew. After the incident at the swamp, my corner of the world seemed to have been forgotten. Once I'd heard Horning below, questioning Uncle if he'd seen the whereabouts of the children. No. No, he hadn't. I'd almost screamed out *Liar*! I didn't. I only lay there on the floor listening to the conversation. Horning asked if Uncle would come and lend a hand in the search. Uncle Edgar's concern had been for his farm. Children would, after all, be children. Oh he'd sounded so sure, so free of transgression.

Instead of crying out, I succumbed to the weight of his power and remained silent, bereft of rescue.

My dilemma hung upon me until I felt my head would explode from thinking on it. How was I to get free? If I managed my freedom, then where would I go? I had no other family here, and my association with the Hornings and Vanmears was barely at acquaintance level. Shadow Song was a possibility, but I did not know where to find him, nor even that he watched. He had deserted me, I suspected, no more than a passing interest. Night after night, day after day, I'd watched out my small window for any sign of him but there had been nothing. Periodically a hawk screamed. Where Shadow Song was I had no idea.

Miserable, I sat up upon my bed and stared around the room, my attention at last coming to settle upon those trunks that had caused me such misfortune one afternoon. Not daring to again open the one marked KJO, I shuffled to the nearest, lifted away the broken lid and searched for something to use against Uncle, anything to make him hurt as badly as he hurt me. Thinking on this I again began to cry and that angered me. It seemed so useless a thing to do. No one would comfort me. It solved none of my problems and only blurred my sight and stuffed my nose.

My inspection of the trunk garnered nothing but a pile of memorabilia and a pocket knife that seemed hardly up to the task of prying open my window or door. Truthfully, it seemed hardly useful enough for anything except cleaning my nails, although the thought of a blade long enough to stick in Uncle's ribs delighted me in a horrid way. I would be free if this pocket knife were longer, less rusty. I would be free and Uncle be damned. I weighed that curse in my mind. Damn. It had such a hurtful sound, condemning. Damn him. I smiled, slashing the air the way I might slash Uncle. Yes. Damn him. This blade would look fine lodged between his ribs, timed for a moment when next he stuck his head through the hatch. That was a satisfying thought. I rehearsed the way that scene might unfold, parrying, thrusting, pivoting, my anger rising red and bloody.

A key turned in the lock. I shuddered. The hatch rose and slammed to the floor, revealing Uncle's head. For a moment I froze, caught by the iciness of his stare. Then, as in one of my dreams, I reacted, pushed by my rehearsal.

Slash. Slash. His eyelid gaped; skin drooped away from his brow. I could see something white, bone I assumed in those slowly passing seconds. The bone seemed so white compared to the filthy bandage still binding his head, and then it blurred as blood spouted.

It was accomplished just like that. Everything seemed to move so slowly, as if caught in jelly. His face registered shock, muscle by muscle, and then pain. He slipped and fell to the floor and then time seemed to return to speed. I jumped from the hatch, heedless of the blade I still held in my hand. Pain crashed up through the arches of my feet. I rolled. The knife skittered across the floor. I had my legs under me now. Hot pain slashed across the sole of my right foot. I screamed, rounded on him, baring my teeth in a snarl and then bolted for the door, pain crashing up through my leg with every footfall.

Uncle's screams were still reaching for me when I hit the trail that would take me to Horning's house. I knew of nowhere else to go. Only that I had to run, despite the pain, despite the fear. Run. Just run and don't stop until I was safe. Branches slapped my face and arms. I was only barely aware that the ground was cool and damp my senses were so absorbed with my injured foot.

By the time I reached the village I could barely walk and felt as though I would vomit at any moment. Feverishly, I looked around, oblivious of people, aware only of buildings. I limped to the gristmill with the hope Horning might still be there, all the while listening to the voices in my head that whispered like the wind.

Inside the mill my panic subsided somewhat, although not greatly. I let out a cry of pain. One of the late workers looked up from his sweeping. I checked my outburst, straightened, tried to look brave.

"Is Mr. Horning still here?" I asked.

I could see the man glance down to my foot and I wondered if the injury were visible. He frowned, nodded to the stairs. "You're hurt, young-un?"

I tried out a smile, gave up. "Scratched." I took a step. Pain flared. I felt myself tumbling and then lifted as the hired hand pulled me up into his arms, shouting for Lewis Horning.

I could hear footsteps on the stairs, rapid, and then Horning's rough voice near to my face. "What happened, girl?"

"I fell," I managed to answer, hoping he would make no further inquiries. I heard a hawk scream. And then I remember nothing.

Chapter 8

Bedlam. It was the first thing I thought when I awoke in Horning's kitchen. The air was filled with shrieks, all the debris of domesticity flung from entrance throughout, and here, in the kitchen, amid a cacophony of voices and a spectacle of confusion Horning's eleven-year-old marshalled her forces. It occurred to me we were of the same age, yet she seemed so young.

She had the eldest brother, Peter I assumed from what Jane had told me, chopping vegetables – hacking would have been a more appropriate description. Who appeared to be her younger sister diced salted pork while the next youngest, Robert, attempted to shovel some form of vile mush into the mouth of the youngest, who in turn spewed a continuous stream of pea-green at his attendant. Even the family dog assisted by sampling the meat intended for the stew while the cat had her head entombed in a pitcher of milk. All of this carried on with a grim sense of determination that spoke to me too clearly of the family's loss.

It all froze when they became aware of their father standing in the doorway with me in his arms. Dizziness threatened again. I was aware that the eldest girl's mouth opened into a wide oval when she looked at my foot.

"Don't gape, child," Horning said. I could feel his voice rumbling in his chest where my head lay. "I'll need some help."

"Who's she?" Peter asked, rising. I could see the way the muscles of his jaw corded that he was preparing for an offensive. I only hoped this wouldn't drag on. My foot throbbed hellishly.

"She's Danielle Michele Fleming," Horning answered.

"Edgar Fleming's? – "

Horning shot the boy a withering glance. The boy subsided. "You," Horning said, nodding to the girl, "go and fetch a clean cloth and tidy that baby up." To the boy: "Get that dog and cat out of here. I need clean bandages, needle, thread, the bottle of brandy – " And so the orders went.

I was taken to another room, although I was barely aware of it at the time, and made to drink a large quantity of some fiery liquid that made me gasp for air. I heard a woman say weakly, "Mind, Lewis, she's just a child." My head felt as though it spun so badly it would disconnect and set off into orbit. All I could think was I'd be free of Uncle and his malice, his silence, his danger.

I slipped into that place where I thought I dreamed dreams that were real. I didn't. What I heard was a song that came from the shadows, like the sound of wind through moonlit leaves, lisping and distant, rather scary and yet comforting. I wanted to see the owner of this voice and turned my head. He stood there where candlelight couldn't reach, naked but for the strip of leather he wore as his loincloth. Veils of smoke enwreathed him, like blue ghosts, fragrant, mysterious, in his hand a long-stemmed pipe of wood and stone from which hung feathers. I didn't know whether to shriek from fright or delight and found I could do neither. I could only watch through half-lidded eyes, terrified to move, desperate to swallow the pain that throbbed up my leg. I remembered stitches being made, of each piercing prick of the needle and of more brandy down my throat.

He moved. I thought of water, or wind, or something that had no rigid form, something that flowed. From somewhere a breeze touched my face, moist, warm. The veils of smoke shifted, drifted, gathered into a form over my bed that made me think of a hawk, or was it an eagle? I reached for it.

"*Kaikaik*," he breathed.

I shuddered with pleasure, my hand falling to my side. His spell rocked me, my question dying. In the next moment he bent to another bed where a woman lay and to my dismay I saw it was Mrs. Horning, pale, weak, dark rings beneath her eyes like sooty smudges. He slipped one arm under her head, so gently, raised her, held a gourd to her mouth. A trickle of greyish liquid dripped from her lips. His fingers wiped it away. He eased her back. She sighed. He straightened and stoppered the gourd and slipped it into a pouch at his hip.

He turned and his attention was for me alone, as if there was no one else who needed him now but me. I knew there was nothing I could hide from him; I felt his sight. He would know I had dreamed of this scene before. He said as much. I closed my eyes in horror, desperate to hide this sin from him, wanting still, only, to be free.

"Fear not," he said.

I held my breath. Don't be afraid of what? The dreams that had brought me to this state? Uncle's danger? Him? Of what, exactly, should I not be afraid?

He bent to his heels, his palms reaching for the crown of my head where my hair parted. The touch of his hands jolted me. I could feel the knowledge in those hands. Such healing. I could only stare wide-eyed as his palms slid down to either side of my face, my tears blurring my vision of this man.

When he reached for the bandage on my foot I did nothing to stop him. What could I do against power as his? Yet there was none of Uncle's silent malevolence in him. I knew this. There was only this fluidity to him, this sensation he heard things clearly where I heard only whispers. He was a man who dreamed and lived by those dreams.

He hunkered back onto his heels when he appraised the gash on my foot. Again he looked at my face.

"You were in a hurry."

How could he know such things? I could only nod.

"He will come for you."

"I won't go." This I said feebly, more from fear than conviction.

His mouth twitched. "Then you will need this foot for running." He opened the pouch at his side, withdrew a smaller gourd and applied a rich yellow salve that cooled the heat in my foot. I moaned for the pleasure of it. He then raised my leg onto a mound of blankets and pillows so that it was nearly over my head. The throb eased almost immediately.

Lewis Horning stepped into the room at that moment.

"What are you doing?" he demanded. I heard the fear in his voice.

Shadow Song's attention remained on me, his sienna eyes gentle, his fingers massaging in the ointment. "Curatif." I knew he spoke in French for me. Healing. He was doing that. I could feel the miracle of it in his hands.

"It's all right, Mr. Horning," I said, breathlessly, rising from my dream-like state.

Horning looked down at me, back to Shadow Song. "If you harm her – "

"I'm healing her, as I said." He placed the gourd into my hand. "Two days, when the sun sets." He nodded to my foot. I gave him a word of understanding. He rose, almost challenging Horning, his gaze unflinching as he stared. I could feel the thing between them, pulling, pushing, tension and suspicion. Something in Shadow Song's manner suggested danger, hidden, but there like a whisper in his indolent stance. In Horning there was only this caution, bred from the recent events that had taken his son.

Their silent struggle ended when Horning's children set to a row. He turned away. Shadow Song lingered over me.

"Why didn't you come before?" I asked thickly, fuddle-headed.

"You were safe for the moment."

"Safe?" I sputtered.

The look on his face softened. "You heard the hawk?"

I nodded.

"Then you also know I watched you as I promised."

"But – "

"Now is not the time to discuss such things. You have running yet to do and this foot needs healing. Later we will talk."

"But Uncle, he'll – "

"Not come after you yet. He'll be too busy healing the gash you gave him." How did he know? "And when he does come for you, you'll be gone."

My questions died when he folded himself into a corner, a song weaving round him with the smoke of his pipe. I slipped into a place of dreams while someone who called himself Nanabush watched over us all.

Chapter 9

Uncle didn't bother me, just as Shadow Song had said, although I gave him no opportunity. I as much as imprisoned myself in the protection Horning offered, resting those first few days, limping about to do my share of the work in those that followed. The family was kindly, distant, and I felt my loss more keenly for their lack of fellowship. Uncle's outright disregard of me was one thing, easier to accept, but the Hornings' cool acceptance was polite, civilized and nothing about which I could protest, nor had I any right. They had offered succour to one of their neighbours, as the Bible said they should. There had never been anything said in scripture about liking what you did.

Yet, even with their assistance, I knew it was only a matter of time before Uncle went on the hunt for me. He would be unshakable then, like a hound at the kill. While this shelter lasted there was calm.

As for Mrs. Horning, time and Shadow Song's uncanny ways healed her. First came the days she could sit up in bed. She had seemed almost invisible against the white linen, too weak to do anything herself, and I made it my task to feed her the thin broths and porridges, to sponge her, to brush her long, greying hair and pin it up once more. I felt during those days as if I'd robbed her of her significant dignity, for I was clumsy in my nursing of her. More than once what had been intended for her mouth spilled onto her chemise and she would only smile weakly. Horning's girls would assist me when it was necessary to help their mother to a commode, which she would endure in silence, with a shrug and smile. I watched and learned from her serenity, from her acceptance of things she could not change. It was a state of grace I coveted, a strength that overcame illness, loss, hardship, something I knew I needed if I was to survive in this new land.

Mrs. Horning's progress was continuous so that she now took her mornings in the sunlight of her window. Those were moments I enjoyed, for we would sit there and watch the landscape, quietly, and often she would rest her hand on mine.

Shadow Song's visits were numerous, unexpected, often when Horning and the family weren't about. There had been considerable tension between them, and I assumed it became more so because of the disappearance of the children, for people were now blaming the Indians. Both Shadow Song and I kept silent about the truth, something I questioned at first but came to see the wisdom of after a little time. What white settler would believe one of their own had perpetrated such a crime against a community dependent upon one another? It was easier to blame the Indians. They were the foreigners in their own land. They were the heathens, the godless unwashed with their savage dress and savage speech and savage customs.

So it was Shadow Song often appeared at a window, in the cabin, anywhere Mrs. Horning and I might be, in his hands some gift be it berries, wild rice from some hidden cache, or a brace of ducks. The first time I took his hunt from his hands there had been an odd smile on his face, as if he shared some secret with himself, for certainly my action amused him and endeared me to him. It wasn't until later I was to learn this was usually the ritual of courtship.

This evening, he sat to table with us all, in a subdued celebration of two healings, mine and Mrs. Horning's. It was tense, for the family and for him. I watched painfully as he stumbled over utensils although he showed some familiarity and I could only assume it had been some time since he had been in England among the civilized ways of whites. I ached for him, wishing to spare him this humiliation, but he carried on as graciously as he could, even using the linen serviette to dab at his mouth.

Conversation was sparse, and so when he announced, suddenly, he would return to his own lands and people on the morrow it caused quite a stir, within my own heart as much as with others. As the meal dragged on, I found myself no longer able to look at him for fear I would betray my sense of loss, for I had no part of his life yet wished I did. Even so, I caught him throwing me covert looks, his brow furrowing.

"Well," said Horning after some moments, "we shall certainly miss you in these parts."

I nearly choked on his hypocrisy. Suddenly my appetite diminished. I was relieved of toying with the food on my plate when Horning said we'd move to the porch, that the clearing of the table could wait awhile. It was like a declaration of a holiday, although I felt none of the festivity.

When we retired outside I sensed Shadow Song's mood shift, like a change in the wind. Perhaps it was being near to the land. Perhaps it was his full belly. Whatever the cause for his change I marked that he seemed to be more at ease, as if he were in his own element free of the confinement of the cabin.

"I will tell you a story," he said after a moment, leaning against a post. He drew a pipe from the otter skin bag he always carried, the bowl of black stone, carved with intricate details of creatures that seemed to move under his hand. Once the pipe was lit, he offered it to the setting sun, to the earth, and then to the cardinal points. The fragrance of the smoke was sweet, pleasant, not at all like the tobacco Horning used. I inhaled deeply, my tensions unwinding under the sorcery of his charms. His attention settled on me, remained there as he began his tale and I felt as if there were no others on the porch but he and I.

"A long time ago," he said, "after *Kitche Manitou* made this the fourth world, there was only one person living among all the trees, the grasses, the flowers. She was known as Spirit Woman. Although she was busy picking berries, weaving and making clothes, she was lonely. There was no one for her, no mate, no animals, no one.

"*Kitche Manitou* saw this and knew this wasn't good. He sent her a husband and for a time they were together. From her first birth came the ruffed grouse, and on the same day came all the other birds of the earth and sky and water. This gave her great comfort. Soon, however, all but the grouse left. 'I will never leave you, Mother,' it promised. 'I will always stay close to your side,' and kept its promise which made Spirit Woman very happy. She was kind to the bird because of its loyalty.

"When she gave birth the second time, it was to rabbit." His eyes crinkled at the corners as he watched me. "After *wahboos* came, the other animals – *nahbak* the bear, *moons* the moose, *peshewh* the lynx – and they, like the birds, went out into the world away from Spirit Woman. *Wahboos* remained, promising, 'I will never leave you, Mother. I will always stay close to your side.' In return Spirit Woman gave the rabbit gentleness and created a rock in its likeness that we call The Sitting Rabbit.

"One last time Spirit Woman gave birth. Her wanderings had taken her to the inland sea and here it was whitefish came to be, and after *ahtikahmag* came all the other creatures of the water. *Ahtikahmag* remained when the others left, making the same promise.

"And so Spirit Woman, despite her many losses, found contentment with the grouse, the rabbit and the whitefish." He looked away from me then, his gaze upon the hills.

The silence that followed was acute until Peter, the eldest boy, asked, "So what's the point?"

Shadow Song answered while still looking at the hills, "That is for you to decide."

Peter scoffed derisively, but I knew what Shadow Song's tale meant; I felt the gift of it upon me. I wanted him to continue to speak and so I said, "Paul Rogette told me about the thunderbirds. Have you seen them?"

His attention came back to me, all at once, focused and keen.

"Don't be stupid," said Peter. "That's only legend."

Shadow Song seemed not to hear the boy's remark. His attention was for me alone. The only reply he gave to my question, however, was a nod of the head. I shivered. Silence hung around us.

"What did he tell you?" Shadow Song asked at length.

My mouth was dry and yet I couldn't say why, only that his interest in me was like being in the bright sun overlong. I managed to unglue my tongue and answer, "That they live in the western mountains, that their chicks cause the violent storms of summer – "

"– that when the fire snaps it is the burning of the chicks' hearts."

I could only nod.

"And you believed him?"

I looked to Horning's children who were hanging on every word, back to him, knowing if I answered truth they would ridicule me. I nodded to him, confirming that I did believe, with all my heart I believed.

He smiled briefly, his eyes sparkling. It was as if I was singular for him, unlike those others who were with him on the porch. I looked away, down to my lap, unable to bear the intensity of his scrutiny, my cheeks hot. Why did he see me as so different? Why were the things I asked him so important?

I sensed him shift, felt motion flash over his body. I looked up as he beckoned to Lewis Horning, his back to me as he left me swimming in a pool of confusion. All the others left as well, the boys to one chore, the girls to another, Mrs. Horning following them with a slow but steady gait. I eluded them and hid myself into a corner of the porch, straining to hear the conversation between Horning and Shadow Song. They were in the shadows of the large birch near the house, Shadow Song's profile limned with red-gold light from the setting sun.

"I can't thank you enough," the miller said, avoiding Shadow Song's eyes. Nothing in his tone indicated gratitude.

Shadow Song made no response. He only stood there as if he were drawing strength from the very ground.

"I guess it's time for payment," Horning said.

Still there was no response. Only that stillness that I knew would change to action unexpectedly.

Horning finally met Shadow Song's gaze. "Well?"

"Something within your means, I'm sure."

My heart pounded.

"Name it."

"I want you to give the child two sets of clothes for warm weather, two for cold."

Clothes for me? Why a gift for me?

Horning's mouth opened, closed, opened again. "But she's going to stay – "
"Perhaps."
"But that's not a payment to you."
"If I say it's so, then it is." He turned and strode into the shadows of dusk. Somewhere in the distance thunder rumbled. I shivered despite the evening's heat, wondering, why he had asked for something for me?

Chapter 10

I woke. I wasn't afraid. Nothing had alarmed me. It was just as if I'd been called, yanked out of sleep by something unknown. Time to go. Time to flee.

I glanced at Mrs. Horning in the other bed of the room, saw her face pale in a band of moonlight, peaceful in her rest. My sense of restlessness grew. I turned and slipped out of bed, the wood cool against my feet. The gash was still tender, but I was perfectly capable of walking on it for it had healed quite well. I dressed soundlessly as I could, putting on the new dungarees Horning had given me that very evening, the socks, the shoes, the shirt. The remainder of my belongings – the possessions Shadow Song had stolen from my loft at Uncle's, the new clothes, a bottle of lavender water from Paul Rogette, the tin of tea from Mrs. Horning, and the book Captain Earbage had given me – these I wrapped into a bundle made from a shawl one of the girls had given me.

Why tonight, of all nights, I was going to flee I didn't know. I only knew what I did was right. If I stayed with the Hornings, Uncle would come, as surely as one day followed the next, bringing to the family more grief than they already endured. I knew I was an intruder here, a reminder of their loss of Lewis Horning Jr.

Standing there like a fugitive, I wondered where I would go now. It wasn't as if I had a wealth of friends or family. It wasn't as if I could just walk down the street and into an orphanage, not here, not in the middle of a forest as endless as the sea.

My only hope was in Shadow Song. He had left yesterday evening and by now could be well beyond my reach. I'd seen no sign of him since, no hawk, no turtle. Even so, I hoped I might find him, that I might be able to depend upon guidance from the few natives who still frequented the mill.

Would that be safe? And what if I found him? What then? Would he even let me stay with him? He was a shaman. What place was there for a lost white girl in his life?

I glanced at Mrs. Horning. Trying to find him seemed better than what faced me here. I wanted no part of being at someone's mercy, thank you. There'd been enough of that already.

Quietly, I hefted my bundle to my shoulder, bent under its weight, and snuck through the cabin, careful to avoid the furniture, straining to see in the dark. Finally I reached the door, set my hand to the latch, lifted it, sure that small sound echoed through the house, and stepped out into a sultry night.

Moonlight shone brightly so that the trees cast deep shadows. Beyond, toward the river, I could see banks of mist hanging like veils. The crickets had briefly ceased their chirping when I stepped out, now resumed. Feeling both elated and frightened, I left the porch and made my way to the river where I walked upstream toward the bridge where it was likely Indians would be at dawn. With a little luck I'd be on my way toward Shadow Song in the morning.

I was not hurried in my journey; there was nothing to hurry for, and the light within the cover of the trees was such that I had to be careful about where I set my feet. At length I reached the bridge. There was one canoe overturned on the bank. I set down my bundle and settled on it to await sunrise.

It wasn't long before my idleness bred fear and I winced at every small noise, sure that Uncle Edgar, or some creature was about to pounce upon me. Something rustled in the undergrowth. I looked about me wildly, not daring to move from my bundle. There was nothing visible and the noise stopped. I settled back to my waiting. Another rustle stirred me. This time I felt the hairs on my nape rising. I held my breath for fear I would be found and stretched my hearing. Nothing. Only the crickets rasping a song to the heat of the night. Likely I'd just heard the trees groaning the way they often did. Speaking to themselves, I supposed. Again I watched the way moonlight threaded patterns across the river, like liquid silver cast upon onyx that disappeared into mist.

I mopped sweat from my brow that ran despite my inactivity, felt it trickle between my shoulders. All my clothes felt as if they were glued to me. Carefully, I took the few steps to the bank and dipped my hands, splashing water onto my face to ease my discomfort. It was shocking in its coldness and refreshed me for a moment.

The crickets had stopped rasping. I froze. They sang again and I rose, slowly, curbing my instinct to run, for to run in this tricky light, with me so inexperienced, I knew would be folly. Someone followed me. Someone who was sure enough to move so stealthily in the night. What if it was Uncle? My heart thudded at the thought. A hand touched my shoulder and I yelped, whirled to my pursuer. I didn't know whether to cry out for joy or fear.

Shadow Song stood before me, imposing in the moonlight, too powerful in this isolated place. In the silvery light his hair shone blue-black, the harsh angles of his face all brightness and shadow. I looked for an escape, my resolve to travel with him dissolved.

"Peace, *wahboosoons*," he breathed.

I couldn't help relaxing at that sound. Everything about his voice hypnotized me and I knew I could do nothing against his enchantment be it real or imagined. Another part of me preached caution, warned that my action was lunacy. He was an Indian, a savage. I was white. That should have set off alarms. And did for a moment. I backed away.

"I mean you no harm," he said softly, showing me his empty hands. It was then I realized the long rifle he carried wasn't slung over his shoulder. "You should know that by now."

I paused in my flight, watching him.

"You're ready to run," he said. I frowned, thinking him stupid for stating the obvious. My confusion must have been evident to him because he added, "From Fleming."

"How do you know?" I stammered.

He laughed and it was as soft as the night. "Because he will hunt you the way he has in his own house."

"What makes you so sure?"

"I know this man. He's dangerous."

"Perhaps he's dangerous because you've done something to his land, because you took his fiancée."

He watched me for a long moment, almost breathless as he absorbed that accusation, and then: "That would be betrayal."

"Exactly," I said, but without understanding, only needing to throw something at him.

"Had I wanted to do him evil, I would have been more effective."

"What's happened to his farm isn't effective?"

"His farm fails because he believes I've done something. That suits me well enough for what he's done to my people." His gaze never left me, his face set and hard. "It is not my way to do evil. That would be what you pale faces call sin. For me to do evil is sin, a sin against the *Midewewin*."

"And the girl Paul says you stole from Uncle?"

He shook his head.

"What's that mean?"

"I did no evil."

"You stole his fiancée!"

"You speak without knowledge."

Indeed I did for I spoke of things I knew were beyond my experience. I was, after all, only girl, yet I felt not so very young. "Then give me knowledge."

He let go of a breath. "She was one of my people, half white, half red. For awhile she thought she'd be a pale face. The pale faces saw her only as red, just like Fleming. So she went with me to return to her people."

"But it was still a sin."
"There was no sin. I never shared her blanket. She was never my wife."
I gestured to the village. "They all say differently."
"They're wrong."
"I may be a child, but I'm not stupid."
"They're white. They wouldn't understand."
"And what about me?"
"I think you would understand."
"Why?"
"You're different." I glared at him. How dare he throw my difference in my face. How dare he speak of the evil that was in me as if it were virtue. "Would you have stayed here at the river, alone, in the moonlight, with a red man if you weren't different?"

Oh. It wasn't of my dreams he spoke. I felt my cheeks redden. Confusion warred and I turned for flight. Like quicksilver he was at my side, his hand upon my arm, warm, alive, as if he were made of something other than flesh and blood, as if the vibrancy of the land flowed up through the soles of his feet. I inhaled sharply, shocked.

"Please," he breathed. I made no move, rooted where I stood. "Please stay."

I nodded, tentatively. His hand left my arm. I could see hurt on his face and I wondered if he'd be wounded if I left? I wondered if I would really want to wound him. I watched him, sorting out my feelings that were a muddle, and gave up. The only thing I knew for certain at that moment was that I wouldn't want to hurt him. To wound him would be sinful, as sinful as what Uncle had done.

"They say the girl died," I said, smoothing my voice so he would hear no accusation.

"Drowned, fleeing the Sioux near Lake of the Woods."

"And what of the girl whose family you killed near Cranberry Lake?" Pain was plain on his face and I regretted my question.

"Suspicion still?" he asked.

"I hardly know you. I have to ask these things. It isn't as if my life has been full of trustworthy people. What else can you expect?" Even that sounded lame, far too full of the things adults did to one another.

"A little more is what I expect. I did heal your foot, feed you, protect you when no one else would. Had I wanted to do you harm, I could have many times before now."

That was something I didn't doubt. Power radiated from him the way the sun radiated light, and yet not once had he demonstrated any malice toward me. I knew now there would be no danger from him.

"You didn't answer me," I said, pleasantly, but still determined to arm myself with as much information as possible. Information was knowledge. Knowledge was power.

"We were betrothed. I had already made gifts to her parents long before. When I returned for her, I found the others had died." He looked steadily at me. "I did no evil."

"So she was your wife."

He nodded.

"And now?"

"She's dead."

"People around you seem to suffer." His eyes closed and I knew he faced an old wound, that in my naiveté I'd hurt him deeply. It occurred to me that my statement was as true of myself as it was of him. I reached for his arm, paused, withdrew. This kind of pain, this kind of loss, was something I knew too well. "I'm sorry, I – "

"– had to know."

"Yes."

His eyes opened and he looked at me again. "I want you to know."

"Why?"

"Because there are things I must teach you, *wahboosoons*."

My decision now seemed right. "Can I come with you?"

He smiled, half mockery, half tenderness. He answered only by hefting my bundle onto his back and leading me to the overturned canoe that turned out to be his. Later I discovered that it was at this point Nanabush ended his vigil. I was where I was supposed to be.

Chapter 11

We paddled until well after sunrise, me inept and clumsy at the bow although Shadow Song instructed me carefully, calmly, without any anger with my bungling. His kindness did everything to win me, everything to unhinge me, for it had been a long while since I had known such treatment. It almost seemed too good to be true that I was escaping from the nightmare that had become my life since that fateful day in 1830. Two years had now passed. Two years in which my entire life had changed.

Now I paddled my way northward in a canoe with an Ojibwa sorcerer, a *midewenini*.

Shadow Song called quietly to me to paddle only on the right side of the canoe now. I did so, listening to the river gushing against his paddle as he steered us in to shore. He brought the stern around, leapt out and guided the canoe so that I could step out without getting wet. Without another word he shouldered his pack, his rifle and the canoe, indicating for me to follow closely as he led into the forest.

Here the trees were much like the rest of the forest I'd seen, rampant with growth, endlessly green and fragrant. We followed what seemed to be a narrow path that wound up a hill, down the other side, until we came to another river, or perhaps the same, I didn't know. It had been about an hour I supposed, and I was weary from my exertions and lack of sleep. Seeing this, Shadow Song made a small camp in a relatively clear spot, lighting a fire and brewing some form of tea that was bitter but refreshing. As always with him, there was silence. He offered me dried fish and berries while he mixed together a doughy substance and cooked it over the small fire. This he shared with me and I relished it, hungrier than I'd thought.

When we were done he sat with his back against a bare, white log, dappled in early sunlight that filtered through the canopy. He lit his pipe, its fragrance like an invitation to rest. He smiled, slightly, but it was such a look of contentment, and as I had seen him do that night on Horning's porch, he offered the pipe to the sky, the earth and the cardinal points.

"Why do you do that?" I asked, full, warm and deliciously lazy.

He blew smoke rings up to the canopy. A grouse clattered from the carpet of seedling maples. "The Anishnabeg," he said, "were given tobacco by Nanabush, who in turn received it from his father, *Epingishmook*, as a way in which we could give an offering and receive peace. The first puff is one we always give to *keezis*, the sun, who gives it to *Kitche Manitou* the maker of the worlds, the second to Mother Earth in honour of life." He repeated this process with reverence, part of him detached in a world I was only beginning to understand. "Then we turn to *Waubun*, the east, and blow smoke in thanks for the dawn and birth, to *Ningobianong*, the west, where the Land of the Souls lies and where all things must go and fade. A breath must be given next to *Bebon* who lives in the north, and from whom we learn strength by trial, patience by perseverance, resourcefulness from scarcity. Lastly, we smoke to *Zeegwun* who lives in the south, and from whom summer and growth and all the goodness of the earth swells."

He offered me the pipe. I could only gesture to myself, unsure of what to do, to say. He smiled. "Now is as good a time as any for you to learn these things."

I took the lovely thing from him uncertainly, set the stem to my teeth and drew as I'd seen him do. Smoke stung my tongue, bitterness flowing along my gums. I coughed, embarrassed I'd made such a mess of his gift. He laughed, joyously. Encouraged by him I tried another puff and this time offered smoke to *Kitche Manitou* and to Mother Earth, *Waubun*, *Ningobianong*, *Bebon* and *Zeegwun*. My head spinning from the sweet grass, I wondered, vaguely, if these spirits really accepted my gift or if I was only play acting. I hoped, with all my being that they were real, that there was a world where my dreams wouldn't be evil. Surely it was to these spirits that Shadow Song now listened.

Wanting it to be real, I strained to hear what Shadow Song heard, searching for some ripple that might reveal that the spirits were truly listening. There was only the rustle of the green leaves far overhead, the scrape and scurry of forest creatures and bird song. Disappointed, I handed the pipe back to Shadow Song. I had wished so much for entry into his world. There was nothing but silence.

He took the pipe from me, saying, "In time, *wahboosoons*. In time. You are new to all of this and have much to learn."

In my heart I thanked him for the promise; it was a hope to which I could cling, a small light in my bleak world. He returned to his smoking, watching the trees, his sense of listening growing and growing until I felt as though I would cry out from the touch of his power. He was tense now, his gaze roaming over the trees, the brush, the mouldering leaves, sniffing the air as if he were some forest beast. At last he stood, knocked out the pipe and put it away. He walked a few paces away from the fire, down toward the river, watching the ground at his feet. After a moment he bent to his knees, his hand on the earth between his knees.

"He has been here." He said it so calmly, so matter-of-factly I felt chilled.

"Uncle Edgar?" was all I could say.

He nodded, his back still to me. There was silence from him for a moment and then: "He will follow us."

I shuddered, closing my eyes. I heard him turn toward me, heard the leaves hissing under his moccasins. "I will take care of you," he said, touching my head. "There will be nothing to fear from him now."

I looked up at him, at the way he seemed so self-assured, and wondered. Would it be possible for Shadow Song to protect me from Uncle? Uncle had the weight of all the white world behind him. An ocean hadn't stopped him from reaching out and destroying. What was one red man against that?

I was left wondering when Shadow Song kicked out the fire and set us to our journey. Tired as I was I followed, knowing from somewhere inside me I did the right thing. To go with him meant hope.

Settled into the canoe, we headed upstream. Upon his first stroke I could feel power building, real, vibrant and was not surprised when I looked over my shoulder and saw steam rising from the river that had only moments before been clear. He hummed softly, as if in conversation with the *manitous* of the water, his attention somewhere inward. I turned back around. If Uncle Edgar were to follow now I knew he'd have to wait for better visibility. Shadow Song had bought us time. Assured for the moment, I watched the river we travelled, listening to the hissing of our paddles sing a song of hope.

The days that followed were filled with wonder and little by little I shed my dour thoughts. I burned badly from the sun, but was soothed by the salves Shadow Song prepared, watching as my skin deepened in color until I was almost as red as he. It occurred to me after the first three days that my time was spent with a great deal of laughter, with his songs, stories, music and conversation spent as an investment in understanding. I came to understand a little better this wondrous, frightening land. I came to understand Shadow Song a little better. Most of all, I came to understand myself a little better. His laughter buoyed me. His songs and stories held my imagination captive. His music touched those places in me that were still wounded. What he sang and what he said filled my head until I felt I would explode for the marvel and gift of it.

During our portages he would show me plants that were useful, those which were dangerous. I learned about may-apples, the blossoms of which had fallen some time ago and were now fruiting and shone like gold and sat sweetly upon the tongue. He showed me Queen Anne's lace, a pretty weed that was more than flowers; its root was a valuable legume. He picked an odd leafy plant that smelled somewhere between vile and savoury, crushed it and smeared our exposed limbs with its juice. To protect us from stinging insects he'd said. It did. Yet another leafy plant sluiced in water acted as soap. Bouncing Bet, he'd said, giving me the English name. For me that unexpected soap came as a relief at the end of the day when we'd splash in whatever body of water we travelled, be it stream, lake or waterfall.

Even more than this he showed me. I learned that spruce root was used for thread, pine pitch for glue, slippery elm for thirst and sore throats and poultices. I learned that all in this land had some use be it boon or bane. All of it something Shadow Song understood with the familiarity of an apothecary and more. He understood this land as if he were a part of its living force, praying before he took a plant, shot game, offering thanksgiving when a life was taken. His actions went beyond ritual, so far beyond the dark mysteries of the church. With him these rituals were a part of life, a way of life, as important and innate as breathing and eating.

During the day we travelled, from sunrise to sunset, sometimes on water, sometimes on land. I became adept at handling the paddle, learned how to dip it and push the water, how to raise it so there was no drag, listened for the hiss of droplets as I drew it forward level with the gunwales and again sliced cleanly into the water.

At sunset we'd make camp in a place he would choose that was watered, defensible. If the weather held fine we'd make our beds in the open air, he telling me tales as I'd lie upon my back, staring up at the stars. When it rained, we'd erect a wigwam, an odd, portable building of poles and bark that did everything to shut out the elements. Inside of this we'd make our fire and let the smoke travel up through the hole in the roof, although it sometimes did tend to remain with us if the winds were so inclined and that made for uncomfortable sleeping, thick lungs and stinging eyes.

We travelled a good stretch of the Pine River, from there through innumerable lakes and streams, over hills more mountainous than rolling. I'd stood in awe at waterfalls where Shadow Song offered tobacco to the *manitou* that lived there. I paddled through canyons the likes of which I'd never seen. North, north and ever north we went, over bluffs as white as bone, through marshes vast and vibrant. Finally we left all of this and headed out over what I thought was open water, a huge mass like the endless freshwater sea of Ontario. He pushed me hard then, telling me we had to make good time while the weather held. That day we passed three islands, one of which he warned me was forbidden for there were lovers there that had been turned to stone.

Another he said was Bear's Rump Island, so called because a bear had fallen into the water and was now eternally caught there.

I watched it all with wide eyes, sure I would miss some wonder if I didn't look everywhere at once. There were gulls pencilling long arcs on an endless blue sky, swooping down on the shoals they fished. Thousands of them there were. And ducks. And geese. I'd never seen so many waterfowl.

I felt more than heard Shadow Song lift his paddle from the water. In another stroke I followed. The fragrance of sweet grass drifted over me. I closed my eyes to savour the aroma of it, taste the pungency of it. There was everything for the senses here. Water thrummed against the canoe. Birds cried overhead. Colors were of blues and greens and greys and pinks, each in massive shape and form that flowed one into the other, sky into water, rock into trees. Even the sun on my skin had a quality I felt was new, as if I'd never before felt what it was like to be kissed by the dawn. It was warm. It was invigorating. It was a language I was just beginning to learn.

Oh, and it did taste. The taste of it was more nourishment than I could ever hope to have. It tasted of harmony, of balances, of things I now knew how to hear. I looked over my shoulder to Shadow Song. To hear. Yes. This was what he heard, these things to which I'd known he listened but things I had been unable to identify.

His clay brown eyes were shining when he looked at me, deeply, keenly.

I'm glad you know, I felt him say.

I'm glad you taught me, I felt myself answer.

Tears brimmed in my eyes, blurring his face. I couldn't ever remember knowing such contentment.

Shadow Song lowered his pipe, his brow furrowing. "I didn't mean for you to weep."

"It's joy," I answered.

He laughed, set his pipe to his teeth. The canoe rippled as he leaned forward and I felt no fear of its movement. He extended his arm to the nearest, most massive of the islands scattered like pearls across this huge body of water.

"Do you know what that is?"

I shook my head, looking where he indicated.

"We call it *Manedoomini* – the Spirit Island – what the pale faces call Manitoulin. I fasted just past there as a boy on Dreamers' Rock so the *manitous* would visit me. We will camp on *Manedoomini* for a little while."

"How long?" I asked turning back to him. He watched me intently, secretive again.

"That depends," he said. "Likely till its time to move to the wintering grounds."

Again he set his hand to the paddle and guided us round to where the coast of the island parted into a long bay sheltered by this white bone of rock. The water was limpid and blue, utterly transparent to depths I guessed were near seventy feet. It was like looking into blue crystal, into worlds and times I had yet to know. There were underwater cliffs and canyons here, populated by their own people, a shy people I fancied, wise people who hid in the cool shadows. It struck me odd I now considered fish as people, each with a name, each with a story. In some other life they had been merely things to eat, smelly things to clean and gut. Now they were a part of this intricate world in which I was only one small but important part.

At a likely spot Shadow Song angled the canoe into the rocks. I stepped out, with familiarity now because of our long journey, and held the craft in-shore for him. He beached it, overturned. As always I carried my own goods, as Shadow Song shouldered the remainder.

We set off upon a trail barely noticeable to the average traveler, but plain enough it seemed to Shadow Song. Although the forest cover was dense, neither was it as tall nor lush as the vegetation we'd left behind on the Indian Peninsula. Mostly pines grew here, the needles small as if in a perpetual state of spring, smaller, paler, much of the plant life growing on thinly covered limestone pavement.

Of a sudden we broke into a clearing that had been made a village, although nothing like any village I'd seen so far in Upper Canada. Where square buildings of board might have been were scores of domed structures of bark and poles. Racks were scattered here and there, some hung with fish, some with meat, under these smoking coals. Others had rudely constructed mats on which dried a variety of roots and berries. Children scampered between the fires, shrieking in the way of children, left to their play by women bent over leather skins and fires. Fleetingly, I thought it odd I regarded them as children, as though I were older. For the most part the men were apart from the women, some engaged in occupations from pleasure to necessity, some cleaning guns, some gambling.

Shadow Song offered me no word of explanation as we made our way through the village. I walked close to his side, suddenly wary of these wild-looking creatures. Glances were thrown our way, nods for Shadow Song, stares for me. He stopped when we were on the other side of the village, well away from the last wigwam. I looked up at him, needing some direction and thought better of questioning him at the moment. He seemed preoccupied, his face set into harsh lines and sternness. Still, it intrigued me that no one greeted him openly yet all had shown him some form of deference.

The routine we made for camp fell into place without direction. Despite the fine weather I was instructed to set the wigwam and from that I was able to gather we were going to stay in the village for awhile. As he had shown me, I placed the entrance of our shelter to the east. That done, there were chores to do, lessons to learn, some of which were red, some white, and in that regard this camp was no different from others we'd made. Yet try as I might to keep my attention on the tasks before me I found my gaze forever straying to the stares of the villagers. Still Shadow Song said little and this disturbed me more as the hours passed.

A woman approached after some time, carrying a bowl from which steam rose even in the heat of the day. She was of average height for an Indian, slender, pretty, dressed in blue calico and moccasins, her hair in two braids that framed her face. She gave me only a cursory glance, offered the bowl of tea to Shadow Song. She spoke in Ojibwa. He answered. So it went for a few moments. From the expression on Shadow Song's face I gathered he didn't approve of what she said, and that neither did she approve of something he had done.

When a sufficient pause occurred that I didn't think I'd be rude, I said, "*Waenaesh k'dodaem*," the way Shadow Song had taught me.

The woman's attention turned to me, her brow arching. "*Maheengun.*"

"Wolf," Shadow Song interpreted, shooting her a look. "The same as me. This is my sister, called by us Morning Star."

I gave the woman one of my best smiles, sure it was wasted on her and grateful that Shadow Song had taken the time to tell me, and given me the power of her name. With a toss of her head the woman turned and walked back to her own wigwam, never once glancing back.

"Did I do something wrong?" I ventured after awhile.

He shook his head to indicate I hadn't.

"I don't think she likes me."

"Give it time. You're strange to her, a white girl."

A white girl. It hadn't occurred to me there would be this problem. "Is that what the rest of the village will think?"

"Probably." He considered something a moment and then: "My sister has given me news from the trading post at La Cloche. Apparently they are asking questions regarding the whereabouts of an Indian in the company of a young white girl."

"Us?"

He nodded. "It would seem your uncle is more eager for revenge than I anticipated."

My heart sank. All my hopes of creating a new life, a happier life, were now in jeopardy and I began to think there would never be a place for me. Shadow Song sank to his heels before me, the hawk feathers stirring near his cheek.

"You are here as my apprentice. I've already made that clear to my sister. The rest of the village will accept that." He pursed his lips. "Is that something you would like? To be my apprentice?"

His apprentice. To be a student of his, learning all the mystic ways of the *Midewewin*. I wasn't even sure I knew exactly what that entailed, but from what I'd seen so far I was sure the occupation would suit me. I nodded my acceptance. He smiled and pulled a small clay figure from his pouch, gestured for me to take it. It was a doll made of white clay in the fashion of the Anishnabeg, bundled upon a cradle board. It filled my hand, no larger than that.

"For me?"

He nodded. "Every girl needs a doll, and you are still yet a girl."

I grinned, pleased.

"I made this for you," he said after a moment.

That touched me even more, that he had taken clay, that he had sculpted it, baked it and presented it as a gift to me. This small doll touched me more deeply than any fine porcelain toy could have, and I could think of no way to thank him other than to embrace him, to place my arms around his neck carefully and peck his cheek. He laughed, closing me into his arms tightly and I almost cried for the warmth he afforded, for the comfort.

"What will you do when you need to trade?" I asked, not wishing to leave the security of his arms.

"I will find a way." He held me at arm's length. "As long as you wish you will be safe with me."

"But why do this for me? I'm not even your kin."

He looked over my shoulder, a distant look to his face. "Because I have dreamed this."

He rose, closing any further discussion and indicated for me to bring a basket. We set off into the forest, again without explanation of what we were to do, but by now I was used to this. I followed happily, trying to emulate the way he walked, to be as quiet as possible, no more than a breeze in the trees. At a thicket where he paused were tall plants with mauve flowers that rustled in the wind. He motioned for me to pick a leaf from the plant, which I did, to bruise the leaf, which I did. Aroma rose, sweet like vanilla.

"For fever," he said and then taught me the prayer for this, how to pick it, how to hold it, what to do with it back at the wigwam so that its strength would hold. I listened carefully, absorbing everything he had to teach.

We continued gathering Indian sage and cedar bark for some time when I froze, sure I'd seen a small, hairy figure dart through the shadows, a figure neither human nor animal. I looked to Shadow Song. He remained bent to his task, his mouth pulled up at one corner in a smile. Perhaps the whole thing had been my imagination. Or had it? Why did he smile like that?

I returned to my task, watching my surroundings with increasing interest. Again a figure was there, just at the corner of my eye. I whirled. This time I caught sight of the creature and shrieked from sheer fright. Shadow Song laughed heartily, folding himself into the shade of a cedar.

"What was that?" I demanded.

"The *maymayquayshi*," he said, laughing so hard it annoyed me.

Sure. What was that supposed to mean? – *maymayquayshi*. I kept my attention riveted to him. He pressed his lips together to stop from laughing, screwing up his face into mock seriousness.

"He is *maymayquayshiwok*, one of the *manitous* that live on *Manedoomini*."

It was so easy to accept what he said. "Is he harmful?"

"Like any of the creatures of the earth, he can be harmful or not. If you honour him then there is no harm, just as you must honour all spirits –" he gestured widely, "– trees, rocks, plants, water, animals. All of them can do without us, but we cannot do without them. It is because the *manitous* of Mother Earth honour us with the sacrifice of their lives that we live. Trees, plants, animals, rock, water give us homes and heat and sap to slake our thirst, medicines to cure our ills, bark to receive our mysteries, food for our bellies, clothes for our backs, tools. Everything we are comes from them. They even give us our dreams."

"But do we use *maymayquayshiwok*?" We. I realized I had included myself in the all encompassing we of the Anishnabeg. He acknowledged that 'we' with an appraising look.

"We use nothing. What we do is ask the *manitous* to grant us assistance, and for the *maymayquayshiwok*, yes, sometimes they assist us, but never as food or shelter."

"Then for what?"

From the look on his face I could tell I was in for another lesson. I almost groaned aloud. When he told me the stories of the Anishnabeg I was often left wondering, without any answers and no further ahead than when I began. Once I'd asked him why I didn't understand. He told me that I should think upon this. Only then would I understand; knowledge, after all, didn't come just because you searched for it.

Just as I suspected, he began a story: "Long ago, when *Kitche Manitou* first made the Anishnabeg, we could speak with all you see. The *manitous* knew what we thought; we knew what they thought. They knew we needed meat and so *mahgwah*, bear, offered himself to us that we might live. Others – moose, beaver, otter – also gave of themselves. It was that way with them all. Whatever the Anishnabeg needed, the animals provided, to the point the Anishnabeg did nothing to help themselves. When they wanted fish, they sent otter to catch whitefish. When they wanted drink, sapsucker and woodpecker drilled holes for them. One was set upon the other.

"This could only last for so long before the *manitous* grew outraged that nothing they did for the Anishnabeg gained some appreciation. They held council. Wolverine and his followers wanted the Anishnabeg killed. Bear only wanted punishment for the Anishnabeg. Dog wanted only to give us his loyalty and so, in betrayal of his kind, he came to us and told of their council.

"When wolf found dog and dragged him back to council, the council was angered, beat him and others like him until it seemed all dogs would be killed. Bear, however, said, 'To kill the dogs would serve nothing. The damage has been done. That cannot be healed. Instead, let dog suffer for what he has done. From now on he will serve man, hunger because of his loyalty, hurt because of his loyalty.'

"And it was bear who decided what to do about the Anishnabeg. 'Let us keep our knowledge to ourselves,' he said. 'Let us speak a different language to separate us from the Anishnabeg. We must let them live. *Kitche Manitou* made them, but they will learn to take care of themselves. We have taken care of them for too long.'

"Now we can only give them our honour in prayer because we cannot speak with them directly. They hear us, but they will not answer. We take no young. Only males. We take no mates. Only that which won't interfere with the cycle of life. We waste no bones of game. We don't desecrate the water with the bones of fish. All things are Our Elder Brothers. And in return for our appreciation, they give us all we need to survive, and they give us the dreams by which we live."

"But what about the fur traders?" I asked, wondering how that huge harvest that was reaped every year fit into this sacred order he preached.

"I didn't say all Anishnabeg followed this way."

"And you're saying it's all right to dream." This I asked carefully, wanting him to assure me again that what happened to me was something normal, natural, that it had nothing to do with the priests' evil world and that I was not damned for all of eternity.

"Without dreams we are blind," he said. "You must dream."

"And if those dreams come true?"

"Then that is good."

"I don't understand!" I wailed. "Why is it good for the Anishnabeg to dream and sinful for whites to dream?"

He smiled. "Because the white world does not live in balance."

"Do I?"

"Is your spirit white?"

He always did this to me – turn my questions on myself. As always I tumbled through the question until I could come up with something. I thought about the way he and his people accepted body and soul and spirit were different things that lived in balance like sun and moon, rock and water, good and evil. My body was white. But what of my spirit? Was it possible for my spirit to be red?

"I don't think so," I answered. "I don't think my spirit is white. I'm not like other people."

"You're more like us."

I nodded.

"Why?" he asked.

"Because I dream and those dreams come true. Because I hear the life of grandmother cedar under whom you sit, feel the things other people think, know when danger will come."

"Just as you knew in your heart I'd do you no harm when I first met you by the river."

I nodded, remembering that meeting, how like a god he'd been to me and how like a teacher he was now. "But what do I do about those dreams? What are they for?"

"They are for guidance. Wolf, lynx, bear, moose, sometimes *maymayquayshiwok* – they visit you in your dreams. Every child goes seeking dreams. With us, when a boy is about to become a man, he leaves his village and fasts in isolation, sometimes four, maybe five days. He goes seeking an important dream, something beyond what he has learned as a child. When the dream comes, the *manitou* who visits him becomes his grandfather, his guardian, and by this dream the boy will live.

"For girls, when the time comes for them to bleed as a woman, they isolate themselves in a wigwam away from the village, fasting, remembering they are made in the image of Sky Woman who made the land after the flood. This is a powerful time for girls. After this they can do what no man can do. They create. They lie down barren in darkness and rise fruitful in light. At any time they may seek a dream.

"But there are also many other dreams we seek, all through our lives."

"But how do you seek a dream?" Mine had always just come upon me, seized me in the middle of night, of chores, of everyday life.

"By purifying yourself. You cannot seek a dream unless your body is free of food, your mind free of others. This is the only way."

"And you've done this?"

He nodded. "The first time when I was very young, only crawling around my mother's skirts, although it wasn't a dream I sought. Many times since then I have fasted, seeking a dream and found one." He rose, tall and powerful over me. "You are honoured, *wahboosoons*. Not many Anishnabeg are privileged to see the *maymayquayshiwok*." He turned as if to guide me back to camp. I touched his arm. He paused, glancing over his shoulder at me, his face haloed in sunlight.

"Could I stay here awhile? I'll be fine – really."

"You remember your way back?"

I nodded. He hesitated and so I said, "To the east of the tree struck by lightning, down the hill and along the river to the north."

He traced the part of my hair with his fingers, that odd smile on his lips. The only answer he gave me was to turn and leave. Somehow I felt this was what he had planned all along, that I'd followed his clues to exactly this point in my life. Now that I'd followed, I wondered what lay ahead.

Chapter 12

After Shadow Song left I wandered a little way through the forest, noting any unusual landmarks that would guide my way back. Eventually I came upon a bald spot, a section of the grey limestone that was completely bare and exposed to the sun while on three sides was vegetation and on the fourth the clear blue waters of this island.

The strangeness of this place tugged at me. I sat, for awhile watching terns dive and play. This soon lost my interest for I was greatly preoccupied with the things Shadow Song had taught me during the days of our journey, wanting, more than anything, to find a dream of my own.

This was ridiculous. Even sitting here alone I felt ridiculous. What made me think the *manitous* would honour me? I was white, a child of a society that tabooed the pursuit of dreams. It was evil, heinous. Those less pious would have called it lunacy.

Hadn't I always had dreams? Hadn't there always been those unbidden moments when the present reality would tilt, fold and open onto another dimension? Didn't my dreams always come true? Didn't that legitimize what I was about to do?

And I wanted a dream, a purpose, a calling. I longed for something with which I could mould my life into more than happenstance and flight. It was time to leave England, Papa and Maman behind. Not to forget. No. Never to forget. But to go on.

Resolved now, I set about gathering dead-fall and making a fire as Shadow Song had shown me, using the fire bow I'd made under his direction and kept in a pouch he'd helped me sew. This took some time. I was not adept, but with care and patience I eventually created enough heat that the birch bark caught and from there the needles I'd used for the heart of my fire. Carefully I fed in twigs, then larger and larger ones until I was able to add the branches I'd gathered. Once it was well and truly blazing, I scrounged the surrounding woods for more deadfall and dragged it back to my makeshift camp.

Next I seared the end of a stick until it was charred enough to scribe with, chanting as Shadow Song had taught me so that I might offer my song to the *manitous*. With the stick I marked the limestone with a circle of black, and parallel lines running perpendicular from the circle to the cardinal points. His lessons echoed through my head as if he were speaking just behind me, the memory of his voice like a gentle breeze. All he'd shown me now seemed so important.

This done, I stepped into the circle, sat cross-legged before the fire and toward the water and emptied the contents of my pouch. They were my personal charms, items special to me alone – a heron's feather, a crude pipe Shadow Song had helped me fashion out of oak, sweet grass, the tea tin that now held a few grains of dried corn and made a rattle, the empty bottle of lavender water, and my doll. All the time I removed them I chanted, arraying them in a semi-circle around me. For me, in the real world, these items were what I represented.

I was still chanting when *keezis* set and painted the sky, still chanting when all that was left of his warmth was a wash of purple. Stars sparkled above, distant cousins of the Anishnabeg. By now my throat was tight from chanting, my head spinning from heat and thirst. These privations were not new to me, and this time they had a purpose and so I continued on my course as night fell completely and the air cooled.

After awhile I lost track of time, of the biting insects, even of my swaying, even of my chanting and felt myself merge with the fire, the sky, the rock so that I was them and they were me. The snake appeared before I realized what happened, coiled like a length of thick golden rope near the last of my pink coals. It didn't occur to me this was unusual for a snake to travel in the cool of the night. I only chanted and observed it. The snake was diamonded with brown patches, its rattle shivering softly in warning. I heeded the warning and moved no closer, only remained swaying and chanting, now offering my song to the snake. I was not afraid. It moved, winding into the coals, its beautiful skin puckering, crackling, searing away until it lay rod-straight in the embers. All of its flesh sloughed away. A brood of other snakes all tiny and bone white slithered out of its body and in the heat of the coals also stiffened, like a bouquet of arrows. I watched fascinated, knowing the meaning of this would reveal itself soon enough.

When dawn broke there was nothing left of my visitor. Once more I sang, roughly but joyously, lit my crude pipe and offered the smoke to *keezis* who just now showed half his face above the water, to Mother Earth who had watched over me during my night of wonder, to *Waubun* in the east, to *Ningobianong* in the west, to *Bebon* in the north and to *Zeegwun* in the south.

That done, I gathered my possessions and made my way back through the forest to Shadow Song, feeling as though this was a new day in a new life. I heard the pulse of the lives around me, of grandmother cedar, of the soul of the rock, of the breeze sent from *Waubun*. Even the stiffness of my body, my hunger, the waves of exhaustion were all sharp and new, as if I'd not realized at all the importance of these things before. My senses sang to these experiences. I felt clean. Burned clean and fresh as the little snakes had been. A lesson and a weapon.

It was this new knowledge that caused me to cry out when I came upon Shadow Song's wigwam. He had his knife poised to stab a snake for our meal – a golden snake marked with brown. My cry arrested the motion of his hand, brought his attention up to me. He looked at me carefully, intelligence on his face and then question.

I shook my head, smiling. "Let *medawaewae* go today. I will make us bannock and berries."

Shadow Song smiled. He sheathed his knife, the snake slithering back to the undergrowth, and he watched me with a new understanding on his face.

Part 2
Makinauk

Chapter 13

I had fasted and prayed all night. Still no dream would come. I longed for a dream. Needed a dream. For three years I'd been preparing myself for these times of dream-questing. It was a time to be tested by the *manitous*. Days later I would emerge with a keen awareness, a sharper sense of purpose.

I knew how to approach the *manitous*. One did not do so lightly. They were capricious, both benevolent and malevolent for that was the way of things. I knew how to draw the circle for the sun, how to create an image around me of life and time in both the linear and cyclic patterns. To do so was to place myself in the eye of events. I knew how to offer tobacco to *Kitche Manitou*, to Mother Earth and the spirits of the four points.

Yet now, rather than drowning in that place I had avoided all those years ago, I swam, willingly, knowingly, no longer fearing what drama would play out before me. This was a gift. It was what had brought me to Shadow Song.

This time, however, no drama would unfold. I felt bereft, abandoned. Now had come this terrible pain that throbbed in my lower back, blood between my legs and soreness in my small, growing breasts. I wondered if I'd been cursed, if I'd in some way offended this rich world of power.

Once more I drew upon my pipe, offering the smoke to spirits that remained just out of my reach. The smoke hung in the cool, damp air, like a blue cloud amid the pinkness of the dawn. Already I could hear the drip, drip, drip of the thaw. Today would be warm. The snow would scatter like kernels beneath my feet, soaking my deerskin boots. Chipmunks would be seen scrambling, chickadees chirping in a way they did only when spring was imminent. Life would awaken around me but I would remain barren of a dream, dying I was sure.

Trembling, I knocked out my pipe, collected my gear with as much care as if I'd had a revelation and turned my way back through the forest to where Shadow Song and I had made one of our winter camps. The going was difficult for I was weak from three days fasting. This disease that afflicted me in no way helped. Several times I paused to rest, consumed with pain so troublesome I felt as if I might vomit. Finally I came to a tree that had split from rot, my signpost, headed south down the slope and into a small declivity in the steep hills we'd hunted throughout the winter.

Despite my ailment, I must have managed to approach with a degree of stealth for when camp came into view I saw Shadow Song sitting cross-legged before the fire, a wolf fur under him. His back was to our sleeping wigwam, his face intent with thought as he stared into the coals. I wondered if I'd interrupted a dream of his own but realized in a moment this was not so for he was wrapped in his cloak, also of wolf, something he would not have done were he chasing a dream.

Pain throbbed through my back once more and I longed for some heat, thought of summer and the village to which we'd return on Manitoulin. I shifted my weight as I stood there, hesitating, watching him watch the fire. There was no comfortable way to stand. I could feel blood trickle between my legs, soaking the bandage I'd stuck there.

It occurred to me whatever afflicted me might afflict him and so I resolved to come no closer, to wait until he saw me and spoke; one did not interrupt the thoughts of a powerful shaman. As I thought this his attention turned up to me, quickly, as if he'd heard my thoughts. I watched pleasure cross his features, bright as sunlight on the floodwater, watched his pleasure dim and become concern when he studied me.

These years together I'd come to realize he cared very deeply for me. I could not think of him as a father, for he was not fatherly. Nor could I think of him as a brother, for he certainly was not brotherly. All I knew was that he did care, that he watched over me, taught me, guided me as no one ever had and for his love and his protection I was grateful. He had helped me to make a new life out of the ruin that had been my other. There had been peace. There had been contentment. There had even been joy.

"What is it?" he asked, in Ojibwa as we spoke most often.

"I'm dying." I could think of no easy way of stating it. Better just to have said it as I did, to place the horror of the thing before us. I watched emotion cross his face, the way his sienna eyes glittered – pain, loss, apprehension.

"How do you know?" he asked.

"I bleed."

Once more he appraised me, his gaze passing over my doeskin tunic, skirt, leggings down to my boots. "Have you cut yourself?"

I shook my head, hardly able to stand the pain, feeling it wash over me in waves.

To my surprise he smiled, faintly, that odd pull at one side of his mouth. He nodded, rose stiffly as if he'd sat there all night waiting for me, his gaze now averted although he seemed suddenly of very good humour. Something was immensely pleasing to him.

"Do you find it so amusing that I die?" I accused. Oh, if only the pain in my back would subside then I could catch my breath, feel my senses settle.

"You do not die." He disappeared into the wigwam, re-emerged hefting his axe. Still he would not look upon me. He only chanted to the trees, his hands running over different saplings until he found one that was pliant to his call and then chopped.

"What are you doing?" I demanded, hurt that he showed so little concern for my difficulties. How dare he set about felling trees when I stood here before him, bleeding my life away between my legs. Had all these years together meant so little to him? Had I been so wrong?

"I'm building you a lodge," he replied, throwing one sapling to the ground and searching for another.

I felt as though he'd taken the ground out from beneath my feet, that I was falling into a hole I thought I'd escaped. Building me a lodge? Away from him? Exiled? I reasoned that he knew what afflicted me and endeavoured to keep himself free of contamination while still caring for me. Surely that was it. Trembling, I managed to ask him, quietly, afraid to hear the answer, "Have I dishonoured you?"

He laughed. There was such joy in his laughter and he continued his chopping, keeping his gaze from me. "What did Grandmother teach you when we were in the summer village last year?"

I flushed. These things were not for men to hear! "Woman things."

"And I am building a lodge for a new woman."

Foolishness replaced my sense of loss. How could I have been so stupid? A lodge for a woman. A menses lodge. This was what he was building me. "Oh," was all I managed to say.

"Oh, indeed," he laughed, paused to chant once more, chopped and laughed again.

"I'll need my things."

"Haven't I always taken care of you, *wahboos*?"

A gentle reprimand that. Perhaps he had known what I thought all along. I realized he called me *wahboos*. Rabbit. Not *wahboosoons*, little rabbit. "Yes."

"Then nothing has changed except that you are growing."

Things were always this way with him. Simple. Always so blessedly simple. I un-shouldered my pack and dumped it where I stood, joined him in his task although I was careful not to touch him, not to look upon him lest I burn his soul with the power of my womanhood. Already I had risked a great deal when I first entered the camp. Grandmother had warned me of this time, explained this was when both life and death coursed through a woman's body, death in the shedding of a life undeveloped, life in the beginning of another cycle and another hope of life. I could even see the old woman's eyes as I worked, dark under folds of aged skin, sparkling with more wisdom than I felt I could know. Every summer I'd learned from the old woman, the mother of the man who had rescued me from Uncle Edgar. Under her guidance I'd learned how to scrape leather to soften it for the body, how to fashion moccasins – a never ending chore – how to sew leggings. All the arts of drying food had been mine to learn, the care of children. In a few weeks I would see her again when we joined her and Shadow Song's sister's family for the making of sugar. I knew Grandmother would see me in a new light. There would be no need for words.

In a few hours we had the wigwam built and I retired into it happily enough, knowing that for my days of flow I must fast and purify my body. I sang despite the pain, searching again for the dream that had not come during my earlier quest. This time many came to me. One vision, more than the others, touched me deeply.

It seemed as if I were fishing, hanging out over the bow of the canoe, a torch in one hand, a spear in the other. I knew stars were winking above me in a great arc. Below me there were many fish, glinting in the torch-light as they swam near in curiosity. Gray and green, white and silver, they watched me. I took none of them although they all offered me sustenance. What I craved was more, something none of them could satisfy.

Numae the sturgeon swam beneath my pool of light, long, grey, like some ancient warrior plated for battle. I was late in striking although *Numae* moved slowly, gracefully beneath the canoe. He was enormous, his body seeming to go on forever as I shifted from one side to the other to take another aim. The canoe dipped dangerously near the water as I moved. It would have been wise council to have fished with a partner. I hadn't been wise. This thing I'd craved pushed me beyond prudence.

The canoe bobbed, my weight pushing the gunwales beneath the water. As I fell I saw *Numae* drift like a shadow in the last of my torch light. Water filled my lungs. I tried to swim and found I couldn't. Yet I didn't die. I breathed. *Numae* brushed my arm, urging me to hold tight, which I did, and together we swam westward. I still held my spear. Now the weapon softened, writhed, slipped into the form of *Medawaewae* the rattlesnake. I thought of the vision I'd had on Manitoulin all those years ago and realized my guide had come to aid me.

At that moment we came upon *Ningobianong*, the spirit of the west. Withered he was, white hair like a cloud round his head.

"What do you know?" he asked me.

I wondered at that. What did I know? I knew of sorrow from the deaths of people I loved. I knew of evil at the hand of my Uncle. I knew also of friendship, of trust, of skills that might keep me alive should I be on my own. What were these compared to what *Ningobianong* the mighty shaman knew? Nothing.

"I know nothing, Grandfather."

His white eyes were compelling as he stared at me. "Are you strong?"

For my age I was strong, but compared to bear I was nothing. And my will? Could I sacrifice beyond my means?

"I am weak and trembling, Grandfather."

He smiled then. I felt as though I looked into the face of wisdom. His claw-like fingers touched *Medawaewae*. The snake became a white arrow. Then he touched *Numae*. The sturgeon became fire under my fingers and somehow I was not burned.

"Sometimes wisdom is best given to those who have suffered a lifetime," he said, "and fulfillment to those who no longer will live. When you understand these things, I will wait for you in the Land of the Souls."

They were gone – *Numae, Medawaewae, Ningobianong.*

Slowly, infinitely slowly, my gaze refocused to the pink coals of the fire in my lodge. Detached, as if I floated somewhere else and not in my body, I reached for the fire, dipped my hand into the coals, lifted one of the glowing lumps into my palm. It did not burn. I knew it wouldn't. I knew also the moment I stopped believing it wouldn't burn, my flesh would char and blacken. With a prayer of thanksgiving I set the coal back with its brothers. I smoked my pipe.

When I emerged into the warming air of the thaw it seemed to me I could hear sap running in the trees, feel the shoots bursting in the ground. Restlessness. I inhaled, deeply, savouring the taste of the air. Such life around me!

I walked to the river, listening, charged, stripped when I came upon it and stepped into its bone-numbing depths, breaking the thin ice as I did so. Shivering, I sang for the joy of the cold, pleased my body quivered so, that my nipples had hardened so tightly that my breasts ached and my breath came in gasps.

Purified, and no longer in the flow of blood, I returned to Shadow Song with my gear, humming. It occurred to me my life was one of contentment with Shadow Song, that the life I'd known with Uncle seemed unreal, distant, a nightmare I'd had before waking. The shadow of his presence had never seemed real enough despite the fact every spring we'd been warned away from the trading post at La Cloche, and every summer the other villagers had told us of inquiries that had been made not only for the two of us but for the children who had gone missing that day back in 1832. Of the two boys I'd heard news, some good, some not. Oliver Vanmear it was said would forever remain touched by the *manitous*, a disturbed fellow who would be treated with respect by the Anishnabeg. Even Shadow Song agreed on that point. Lewis Horning Jr. adapted well, now a fine hunter with a tribe near Red Lake. Neither of them would be able to return to the white world until Edgar Fleming was no longer a problem. Should they, it was a foregone conclusion he would kill them the way he had killed Susan and Jane Vanmear.

I would not think of these things now. Now was a time for contentment and I would relish it for as long as allowed.

We had made our camp among pines and fir, sheltered in a small valley amid the hills of the La Cloche Mountains. It was a good place from which Shadow Song was able to hunt, the game abundant and traces of white intrusion scarce but for the fur posts at La Cloche and much farther west at the mouth of the Mississagi River. Shadow Song was out hunting at the moment, I knew. His message was in the axe he'd left propped against the wigwam.

This suited me well enough. Stowing my gear, I eventually set to preparing a hide of leather for him. It would be part of a new tunic, I decided, a special tunic as a fee for my first initiation into the *Midewewin*. For the most part it was pleasant work, scraping the leather so it would be soft, feeling it pliant on the stretching frame. Periodically I would rise from my work to tend the fire, a refreshing change to have it out of doors in the warm sunshine. I hummed, chasing the twitters of the chickadees, wondering if Shadow Song would be gone long, if I would be alone tonight as often I was when he had gone to the hunt.

Toward sunset, as I stirred a stew of rabbit he'd left for me, I heard *Kaikaik* the hawk cry. It was early to hear the hawk, and that portended two things: that spring would soon be upon us, and that Shadow Song was near. Hastily, I packed away my work, hid it in my bundle of goods and pulled out a pair of moccasins to finish near the fire.

He trudged into camp shortly afterward, pulling a sled strapped with moose meat. The remainder was likely tied up a tree somewhere, safe from scavengers and unlikely to spoil in the cold. The fringe across his arms and chest was dripping from melted snow, his cloak of fur thrown across one shoulder. That long rifle he prided poked out from behind his shoulder, the powder horn at his hip.

He watched me as he arrived, saying nothing. Only his eyes spoke, crinkling at the edges in approval. With a grunt he dropped the sled and I rose to assist him with the preparation of the meat. Most we hoisted into various trees at some distance from the camp, keeping only one cut which I spitted and roasted over the fire. Tomorrow I would build smoking racks and begin the long, tedious process of drying the meat for preservation and easy transportation.

The head was in this load. While Shadow Song looked to the antlers, I sliced away the bell, adorned it with sweet grass and ribbons and hung it from a tree so that the spirit of the moose would find another.

That night we laughed a great deal, stuffing ourselves till we ached and were glad that the *windigo* had not found us in our little lodge. At length I curled myself under furs and watched the fire burn like autumn leaves. I knew Shadow Song studied me. It was something he seemed to take pleasure in – to watch me fall asleep. In truth, it was something I, also, took pleasure in, to know someone watched over my sleep.

"We will travel soon," he said after a moment. "The sap will be running soon."

I smiled and looked up at him sleepily, feeling drugged with this bounty. "I know. I heard it this morning."

His only reply was to laugh.

The following day I built drying racks while Shadow Song hauled meat into the camp. Together we carved it, laying it over the rungs so that smoke would rise and wither the flesh. It took us near to a week to prepare the entire moose, but when it was done we were assured a plentiful supply of food for the remainder of the season.

When finally we had packed our goods, we broke camp and set off to find Morning Star and Lightfoot, her husband. The season of the sap was one of my favourites, a time of hard work rewarded with sweet treats and the beginning of the congregation of families. At least, it was for those who hadn't been relegated to reserves. For this reason Shadow Song and I remained on the north shore of Lake Huron during the winter, returning to Manitoulin and the village of Manitowaning every summer, thereby escaping confinement and the scrutiny of whites.

It took five days of travel to reach the maple stand where Morning Star camped. Grandmother was there, as were Morning Star's children, Deer-Coming-Down, and the youngest boy and girl who had not yet earned their adult names.

Greetings, as always, were tacit. It was simply the way of the Anishnabeg. We erected our wigwam, stowing our goods there, and brought our furs into the larger wigwam of the family, as it was our custom to share one lodge for the season. There was safety in numbers, there was warmth, although there was little privacy, a factor that was to rankle me soon enough.

I set to work quickly, pressing into service every available pot while the children foraged for wood. Morning Star, Lightfoot and Shadow Song hauled sap. The fire trench I built was long, rectangular, to allow for easy access from either side of the row of pots. Grandmother was made comfortable on furs near the fire. Often she would both entertain and instruct me with the stories she told and I honoured her by making sure she was warm, that she had a hot drink. At night Morning Star and I banked the fire to be sure the pots stayed hot, and we slept in shifts.

The second day I told Grandmother of the news of my womanhood. That evening she arranged a separate feast that involved only we three women. It was over the glow of the fire that Grandmother said, "You left us a girl. You return a woman. We sorrowed when you departed, leaving behind a girlhood we had grown to love. We rejoice at your return, new and different. Through you, will the people live and live on."

The old woman bent to me then and enclosed me in her arms, like wings round a fledgling. Morning Star did likewise and the ceremony ended.

All through those following days I worked happily at my post, stirring, stirring, constantly stirring the sweet, clear brew that would give us syrup and sugar. I knew the older women passed me glances. This disturbed a little, for there was something more to their attention than idle curiosity. When Lightfoot watched me intently, I wondered briefly if there was some problem. None seemed to surface and so I ignored their scrutiny. I was a new woman. I was safe. I was happy.

This contentment, however, was not to last. That day we had decanted sap into fewer pots, the liquid having boiled down considerably. One pot had been too heavy for me to lift and Lightfoot, nearby, came to my rescue. His touch had been lingering, his attention intense so that I felt uncomfortable. He did nothing overt, nothing to raise an alarm, yet I was very much in a state of alarm. I kept my peace.

When night fell we, as always, huddled into the one lodge, a fire in the center. I lay across the fire from Shadow Song, to the right of where Lightfoot and Morning Star slept and left of the children and Grandmother. A moan woke me. It was a sound with which I'd become familiar over the years, and as always, I shuttered my lids to spy on the activity I knew was taking place.

Lightfoot was propped on one elbow over Morning Star, the furs dislodged. He was unlacing her tunic, his actions urgent. In a moment he had exposed one breast, red-gold in the embers of the fire, the nipple dark as walnut. He closed his hand over her breast, pinching the nipple and again she moaned. Now he leaned into her, his tongue flicking over the nipple while his hand travelled down beneath her skirt. She parted her thighs eagerly, rocking her hips to his ministrations. In a moment he had flipped her onto her knees, shoving her skirt back from her buttocks. With one hand he pulled away his loincloth, revealing the dark rod of his manhood and then plunged deeply into her. It wasn't long before their movement was sweaty, thighs slapping wetly together. Although I had watched them couple many times in the sugar camps, I had never before felt this pulsing between my legs, the swelling of my breasts. I closed my eyes when Lightfoot grunted and shoved one last time into her, feeling my heart race, my body tremble. When I looked again I saw Shadow Song watching me, an emotion on his face I'd never seen before. Power, yes, but power I did not recognize and this frightened me. Confused, I turned in my furs and faced the wall of the wigwam. I could hear Lightfoot and Morning Star snuggling down.

I was up before dawn, stoking the fires under the sap pots before anyone else stirred. When the remainder stumbled into the morning, I worked diligently, avoiding eye contact with any of the adults. Shadow Song sat near the fire briefly, cleaning his gun. It wasn't long before he moved, although I knew he watched me throughout the day.

That evening I retired early. The others lingered over the sugar fire rather than take the shelter of the wigwam. Their voices rose and fell, my name rising often. Curious, I listened a little more carefully.

"It's not seemly," Morning Star said. She had said that quite a few times before I realized the conversation revolved around me. I stirred in my furs.

"Why not?" Shadow Song said. I could hear the underscore in his voice, like distant thunder.

"Because you're a man," Lightfoot answered.

I crawled to the edge of the wigwam, lifted the birch bark carefully so they would neither hear nor see me. All four of them sat hunkered round the fire, their faces golden in the glow, Deer-Coming-Down returning from a forage for firewood. He dumped his load with a clatter and sat cross-legged with them. Behind me I could hear the children stir, settle. Shadow Song had his back to me. I could tell by the rigid set of his shoulders that he resented their interference.

"I have never denied that I am a man," he said.

"And what do you think people will say when we go to the summer village?" Morning Star asked. "Now that she's a woman."

"I know what they'll say," her husband furnished, "that our *midewenini* has raised himself a woman."

"I would advise you to take that back."

"She should stay with us now," Morning Star interjected.

"Yes, she should stay with us," Lightfoot said, his eagerness not quite concealed.

Stay with them? I felt cold.

"She has had enough of being handed from person to person," Shadow Song said. "She stays with me."

"And what of your reputation?" Lightfoot asked.

"I am pure of heart. Nothing changes."

"It will when people stop coming to you."

Silence for a moment, so intense I could hear the hiss of the fire, Grandmother's laboured breath.

"What makes things any different if she stays with you?" Shadow Song said finally. "Nothing. She would still live with a man who isn't her kin."

"She'd be safe with me," Lightfoot growled.

Anger then. It radiated round Shadow Song. "She's been safe for three years."

Grandmother spoke then for the first time, her cracked voice carrying across the fire. "Then, my son, perhaps it is time for you to wife."

"I have had a wife."

Such sorrow in his voice. It was thing of which he wouldn't speak, and of which I chose not to question him. I knew only a little about his wife from what Paul Rogette had said and from the things I had gleaned from him – a girl from near Cranberry Lake who had died. How could they wound him like this?

"You are yet young, my son. Wise, yes, but not so wise as your elders although you have accomplished much. A wife would solve many of your problems."

He rose then, stiffly. I could tell he was wounded, shamed, affronted. "I will consider it," and he turned for the wigwam.

A look passed between Morning Star and Lightfoot. I didn't like it. I slid the bark home quickly and scrambled back to my place, feigning sleep when he ducked in. Tonight, for some reason, he did not undress. He slid into his furs, lying on his side, his earth-brown eyes turned in my direction. I would not deceive him and faced him.

"I'm not asleep."

"I can see that."

There was little I had ever been able to hide from him. Nothing about his face softened. I didn't know how to react to this. It only now occurred to me I complicated his life, forced him into restrictions I had no right to impose.

"Shall I leave?" I asked.

He closed his eyes. Was it hurt? Resignation? "Is this something you choose?"

"No." He was the only life I had. What would I do without him?

"Then you shall stay," he said and rolled away.

It was not to be that simple. This I knew. In this one matter his easy way of dealing with life would not hold. I wondered what would become of us then? For now I would accept this. There was nothing else for me to do.

Chapter 14

All year long I'd been gathering gifts for the *Midewewin*. It was my most earnest wish that I would be allowed to take the test, that I would be deemed worthy enough to pass and step into the mysteries I'd until now only been skirting. Shadow Song was an excellent teacher, but, bound by the traditions of the society, he could not give me insight into the deeper mysteries. The only way to begin this process was to offer gifts to the *midewenini*. This was not an easy thing, for the gifts had to be considerable and I was a young woman without much in the way of means. Further, I lived with the *midewenini* I wished to study further under and so for me to keep my hoard a secret proved a test of its own. At long last I had gathered enough that I felt confident my offerings would not be scorned. If I was refused the test it was because of judgment of my character, not my gifts.

Now, standing there in the grey morning of the summer village, a year after having become a woman, I was unsure of myself. I had seen the kinds of things those older and of better means had presented previous summers to Shadow Song and the other lesser *midewenini*. Perhaps I was too young. Perhaps Shadow Song might not accept my gifts. Perhaps I would simply be found unworthy of the rite.

I looked to where Shadow Song fletched a set of arrows he'd made. While he used the rifle, he often hunted with the bow, powder and shot requiring expensive and potentially dangerous trade at La Cloche. If he couldn't find someone trustworthy to transact the trade for him, he would do without. It was because of me he avoided the trading posts. The inquiries there had changed from merely locating us to bringing us both in to answer for crimes we had not committed. Uncle Edgar, after all these years, kept to the trail, never letting us go.

I swallowed a breath, smoothed my best dress of doeskin and lifted a wooden cup filled with strawberry tea, Shadow Song's favorite. With care I approached him, for he bent intently over his work. Village children squealed nearby, diving past me like a flock of birds and then disappeared among the wigwams. Smoke hung heavily in the clearing, caught by fog that came in off

Shadow Song

the bay and cloaked everything in sight. Once I glanced up at the tall white pine that swept the grey air of our encampment, took courage from its solitary beauty.

Shadow Song looked up not at all when I approached with the fragrant tea. I set it upon the edge of a rock near him. For a moment I watched his intent face, the way his eyes narrowed as he looked at the shaft in his hand, the fragile feather. A frown caught his brow, puckering the scar there. That odd feeling I'd had recently again throbbed through me. Not now, I thought. I didn't want tension to destroy our easy way together.

"I come seeking your consent, *Kekinoamaged*." *Kekinoamaged*. Teacher. That brought his attention to me, his sienna eyes sharp with interest. I swallowed another breath. "Would you do me the honour of sharing my food this evening?"

His brow arched. "It's my food we usually share."

Heat rose to my cheeks. My gaze dropped. If he continued to look at me that way I was sure I'd lose my nerve, tremble like a child. "I've been hunting. A new lodge has been prepared – "

He caught my chin in his thumb and forefinger, his face hard, the way it would be when he taught me something vital. Another emotion flickered there a moment, a thing that had brooded in him ever since Morning Star discussed my future a year ago. It was just a pulse of motion, but I felt his hand tremble, freeze. Calmness again returned to him.

"Are you sure of what you seek, *wahboos*?"

"I am sure."

"You know the life I lead."

Indeed I did. There was such austerity to much of his life. When other men gambled in the summer village, indulged in raids on settler camps, or took to whiskey, Shadow Song held himself apart and beyond these things. Even when the single men found willing girls to rut with, Shadow Song refrained, although I knew he did make careful liaisons, that he would remain out at night periodically and return smelling of sweat and sex. He was only a man, as he'd said, but he was a careful man. His laughter was restricted to the humorous stories of Nanabush, or to the little everyday occurrences that were absurd. When others were profligate in the hunt, he stalked in the old way, chanting the rites. Through all of it the village people held him aloft, a holy man whom they both revered and feared. Even children were careful not to laugh too near him lest they make him think their laughter was at his expense. It wasn't wise to annoy the village shaman.

I looked down at my feet, unable to face him. "It is because of the life you lead, *Kekinoamaged*, that I ask." I had found surety in his lifestyle. I had found comfort. His was an ordered world and I wished to always have that order guide me.

I knew he watched me closely. His fingers left my chin, traced the lids of my eyes and the lashes, my lips. I felt him still, harden. His hand fell away.

"No," he said hoarsely and centered his attention once more upon the fletching.

My mouth dropped open, my hurt plain for him to see if he would. "But...." I let my protest die. The *midewenini* had spoken. His word was not to be challenged.

Shame heated my face, tears hot upon my cheeks. Didn't he know how hard I'd worked? I hastily lowered my face from his scrutiny and turned on heel, striding for the wigwam I had built in the early morning.

Throughout the day I continued just as if he'd accepted my invitation. By noon the fog had burned off. Heat mounted until black flies carpeted the air. I stripped off my long tunic and worked only in a laced vest and skirt, my limbs smeared in fleabane, my hair plaited in braids with blue ribbons.

I was oblivious of the activities of the village. All my being centered on claiming this one place for my own, of controlling my emotions so that I would not shame myself before my peers. I was sweeping my wigwam with fir boughs when Morning Star stopped by. Ducking, I emerged from my task. She looked smug, clearly feeling triumphant.

"Building yourself a wigwam?" she asked.

I gathered the basket of cedar chips and fir boughs I'd collected and stepped back into the wigwam, scattering them about the edges to keep the place sweet.

"About time," I could hear Morning Star say. "I'd not live with a man who's in love with a ghost."

Again I emerged, straightened, feeling my jaw clench. "This is none of your concern."

Morning Star laughed. "But it is. Being the nearest elder female, I'm responsible for you."

"I'm responsible for myself." I left her and took the few steps to my fire where a beaver carcass awaited preparation.

Morning Star, however, wouldn't be shaken. She followed and hunkered near. "He found his wife at Cranberry Lake one year, you know – "

"I've heard the story, thank you." Paul Rogette's voice returned to my memory, an almost forgotten voice from some other life, telling me a tale of mystery about a man who had reached through the forest and killed an entire family because he had been dishonoured.

"Did you know he asked for her as payment for curing her father?" Morning Star asked, not expecting an answer.

"And she went willingly enough."

"You would too if your family were killed off."

"It seems to me the shaman's sister knows little of respect." That one cut. I felt Morning Star's anger rise.

"Why don't you ask him?" she prodded.

I looked up from my bloody work. "I don't need to."

"Oh, don't you? Then maybe you should ask him how she died."

I returned my attention to the beaver, unwilling to let Morning Star see how that last barb struck. It had been a question I'd longed to ask Shadow Song, but never had. Just to see the old wound in him open was enough to seal my curiosity. I'd not hurt him.

"Or don't you want to know that he left her camping near a Bay trading post while he went off searching for plants, that while he left her without protection the men of the post raped her, that she ran naked through the woods screaming for Shadow Song and died before he found her? That's the kind of protection he can give you."

I stopped now, seething with anger. All I knew was that I wanted Morning Star's smug look to disappear. I hit her across the face with the back of my hand. Morning Star reeled. I hoped she saw stars. "Get out!" I snarled. "You are unworthy to share his totem – you who attend the white man's church, wear white man's clothes, use white man's things. Get out!"

She massaged her cheek with her fingers. "Look who speaks? The white girl trying to be red," and turned to where a flock of women had gathered. I had mishandled the situation. Brought shame upon us all. Morning Star was received into the embrace of the women. Trembling, I gave them all my back, bent again to the beaver and continued to prepare a feast for a shaman who would never attend.

By evening I had roasted strips of beaver meat and prepared the tail, had blackberries to please the palate. Whitefish had been added to this. There was an assortment of greens, lily roots and wild onion, tea made from strawberry leaves. These were arrayed in the wigwam with the gifts I had collected – a blanket of rabbit fur made from rabbits I'd trapped throughout the winter, a new shirt beaded with *Makinauk* the turtle, *Kaikaik* the hawk and the circles representing *Kitche Manitou* and the sun. A pair of moccasins was included, squeezed out of the deer hide I'd used for the shirt. There was also a pouch of dried, powdered rhizomes from the red trillium, a powerful medicine against internal bleeding and heart troubles, also hoarhound plantain for snakebite. And, as always, sweet grass. The gifts were few. They were all I had. They contained my heart.

As I looked at this array, I chastised myself for ever thinking he would come. His response had been a firm denial. Knowing this I'd even gone to the trouble of preparing his own meal as usual, except I wouldn't be there to serve him. This feast before me was surplus, a foolish waste of food, time and emotion. So I sat there upon the furs, empty and desolate, indulging the tears I had staved off all day.

Spring peepers were calling when Shadow Song ducked into the wigwam. I felt my heart flutter with wild hope, watched him carefully for signs. There was nothing to read on his face. I felt my lower lip tremble like a child's. He was closed to me.

"I have brought four others," he said roughly.

I gasped a little. There were no other members of the *Midewewin* in the village. This could only mean he'd been paddling all day. I nodded. "I am honoured, *Kekinoamaged*."

Four others stepped in behind him, placing themselves in a circle around my fire. My hand touched my hair. It was in disarray, wisps fringing my face. There was no time now for myself. Ritual was about to unfold.

Shadow Song lit his pipe and began the ceremony. I yielded to his power, letting the bittersweet aroma of sweet grass leave me dizzy. My senses stretched, reached out and out into the green forest, the rocks, the water. We ate and I barely noticed. Stories wove through the night, tales of how bear had traveled through the four worlds to bring the *Midewewin* to the Anishnabeg, of how *megis* the clam had been pressed into service. When it came time for me to give Shadow Song the gifts, I could barely meet his eyes, keep my hands from trembling. His mouth twitched once when I finished. No more than that. A twitch. He was pleased. Perhaps even touched.

"Tomorrow you begin purification," he said.

Joy shot through me. I felt light-headed, sure I could float let alone fly. He had accepted my petition. Tomorrow I would begin the first of four days in the purification lodge where I would sweat the unclean things from my body.

Chapter 15

On the morning of the fifth day I was convinced I should have heeded Shadow Song's advice. For four days I'd endured sweat lodges, shedding my body's water and impurities in prodigious quantities while Shadow Song ever increased the heat, the steam and the temperature. The heat made breathing difficult, my lungs labouring for air that wasn't there. My skin was sore and burned from sweat, open wounds now chaffing under my breasts, between my legs, the folds of my arms so that any physical action made me want to cry out. Thirst, however, was now my worst enemy and my greatest difficulty. I was allowed only the barest trickle of water, enough to prevent me from dying, this initiation being only the first of the rituals the *midewenini* endured. I wondered, vaguely, how Shadow Song had survived the rigours of the higher orders.

These trials were only those that plagued me during the day. In the evening, exhaustion growing, I was required to feed the shaman who had come to test me, to stay awake while they told their centuries-old legends and mysteries. So, in combination with all of the rest I also was required to suffer sleep privation.

I endured. Somehow I'd found the raw determination to defy my own body and make it to this the fifth and final day. My pride had broken long ago, now there was only grim purpose, a sense of humbling, of weakness I had never known I had.

To rouse myself on this auspicious dawn proved difficult. The deerskins beneath me were soft, my limbs soothed by inactivity. I knew, however, this was the greatest temptation of all, that they let me sleep this fourth night. It would be so easy to lay here, to let exhaustion sweep over me and refute all I'd done. I'd come so far. To throw it all away today seemed a greater sin than lying here in comfort. Today, if I succeeded, would be the fulfillment of all my study thus far, of all my sacrifice.

Stiff, groaning, I lifted myself to my elbows, my hair in my face so that I could not see the poles of the wigwam. Still, it was a beginning. I pushed my hair from my eyes, plaiting it with fumbling fingers. From there I found the strength to crawl out of my wigwam and rinse my face of grime, scrub my teeth with a dogwood stick. An apprentice watched me in my ablutions, ensuring that I took no water to drink. We exchanged no greeting. I turned and looked to the east where the sun rose, a band of turquoise stretching across the horizon. Giving a silent prayer to *keezis*, I returned to the interior of my lodge and put it in order for it was from here I would be summoned to the *Midewigun*, the ceremonial wigwam where I would meet my final test.

I waited cross-legged when done, hoarding my strength, letting meditation set me into a calm state of being. Presently, Shadow Song stepped in, dressed only in a white loincloth. He hunkered there on his heels a moment, studying me, frowning. I returned his gaze steadily, trying not to break.

"Are you sure about this, *wahboos*?"

I nodded. It unsettled me the way he watched me.

"Your life will never be the same."

"My life never is the same."

He snorted at that and gestured for me to follow. I did so, bending through the opening. By now the sun had risen, throwing long shards of brilliance into feathered clouds. As I watched the colours shifted. Distantly I was aware of the villagers stirring around me, gathering to witness my initiation. More and more the patterns in the clouds changed. A cry rose from the villagers. I could only stare at the spectacle above me. A hawk seemed to form from the clouds. *Kaikaik*, the elder brother of Shadow Song.

What omen was this?

Shadow Song shot me a sharp glance. With a grunt he beckoned for us to continue, and, slowly, I turned away from the portent in the sky to walk beside the *midewenini*. He chanted behind his teeth, softly, no more than a wheeze. I heard it as a song of thanksgiving to *Kaikaik*.

So he thought it a portent as well. This did nothing to settle my unease.

I looked away from him, now to the *Midewigun* we approached. It had been constructed at the edge of the village, an unroofed lodge within a lodge, its doors aligned to the east and west. The four men representing the four bears waited there at the east. Four other men, tempters, would soon join them.

As required, I exchanged a ceremonial greeting with them, turned and began my circuit around the outer wall, encouraged as I went by my escorts.

The first bear of temptation came upon me. "Come to your lodge. The skins are soft. To sleep would be good."

Indeed it would. To sleep? Oh, how I longed to accept that invitation, to sink back onto the doeskin, let the cool shadow of the lodge soothe all my aches. But, no, I had this one final test to pass. That was all. Ignoring him I found the will to continue round and round, to deny my body to purify my soul. Another bear of temptation came upon me, offering me food to break my agonizing fast. My stomach cramped with want, my mouth watering prodigiously. He held in his hands succulent strawberries. When I made no move to accept his offer he bit into one. The aroma swept over me. Juice dripped from his lips. I reached out. A look of triumph crossed his face. I dropped my hand and continued my walk, wishing for just one of those berries on my tongue. I didn't think I could survive the next two temptations. They offered me water. They offered my salves for my sores.

"No!" I wailed, cracking my lips, stumbled, hauled myself up and somehow gathered the strength to walk again.

Now, again at the eastern entrance, I completed my fourth circuit and was welcomed into the *Midewigun*. Trembling, I stepped within the lodge.

If it was possible, this was a world apart, a place where time stretched, where spirits dwelt, where wisdom lurked for the unwary. Just to the south of the entrance stood the *Midewatik* for the plant beings, a live cedar post representing the tree of life. Beyond this was a fire for one of the basic elements of the worlds.

I looked at each of the other *Midewewin* members who sat in rows, took note of how many had been drawn from other villages, some women, some men, some aged, some young. Shadow Song sat near the fire, cross-legged, his hair polished and loose, bound with the headband he wore when I'd first met him. Now I knew the meaning of the design there – the nine digressions and seven paths that led from life's main trail. This was the trail upon which I now embarked.

I held his gaze, suddenly calm. "I come, trembling, weak and unlearned. Teach me."

The other *Midewewin* members replied, "Behold, a new sister. Let us welcome our new sister."

Shadow Song lit his pipe, offered the smoke to sky and earth, the cardinal points, and then passed it to his right so that its mystery would be shared. Only then did he turn to me and motion me to sit. I did.

Next came the hours of questioning. I answered all they asked of me, all to demonstrate that I'd mastered the knowledge I'd been assigned to discover. Periodically the members leaned toward one another, whispering. Whether it was in approval or not I was unable to tell. I only did the best I could, remembering all the things this powerful man had taught me over the past years. Even so, I knew if I faltered even once, erred once, I would fail and never know until it came time to shoot me with the *Midemegis*, the otter skin bag filled with shells. Only then would I know if I was worthy or not of renewal and the *Midewewin*. The *megis* could either stop my life forever, or cause me to be reborn.

Around mid-afternoon the endless barrage of questions ceased. My head was light, my senses adrift. I had to pee badly, so badly I could taste it. Hunger and thirst were almost more than I could bear, my throat hoarse, my tongue thick. It was then Shadow Song rose, holding the *Midemegis* and aimed it at the point between my brows.

I was sure my heart stopped beating. This was the ultimate test. The *megis* would magically leave the bag, shoot through the air into my body and test me. At that moment it seemed as if everything dissolved except Shadow Song, the ornate bag he held and my own body. The moment the *megis* passed into me was real, painful, a hot explosion of light inside my head. I cried out against it and the world closed over me.

The pain passed. My vision cleared. It felt as if every bone inside me had been burned clean, my flesh stripped of excess. Somewhere out there I could hear Shadow Song's voice reaching for me, catching me, pulling me into a new world.

"We welcome our sister who has been born anew, who shall be called by us *Wahsayause-Newadjindim*, Shining-in-the-Water. It is yours. It is our gift to you. You must uphold this name. You must espouse the ideals in this name."

The others rose and left through the western door, a closing of matters, sunrise and sunset. It all followed a natural cycle and only now I saw it for what it was.

Shadow Song remained with me, towering, immense in his power, beautiful in his purity, terrible in his strength. For a moment I thought he would bend to me, touch the part of my hair the way he had for years past. He caught himself just then, straightened, turned and left.

The joy of my initiation fled. He hurt me then more acutely than if he'd cut me. Why was it he closed himself to me?

All I could do was cling to the name with which he'd honoured me, Shining-in-the-Water, and hope that its promise would be enough to carry me through until the storm between us broke.

Chapter 16

All of my days of trial were to culminate with a village celebration. There was to be no rest. There was, instead, a huge feast. A deer had been brought down. Butchered, its parts were now spitted over fires. Legumes and fruits were boiling or being served raw, these with bannock and even cornbread. I surveyed all this cooking dizzily, sinking down at last outside the *Midewigun*. One of the men staggered by. I realized there was also to be an abundance of whiskey; as the night wore on events might get dangerous.

I was beyond caring about any of it. All I wanted was to sleep. I was willing even to sleep through the highlight of tonight's festivities, the *jeesekeum*.

Only twice before had I witnessed the *jeesekeum*, the Shaking Tent ceremony. Both times I'd come away stunned. Both times Shadow Song had been the shaman to perform the rite. Some of the villagers said the special wigwam shook only because Shadow Song made it. Others, especially the elders, maintained that when the spirit of the shaman entered the wigwam, the tent shook in acknowledgment, driven by the swirling of the four winds. Me – I didn't know what to believe. All I knew was that even as Shadow Song would approach the special wigwam it shook, that voices unlike his own issued from the place, voices claiming to be *Makinauk* the turtle, *Kaikaik* the hawk, *Numae* the sturgeon. The spirits found missing objects for the villagers, visited their loved ones in other places, and often issued warning or advice as it was required.

As I sat there, fighting to remain awake through the last few hours, I knew in my heart I would regret missing this *jeesekeum*. This time it would hold special meaning. These powers were powers I would learn when the spirits found me fit.

Dusk settled over the camp. I watched as the campfires burned higher, watched as the villagers brought wood for a larger, central fire around which they would gather. Beyond this I could see Shadow Song's dark shape as he made a final inspection of the special wigwam just beyond the fire. This wigwam, like all *jeesekeum* I'd seen, had been constructed according to his specific direction. Yet he never touched any of it until it was time to enter. It was small, barely large enough to admit him, its poles so close a child couldn't squeeze through let alone a full-grown man. There was no entrance.

Why he went to such elaborate lengths this time I didn't know. Perhaps it was because of talk among the villagers that their shaman had strayed from his intended path, that he kept a woman in his wigwam who was neither his daughter, his sister nor his wife. By testing himself so severely I supposed he would prove both to himself and the people that he was still pure of heart, that he still walked the path.

Grandmother shuffled near to me and beckoned. I rose as respect demanded, although I felt my legs weak beneath me, and followed her to the fire. Someone shoved a hunk of meat into my hand. I looked at it for a moment, the puckered, dark flesh, wondering what it was? I had not had food pass my lips for days. My mouth watered. My stomach cramped. I bit deeply, juices squirting down my chin.

"Slowly," Grandmother cautioned.

I looked at her over my hand, saw the concern on her face and checked my ravenous tearing. Slowly, I chewed, reducing each small mouthful to pulp before I swallowed. Tea appeared before me, brought by another of the villagers as a way of showing deference. Distantly, I wondered if it would always be this way now.

"It's only because of him," I heard a woman say behind me. "It helps to share the same lodge as the *midewenini*."

I felt my blood run cold. Is that what they thought? That Shadow Song allowed me entry into the *Midewewin* because I supposedly coupled with him?

I caught Grandmother looking at me. She shrugged.

"You know that's not true," I assured her.

"People will think what they will think." Her attention turned to the fire.

The last thing I wanted was this. True I was not kin of Shadow Song, but for all that had been between us I might as well have been. I was easily fifteen years his junior. As I looked around I realized that age difference meant little. All manner of men Shadow Song's age and older had taken wives as young as I, some even younger. Women wore out fast in the backwoods. A young wife meant longer years of service.

By now my thoughts were as dark as the night. I felt like an island amid the festivities. Children shrieked. Laughter was everywhere. One of the men had started a drumbeat, his hair braided and his face red-gold in the firelight. Another joined in and the chanting began. The drums echoed my heartbeat. Dancers arose, moving their feet through the shuffling beat, backs bent, arms waving. The pace increased and my head spun just watching them. Heat from the fire was intense. I thought for sure I would explode.

The air stilled. All action ceased. Power rippled up my back like the brush of fingertips. I knew this. I had felt this time and again in my years with the Anishnabeg. Shadow Song approached. It was as if in stretching his senses to the spirits of rock, wind, tree, he carried with him this eerie calm. He emerged through the crowd behind me so that I had little time to see his face. His back was to me quickly, rippling as he walked, every line of him glazed with gold from firelight. He affected me as profoundly now as he had that first time I'd seen him by the river. My love for him I knew was akin worship. I cared little that the priests of long ago would have called my love sinful.

Even as he approached the wigwam it trembled, first like a shudder, again, now growing. A hiss rose from the people when he stepped through the birch bark. It just seemed to part, poles and all, closing after him when he was inside. I held my breath, my every fibre attuned to the *jeesekeum*.

Now the wigwam shook violently. A wind from the west swirled through the area, powerful, another from the east, cold from the north, warm from the south. The wigwam bent so dramatically I was sure it would fold in two, swaying back and forth, round and round. Then a voice, disembodied, hollow, rose from the structure.

"*Makinauk!*" the people cheered.

It amazed me they who presented themselves so piously to the white preacher in *Manitowaning* could be among the most enthusiastic at a *jeesekeum*.

"How close is the white agent?" a woman in the crowd asked.

The white agent. I was disgusted with the question. How could any of them ask after the government agent who visited Manitoulin annually? Only once I'd witnessed the pomp and degradation of this visit. Shadow Song would have left the village but I'd begged him to stay, pleaded with him that I wanted to see what all the fuss was about. I wished I'd never talked him into it.

So condescending the agent had been, patronizing, dressed in British reds and years as the conqueror. His face, to me, clearly expressed what he thought of this mass of unwashed heathen. They were simpletons, savages, unworthy of recognition or respect. My children, he'd called us. I wondered distantly if he'd brought leashes for us all so that on command he could make us walk, sit, beg. I'd stalked away to prepare my things for a fishing camp.

"In four days the white agent will be here," the voice answered. I made a mental note to prepare so that we would be gone in plenty of time. "But this is not a thing for rejoicing," *Makinauk* added. I could feel tension mount around me. They didn't like the warning, it was plain. This wasn't what they wanted to hear from the spirits. "You defile not only yourselves when you deal with the white agent, but Mother Earth. What are we without her?"

"Let *Makinauk* speak!" a man shouted nearby, plainly convinced his shaman lectured. Others spoke out in support of the man. In the next moment he cried out in pain. It seemed a snapping turtle had bitten him. That brought the crowd to silence. Makinauk had issued a warning. Despite myself, I smiled.

"How is it?" *Makinauk* continued, the wigwam trembling, "that the proud Ojibwa fought the Sioux for years when the land was taken, but they fight not at all to save the land from the whites?" No one could reply to that. "All through the lands to the south game has fallen or fled. The rivers dry because the whites don't hear the trees. They cut them instead, burning whole forests. They cast their nets in the waters, reaping harvests more than they require, all so their chiefs may eat of twelve courses every day. They grow fat while the land grows lean. I tell you, there will come a day when the white man will have silenced Mother Earth so that it will be difficult even for the Anishnabeg to hear her. It is then the whites will come to us. The world will cry out. And we had better remember the song of Mother Earth or this, the fourth world, will also die, as will also the children of Mother Earth."

I could feel the people fidget around me. Silence was so acute I could hear them breathe. This was not what they'd expected from the *jeesekeum*.

Nothing more was said for some time. Grumbling, they dispersed, halted when another voice, that of *Numae* the sturgeon called out, "Come to me, Shining-in-the-Water."

Fear shot through me as sharp as a knife. I felt every gaze upon me, felt their speculation, felt their anger, even jealousy. At that moment I was grateful for the darkness.

All I could think was, why did *Numae* call me? I'd never before heard of this happening.

The voice again reached out for me. I rose, obeying the summons, not knowing what else to do. A murmur passed through the crowd. I walked, placing one foot before the other, my pulse pounding in my ears. The crowd parted before me, their faces full of question. I was before the trembling wigwam now, unsure if my knees would buckle or not. Behind me I could hear whispers, gossip.

"Come," a voice said. Had it originated from the wigwam or the air itself?

I reached for the birch bark with my hand, not knowing how else to enter. The bark melted away, parting. The crowd stirred. I withdrew my hand, afraid.

"Come," the voice said again.

Once more I reached for the birch bark, watched it fold away, the poles bend into an opening for me. Vaguely, I could make out Shadow Song, bent over upon his knees, face to the ground. I had always supposed it was his body the spirits used, but he remained so still.

I stepped in. It was like thunder cracking at my back when the birch bark closed. I blinked. The hammering in my ears stilled. Logic told me this should have been a dark place enclosed with poles and sheets of bark, that Shadow Song should have filled the tiny space of ground. What I saw had nothing to do with that preconception. Shadow Song was there, yes, bent upon his knees. But the world around him was a vast plain, an arch of stars above, and in a ring round the prostrate midewenini were the manitous who had come to share the *jeesekeum*, thin of matter, ghostly, almost gold and blue in color. *Makinauk* was there. I couldn't mistake him. So also were *Kaikaik*, *Numae*, bear, wolf, lynx, others so numerous I could hardly count them. At the cardinal points sat shy *Zeegwun* of the south, wise old *Ningobianong* of the west, warlike *Bebon* of the north and young *Waubun* of the east. *Nanabush* the trickster sat at a distance, across from him his father the great *Epingishmook*, as were the other sons of *Epingishmook* and *Winonah*: *Papeekawis*, *Madjeekawis* and *Chichiabos*. The storyteller *Daebaudjimod* sat there also.

Such a host filled the *jeesekeum* I could hardly believe my eyes. I sank to my knees, clumsily stuffed sweet-grass into my crude pipe and smoked to them. Through it all Shadow Song watched me with that cool, aloof way he had, all stillness and observation.

When he moved to take my hand I flinched, but allowed him to guide my fingers around one of the lodge poles that were still visible. Not a word had been spoken, and yet I understood everything every being in this world of the shaking tent thought. To place my hand upon the lodge pole was to connect myself with this mystical place. Little by little his hand left mine, as if to allow me to adjust. Power surged through my fingers, almost burning, as if it coursed not through my blood but through my marrow. I almost cried out against this heat. I held myself firmly, my gaze upon Shadow Song's, lost somewhere in the depths of his wisdom. It wasn't until then I realized how old he was for his thirty-some years, as if he were the old man under whom he'd tutored, and the tutor before, and the tutor before. I wasn't the first woman in this line of wise ones, but I was the most recent. This was a direct connection to Mother Earth. Here I could understand all the mysteries of the world.

The moment ended as abruptly as it began. I released the lodge pole, quaking with power. Too much. This had been more than I felt myself capable. This was power for a future time. For now, at least, I understood the way of it, how much would be demanded of me: absolute purity. Nothing less.

The poles at my back bent. I was as much as spit out of the *jeesekeum* into the astonished villagers. My skin still tingled from the experience. I was aware of hands upon my arms, of people assisting me to my feet, of voices rising in question.

I waved them all off when Shadow Song bent through the wigwam, his attention for me alone. What was it he said to me? I started to ask but he turned and strode off for the wigwam. I did the only sensible thing. I scrambled after him.

Chapter 17

The weeks that followed did nothing to ease the tension between Shadow Song and me. Not that we argued. We didn't. It was just that he studied me and it was as if his realization unsettled him. I was careful. I did not wish to lose his affection or the haven I found with him. He was, after all, a shaman. That in itself accorded some caution.

I studied under his tutelage, careful to be precise in all my reproductions of his lessons. Combined with this I shouldered the usual tasks of a woman. I cooked. I fished. I made sure we had clothing and that endless task of making moccasins, cured and worked pelts and hides. There was the smoking and drying racks to attend, and of course my services to Grandmother that were her due as the matriarch of the family.

So it was the weeks passed and we managed to evade discussion of the difficulty between us. There was always some job that needed doing. It was enough excuse.

For Shadow Song, there was yet another occurrence to preoccupy his thoughts. When we arrived in the spring this year there were white settlers just beyond the traditional village grounds, headed by a Captain Anderson who, Shadow Song told me, had been appointed by the British government as the first Indian superintendent. With him had come a fellow by name of Orr, apparently to educate we dull brutes, and none other than the Reverend Adam Elliot.

All of us could see the bald spot they'd created for the purposes of their settlement. The beginning of a building was rising, which, we were told, was to serve as school, church and storehouse. A house had already gone up. Orr was attempting to herd children off to school, and Elliot to church us all. All of this was in preparation of an alleged mass exodus of Odawa from the United States.

The hand-bell for church had been shaken heartily some hours ago. Apparently dissatisfied with his paltry congregation, Elliot took it upon himself to come out and recruit members. He made the sorry mistake of stopping to see Shadow Song.

"Are you not coming, my son?" he asked.

That was the wrong tact to take with Shadow Song, I could tell easily. I looked up from where I sat scraping a hide, to where Elliot stood. A fastidious man, he was dressed impeccably this hot August morning, right down to his Anglican collar. This, rather than making him appear a fine gentleman of the church, left him only ridiculous amid all the bare, sun-reddened skin around him. His face was flushed. He sweated enormously, mopping his face, where fine blue veins showed, with a white linen handkerchief. Although pleasant of demeanour, I sensed his discontent. This man was forever at war with himself. Amid the backwoods he found no laughter, no tolerance and no understanding for anything that didn't fit into his sterile view of the world. No doubt he'd be planting a garden of fine English roses amid all the wildness of Manitoulin. I couldn't help thinking of my uncle, of how he'd read from a Bible and lived in a hell. I wondered, vaguely, if it was the same for Elliot.

I turned my attention to Shadow Song. He hadn't even acknowledged Elliot with a glance, instead, keeping his attention upon working a new bowstring. I felt nothing but annoyance around him, the way he might feel about a plague of mosquitoes or an unbalanced arrow shaft.

"As the leader of your people I would have thought you'd take more interest in what they do," Elliot said.

Shadow Song replied, without looking up, "I told you before. They're not my people. I don't own them."

Elliot laughed, one of those short, polite British things. "Of course not. I didn't mean to indicate that. None of us owns God's creatures –"

"Neither are we creatures."

A breath of exasperation. "Don't evade the point. I'm sure you'd be interested in what the villagers are learning."

"Not really."

"But you don't even know – "

"Don't I?" Shadow Song looked up from his work, his face hard and uncompromising. Elliot fidgeted. Shadow Song gave no quarter. "You will teach them they are sinful. You will teach them that seeking dreams is heinous, that to hear the voices of Mother Earth is nothing less than demonology, witchcraft, that to fell the trees and strip the land and drive the animals from their homes is civilized. You will tell them Christ died to forgive them once and for all, and then have them forever repenting of their sins. And all the while you will loathe them for their red skin and their simple ways, think of them as simpletons to be guided and instructed in the way of any bovine, but never, never, do you want them truly educated so that they realize they are a proud people, a people more in harmony with a creator than you could ever be, because then we would stop allowing in the white man." He stood, handed me the bowstring. "I know. I know from all of your best English educators." He stalked off. Elliot was left sputtering where he stood.

In a moment, plainly in an attempt to save face, he looked down at me and asked, "You?"

I smiled and shrugged my shoulders, feigning non-comprehension. It was safer to play the part of an Ojibwa-speaking Indian than to acknowledge him. I was always aware his world would take me back to Uncle Edgar. There was nothing left for Elliot to do but make an about-face and return to his open chapel.

I looked out over the village, only barely able to make out Shadow Song retreating toward the water. He was in a mood. Likely he wouldn't return until later in the day. He'd hunt. I looked at the bowstring in my hand, at the rifle propped against our wigwam. Perhaps he'd play at hunting. In my heart I knew he'd attempt to soothe the thing the preacher had opened. Yes, Shadow Song remained as true to the ancient ways as possible. There were, however, glaring inconsistencies in his life. He used a rifle. He carried with him a few books. Carefully bound in leather he kept a few personally signed poems from Byron and Tennyson. The poets and he had apparently all been at Trinity together.

Then there was a silver flask smelling faintly of old brandy, engraved with the names Peter and Iris. Peter had been the name given him when he was schooled in Britain. This much I knew from my conversations with him when he would insist on instructing me in matters literate. Who Iris was remained a mystery. I suspected very much she had been the sort who flew after the exotic, a woman who had cultivated a very intimate relationship with her Peter for the sake of being avant-garde. This was, I knew, an unfair evaluation of a completely unknown woman. It was an evaluation I felt accurate when watching Shadow Song handle the flask. Grim was his face, troubled. I suspected he kept that one shining object as an icon of the life he'd left behind.

Yes, Shadow Song would hunt today. It wasn't game, however, that he stalked.

I watched him until he disappeared in the distance, paddling with precise strokes. With a sigh I turned my attention to the village. Now Shadow Song was gone his duties would largely fall to me, being his apprentice and a member of the *Midewewin*.

The rest of the village was sparsely populated, many of the people following Elliot out of curiosity. I knew what would happen with the remainder of this day. People would return from church. Instead of being uplifted they would be despondent, chastened for their sins and their sinful ways. Whiskey would flow. It was an easy way to drown sorrow. The brawls would begin. It would be dangerous to be an unprotected woman. It would be dangerous just to be. I wondered if Elliot had any idea just how much damage he was doing in the name of God?

As much for the sake of safety as to clear my own thoughts, I remained quiet throughout the day, going about my tasks unobtrusively, trying not to draw attention to myself. The villagers returned from church. I could hear talk among them, sharing the Word they'd received and spreading its discontent. It was like a disease. Everywhere it fell it infected. Three of the men sat gambling. A whiskey jug appeared. They drank. A wife served food and she drank also. Soon the foursome was laughing loudly. Others joined. More whiskey appeared.

The sun was low on the horizon when the first brawl broke out. I turned my back, listening to the sound of fists smashing into flesh. The yells followed soon after. I ran my oval scraper over the moose hide, softening it. There was only the work. Alone, I could do nothing about the discontent around me.

Not long afterward one of the young women approached me, clutching a rag to her face. I recognized her. Newly wedded to a fine hunter if a bit of a braggart. Her name was White-hand, called so because of the white spot on the back of her left hand. I gestured for her to enter my wigwam, her three adopted children in tow. I bent in after them, smoked and cleared my head so the spirits could work through me. In the gloom of the lodge I probed her cheek, appraising the ragged gash that snaked from the corner of her eye to her nose. Messy. Likely from a knife let go to rust. I worried over the latter, remembering the things Shadow Song had told me about infection.

I clucked my tongue. Grandmother had once chided me that was something very old to do for one so young. "How did this happen?" I felt White-hand stiffen.

"I cut myself."

"Or you were cut."

She flushed, lowering her gaze.

"By your husband when he was drunk."

She nodded. The youngest child, no more than two, tugged at White-hand's sleeve, plainly afraid. She wrapped her arm around the girl. I knew the only reason White-hand allowed me this liberty was that I was *midewequae*, young but powerful. Everyone for miles around had heard about the episode with Shadow Song's jeesekeum within the month, the way I'd been allowed in by the spirits and then allowed out. These kinds of things happened only in legends.

I turned my attention to the small coals in the center of the wigwam, blew on them, fed in a few twigs so that I had a cheery blaze. Next I sorted through a series of gourds I kept stoppered, searching for the right one and then found the yellow salve. This I placed near to the fire. I unsheathed a small stone knife

I'd made during my most recent dream. It gleamed whitely. This, also, I set beside the fire and then chanted, letting my spirit slip into the fire, into the knife, passed the white blade through the flames until it gleamed gold. White-hand's eyes were wide with wonder that I didn't burn from the heat.

It was a simple procedure to lance the wound, to let it bleed and clear any infection. I washed it with a clean rag and then covered it liberally with the salve, giving a small quantity to White-hand when I finished.

"Every day when *keezis* returns to the west," I instructed, remembering a time I'd been told to do the same thing.

White-hand nodded. She offered me tobacco and print. I accepted the tobacco, refused the print. It was part of the world I'd left behind, and, to tell the truth it was not very durable for the kind of life I led. Skins were far more practical for my purposes.

"My medicine will heal your face," I told her. "It will do nothing for the next time."

"Perhaps he won't drink," she said.

I looked over at the three silent children who sat to her rear. They had known beating, terror. The truth of it was in their eyes. "What does your grandmother say?" I asked her.

"That I should leave."

"And your grandmother is wise. Perhaps you will be if you heed her council."

"But that's not what the preacher says."

I smiled. "Is the preacher a woman?"

White-hand shook her head.

"Then what can he know of woman things?"

She thanked me and backed out of the wigwam, her children with her. In a moment I followed. I arched my back when I straightened, letting my hands rest against my hips. The leather felt good against my skin, soft, supple.

Out in the village events seemed to have settled somewhat, although I had no false illusions. Bracing for a busy evening, I checked my racks where fish were smoking, berries drying. Judging by the early color of the shrubs, perhaps another moon, it would be time to harvest wild rice. We would have a good winter supply. It was always a secret dread with me to stave off the *windigo*, the evil creature that could seize your body and feed from the flesh of your loved ones.

Commotion at the water's edge took my attention. A man had beached his canoe, gesturing in sharp motions that spoke of haste. From the look on his face I judged that he'd paddled for some time without rest. It was evident in the way he bent, nodding to the woman who pointed in my direction.

Someone sick, I assumed, in need of immediate attention, sent to summon Shadow Song. I watched him approach at a trot. I motioned him to the fire and fed him from the fish stew I had bubbling, as it would have been discourteous to have asked after his business before making him comfortable. I would have done no differently for anyone else. He was hungry, that was plain. Indeed it had been haste that had brought him here.

I felt a flutter of panic knowing this. I inhaled, let it go, steadied myself. This was his urgency, not mine. I lit my pipe. We smoked together. Now, custom satisfied, he could speak.

"I bring news from Hornings Mills," he said.

Ice fell down my spine. How long ago had it been that I'd fled from that place? A lifetime? I nodded for him to continue.

"Word is being sent to all the trading posts to capture you and the *midewenini*." I arched a brow in question. "The whites are to judge him according to their laws for kidnapping and murder. You are to be returned to a man called Edgar Fleming."

I blew smoke, letting silence feed me calmness. Then: "You are welcome to share our fire this night". He fidgeted, plainly uncomfortable with this form of gratitude. "Of course, if your family is waiting, I would rather you were on your way. Perhaps I could offer you tobacco for your journey."

That pleased him. He accepted, adding, "White men will be here in five days, perhaps six the way they travel. They will stop here on their way to La Cloche, to warn us."

I nodded, offered him another small token and he left. Five days. Maybe six. My whole world could fall apart in that time. It had never occurred to me that Uncle would hunt us so diligently, that his passion for revenge would feed him all this time. I should have known better. Hadn't we been warned away from trading posts almost from the outset? Anywhere whites were located there would be trouble, and now they were at our own backdoor.

At that moment Shadow Song strode through the village, a basket over one shoulder, a brace of geese over the other. There was that sensation around him I'd noticed after my first cycle, a sensation that kept me at a distance. Nothing malevolent was in him. It was just that he seemed wary about me, or more with himself, as if he might stray if he didn't keep himself under rigid control. Again I tried to discern the reason for his change. I could think of nothing. I had done nothing different to bring this on. The news I had would only add to his tension.

"Geese," he announced when he was near, lifting the brace. "Dry these for winter."

I marked how he didn't offer me his hunt as he used to, in fact hadn't for some time. Not even Grandmother would answer my circumspect inquiries about this.

"There isn't time," I said, offering him tea. He took the bowl, watching me although I tried not to meet his gaze. "I've had news."

He squatted. "What news?"

"Uncle's sent agents after us – for your arrest, for my return. Still I kept my attention upon the ground, desperate not to look at him, not to let him see the hurt and fear that must surely show on my face. "Perhaps we should leave separately, go in different directions."

"Sit."

"But – "

"I won't discuss this with you standing. Sit."

I sat. I heard him sip, again, inhale and then, "I will ask you as I've asked you before: Do you wish to leave me?"

Leave him. It sounded so personal, so intimate, and I had to admit so frightening. Why when he spoke to me like this did I tremble from something not quite fear? I shook my head in answer.

"Then I will answer you as I have before. You will stay."

I looked up at him. Held my breath. I wasn't sure I wanted to see what he revealed in his face, something I didn't understand and didn't know how to respond. "As long as I stay with you he'll hunt us. You said so yourself when I first came away."

"Has he caught us?"

I shook my head.

"Then there's nothing to worry about."

"But the agents will be here in five days."

"Only a coward would run."

"Then I'm a coward."

He smiled, a wry twist to his mouth, his clay-brown eyes dancing with light. "This from the one who has faced so much?"

"But they have guns, they have power – "

"They have nothing. I am not afraid, *wahboos*. They will come, they will threaten, and they will return empty-handed. He gestured to the geese. "You had better see to these if they're to dry."

Chapter 18

Just as the messenger said, the agents came six days later, around mid-day, no more than a rough crew of mercenaries working on the fringes of the law. Bounty hunters they were. Three of them. One dark, bearded, that look to him that said he was wild, a casual killer. Another silent in the way he trailed behind the dark, his earth-brown hair unkempt, long. There was viciousness to this one. The third seemed more an idiot than anything, an outcast these two had picked up for no better reason than sport when bored.

They stood in the midst of the village, ringed by a gaggle of curious children who tugged at their clothes, inspected their packs. The rest of the villagers remained with their work or their leisure, uninterested in what this motley crew had to say.

"Get them off," the dark growled, gesturing to the children.

"They are children," Grandmother answered. "This is how they learn."

I stood beside Shadow Song, measuring my breathing.

"We come looking for – "

"We eat," Grandmother said. "Then we talk. She offered them a bowl of fish and wild rice.

The dark slapped it from her hand. It tumbled in a whirl of scattered food. "The hell with that shit. We've come for the medicine man and the girl."

"Which medicine man?" Grandmother asked.

He snarled, raised his hand to her. Shadow Song stepped in the way all of one fluid movement, caught the dark's arm so quickly I wondered if it had happened at all. They stood there like that for several moments, the mercenary unable to break Shadow Song's hold, Shadow Song with that mocking look to his face. He released him only after the dark's gaze dropped.

"We offer you our food," Shadow Song said, "our tobacco. Then we will talk." He gestured to the ground near our fire. We'd moved our encampment near to the center of the village, to disguise the customary placement of the shaman's wigwam.

The mercenaries passed looks between themselves. The dark sat. The others followed. Shadow Song lowered himself to the ground, indicating for me to help Grandmother fetch more food. I scurried about my business quickly, ladling rice and fish into bowls. Into three of them I surreptitiously squeezed the juice of red berries from bittersweet nightshade. In sufficient quantity it could kill, but there was only enough here to make a person ill for a few days. I handed them their bowls. They ate. They smoked. I watched both them and Shadow Song.

The dark smiled, a slow curling of his lips across yellow teeth. "So you're the medicine man."

Shadow Song didn't even flinch. "If that's what you think."

He nodded toward me. "And she's the niece."

"Does she look white?"

The dark's eyes narrowed as he watched me. I knew my skin was as red as any Indian's, that with my doeskin dress and my dark, braided hair I could pass.

"She'd be burned, wouldn't she, after all these years." To me, "Wouldn't you?"

"*Nind kah exhechega nebwahkahwin.*"

"She doesn't understand, she says." Shadow Song smiled. "How could she?"

"She could also be acting, like you."

"I'm not holy enough to be the man you're looking for. Ask anyone in the village."

"I'm asking you."

"I'm just a man."

"And her?"

Shadow Song grabbed my wrist and yanked me down to the ground beside him. My skin tingled. "She's mine." Why did his statement tie knots inside my belly, set my pulse to hammering? He turned to look at me, his lips close. "Aren't you?" And then he kissed me, hard, swiftly, but with more feeling than I expected. My head spun. He shoved me away and I almost fell into the fire. "I like my women young." He grinned. "But if you've whiskey I'd trade her."

I tried to keep from looking at him, to keep all emotion from showing. What was he doing?

"We didn't come to trade," the dark said.

A few of the women nearby had stopped their work, their attention upon us. Even a few of the games the men pursued came to a pause. Their tension was so real to me that my bones ached.

"If you're not interested in trade," Shadow Song rose, dragging me with him, "then we have nothing to discuss."

"Wait!"

Shadow Song remained with his back to the man, his hand still gripping my arm.

"Perhaps we can trade information."

"On?"

"This medicine man's whereabouts."

Shadow Song laughed. "He's gone. Do you really think he'd be stupid enough to stay around here? He took his witch-woman with him a month ago, headed for Atikokan." A few murmurs from the villagers confirmed his lie. He pushed me into the wigwam, ducked in after me.

We sat there across from one another for a few moments, watching each other. The commotion outside subsided. Paddles could be heard pushing a canoe out from shore. In the afternoon heat I could hear the women again about their business, children playing, men laughing over a moccasin game. In here nothing returned to normal. My pulse still hammered. My mouth still tingled from his kiss. His gaze never left me. There was such conflict in him.

"I'm afraid," I whispered at length, needing to let him know he was frightening me, that the situation was frightening me.

His face softened. He reached out and touched the part of my hair, withdrew as if he shouldn't do this thing. "You're safe with me, *wahboos*." He looked over at his medicine bag bulging from underneath a deerskin. "I'll be gone a few days. When I return we'll begin the harvest of rice." And left.

I knew he was off to seek a dream, to fast, to purify himself. Knowing that did nothing to settle my pulse.

He was gone fifteen days. I thought I'd go wild with worry. Some of the women said he'd left for good. One young man, Red Cloud, was so convinced he began to make overtures, leaving gifts with Grandmother. When I made a protest about this behaviour, Grandmother merely shrugged her shoulders.

Again Red Cloud approached me, his eagerness disgusting. I continued to repair Shadow Song's heavy wolf-fur cloak. "When Shadow Song returns," I told him, "then you may discuss the matter with him."

"I'd rather discuss with you how I'll lift your skirts."

I stiffened. This kind of cross-talk always angered me. It was normal enough for ribald flirtations to take place between cross-cousins, but I didn't want any part of it. That was the problem. I was of marriageable age and it was plain not only Red Cloud took an interest, but several other young men for they hovered nearby. Even at this moment they ogled me, bending together in laughter and whispers. Probably speculating on Red Cloud's success.

It wasn't that I didn't want to marry. God knows I did. I wanted a man to touch me. I dreamed of a man touching me. So often I fantasized what it would be like to couple the way Morning Star and Lightfoot did, wondered what it would be like to sleep under the same furs with a man. I thought of these things so much my loins ached with the thinking. If I didn't do something about it soon I was sure I'd explode. I just didn't want to do it with Red Cloud. He was too eager, too sloppy, like a dog that pants after a bitch in heat.

"You'll discuss this with Shadow Song," I said firmly, determined to give him no quarter.

He shrugged, grinned and turned away to his group of cronies. They closed around him like waves, gesturing in my direction, firing me looks. Laughter erupted. I shifted, giving them my back. When they wouldn't leave I rose and took my mending over to where Grandmother sat before Morning Star's wigwam.

She was bent, wizened, her fingers flicking at her stitching like spider's legs. On the grass mat was a profusion of baskets, some filled with threads, some with beads made of shell, more of glass for which Lightfoot had traded. Like most of the women she'd taken a liking for white things. Her beadwork was filled with flowers made from the glass beads. I wondered how long it had been since she had embroidered with shell in the geometric designs of the Anishnabeg.

I lowered myself near to her with deference, clutching my own work. We worked there side by side pleasantly enough. I thought there might be a reprieve until Grandmother said, "You don't like the way they talk," never once looking up from her work, her deft fingers stitching, stitching.

I yanked the thread tight, more in frustration than to secure my work. "No."

"It shouldn't surprise you that they do."

"Why not?"

"Everyone wants to own something beautiful."

Beautiful? Me? I lowered my work, heat rising to my cheeks. "I'll not be owned. And I'm not beautiful."

"Red Cloud is a good hunter."

"That makes him a good husband?"

"You'd never go hungry."

"I'd never go hungry even if I had to take care of myself." That I knew was true enough, not just braggadocio. Shadow Song often wandered in search of a dream, leaving me to fend for myself. It had never bothered me. I knew I was capable of survival. That much had been proven when in the streets of England and when in Uncle's company.

"It's not seemly," the old woman said after a moment, relying on a lame, tired argument.

I silenced the sharp retort on my tongue. What Grandmother was heading to I didn't want to hear. I would. The old woman wouldn't relent.

"How long do you think you can stay with my son?"

I didn't answer. I worked furiously with the repairs, stinging from the situation.

"He is a man."

I could feel anger rising. I mustn't speak lest I say something rash. I took another stitch.

"And you are a woman. Why do you think he has gone away?"

I shoved the cloak into my lap, heedless of caution. "He hasn't gone away. He's coming back." Deference to my elders be damned!

"No dream-seeking takes this long. He's gone because he knows that to stay with you is wrong. There are only two choices left to him – to stay and wife you or leave and hope my daughter will take you in as her own."

I rose, trembling with rage, longing to hurl hurtful words at the old woman. "He's coming back," was all I managed to say, turned and stalked to the bay.

Ever since my dream of *Numae* I'd taken to swimming. I felt at peace in the water, pleased when I emerged clean and vermin free. The sheltered cove I usually swam from was a little way along the white cobble beach and I walked there, shaded by pines that swept the shore. Alone, the sounds of the village gone, I undressed and slipped into the aquamarine water, diving down until my lungs burned for air and then rising with a gasp. A warm current shifted around my legs. I hovered in it for some time, trying to let my most recent conversation wash away, to let the water work its magic. Peace, however, was to evade me. Just the feel of the water on my skin, the way I imagined a lover's hand would feel, aroused me. My breasts ached with desire. I didn't want to feel this way. It only complicated my life and my thoughts.

Frustrated, I swam back to shore and dunked my skirt and vest into the water. There was no use having a pest free body if one's clothes were inhabited. I took malicious pleasure watching those tiny creatures rising to the surface of the water. The leather would be hard when dry. In my grim state of mind I welcomed the chafing that was to come.

Dressed once more, I returned to the village and my wigwam. Throughout the day I brooded in the lodge, sweating in the heat, chewing on my tears. I'd not show my face to the village. That would only give them reason to gossip about the *midewequae* who lived with their holy man.

In another attempt to divert my dour thoughts I brought out the precious pen and ink Shadow Song had traded for me and wrote in a journal that had cost him too many pelts. This was one of the few things of the white world Shadow Song allowed me to keep – knowledge, the ability to write, to read. He said they were powerful tools that would eventually free the Anishnabeg.

Even when evening came and people began to dance the Partridge Dance for fertility, I remained in my wigwam, journal set aside, still brooding over my situation. I wished with every fibre of my being Shadow Song would come back, that Grandmother was wrong.

Laughter and songs rang through the night air, the deep rhythms of the drums thudding in my heart, the stamp of feet upon the earth an invitation I wanted to accept. The air itself quivered with voices, that high, nasal chant I had come to know and relish. Laughter grew boisterous as the night progressed, evidence someone had made a trade for a quantity of whiskey. They always drank like this when Shadow Song was away. He was the only reason they still clung to a few of the old ways. If things continued, there would be a brawl tonight. No doubt I'd be busy tomorrow setting right the wounds of tonight.

Exhausted, nerves flayed, I undressed and lay myself upon the skins, inhaling the sweet scent of fir boughs that cushioned the earth beneath me. At the height of the dance I felt myself slipping into sleep, that delicious state of drifting in a place where one is not really asleep, neither really awake. Then I must have finally slept for I awoke to silence and the deep darkness of the night.

What woke me I was unsure. A ripple. A sensation something was not quite right. I lay there, blinking into darkness, heat clinging to my skin like a sticky blanket. Was that a movement in the wigwam? It was then I was aware of someone breathing beside me, of another body near to me. I stiffened, trying to judge how close my knife was to hand. Fingers slid over my breast. I tried to cry out but was stifled by a hand closing over my mouth. Panic jolted through my limbs. I raised my foot to kick, was caught and pinned to the ground. Beneath this stranger's hand my heart beat wildly, his breath heavy with whiskey. I cried out again, heard it muffled and felt the strength of the hand over my mouth.

"No skirts to lift," the stranger giggled.

Red Cloud. I struggled frantically now, kicking and clawing. I'd wanted to couple with a man but not like this. His fingers were between my legs, rough and unkind. He thrust one inside me and I thought I would faint from the pain. I bit his hand. He snarled and flung himself on top of me, forcing my legs apart with his, holding one hand over my mouth to prevent me from screaming as loudly as I tried. I could feel his lips on my breasts, the wetness of his tongue and his mouth, the sharp intake of breath. His manhood was hard and frightening as he probed for entry into my body. I was afraid as I never thought I could be, gasping for air, tears stinging my eyes.

"Please, no," I moaned, hoping he would be merciful. I heard the faintest of sounds outside the wigwam. Then suddenly Red Cloud wasn't there. His weight vanished.

I curled into a ball, listening, listening. There were the sounds of scraping feet, of flesh impacting with flesh. A cry then. Pain. Then the sound of shoving, of someone grunting with exertion. Silence. I shivered so hard I thought I would bite my tongue, whimpering in my fear.

Still I could hear the breath of someone else. Despite my state I tried to discern in the darkness who now shared my wigwam, terrified that my rescuer might only be another assailant. I could feel his presence, palpable, powerful, very male. I flinched and cried out when his hand touched the top of my head, slid down to cup my cheek. Try as I might I couldn't stop trembling.

"Did he hurt you, *wahboos*?"

Just the sound of that voice was balm. I wept then. Thanking the *manitous* that he had come back, that he was here with me, that I was safe, safe, always I would be safe with Shadow Song.

"*Wahboos* .... "

He was here. Grandmother was wrong. Everything would be fine now.

"*Wahsayause-Newadjindim*, I beg you, please – are you hurt?"

"A little," I managed to say, unable to speak clearly I gasped so badly.

"Did he – "

"No."

His hand left my cheek and his arms were around me, gathering me to his chest as if gathering something fragile. I wept then as I'd not wept in years, all the while rocked in his arms, his lips moving over my hair as he whispered soothing sounds into the darkness.

When at last I was able to compose myself I remained in his embrace. It was then I realized he trembled also. I could feel the quivering of his arms, the way he held me tightly.

"We must go," he said after a moment, no more than a breath of words. "We must hurry."

I looked up from where I pressed my cheek to his chest, trying to make out his face in the darkness and couldn't. I heard fear in his voice. Cautiously, I reached up and touched his face, felt the frown. He released me then. I heard him shuffle about, heard flint on steel, saw the bright, hard sparks fly and catch on birch bark in the fire-pit. In that small light I saw the tension on his face, watched him feed twigs into the pit until they flamed enough to add larger branches kept in a cache to one side of the lodge. He began rolling skins, tying them, his actions jerky.

"What is it?" I asked, clutching a fur to my breast, feeling very exposed.

He stopped his work, turned his face to me slowly, as if what he knew was too terrible to speak. His face was gaunt from fifteen days of fasting, his eyes bright, almost fevered. All along the length of his body I could see his muscles had knotted into hard bundles, as if ready for flight.

"A man comes for us," he said.

I frowned, not able to understand why he would run from one man when he wouldn't run from three.

As if in answer to my perplexed look he added, "A man like me but who sends out bad medicine."

I began shivering again. "How do you know?"

He only looked at me as if should know the answer to that. It was then I realized this was the reason he had been gone so long. He'd sent out his soul on a journey, a very long journey few would undertake. Shadow Song had been soul-travelling.

"Who is this man?" I asked. As soon as I asked I regretted it. Such sorrow swept across his face, a wound long unhealed.

"The father of my dead wife."

It took everything I knew to ask, "Why does he come for you?"

"For us. He comes for us." That chilled me even further. "For me he comes to seek vengeance for the death of his daughter. For you he comes because he has been hired by your uncle. The latter serves the purpose of the former. I should have realized your uncle would stop at nothing. I underestimated my enemy."

That was when I asked him a question I'd long considered. "What happened to her?"

The feverish look in his eyes dimmed, clouding, as if he were back in that time. "I was seeking a dream when white traders raped her. I dreamed of a young girl who would come across the Atlantic and seek out my guardianship, I dreamed of *Nanabush* guiding her. While dreaming my wife suffered. She ran. They hunted her for days until she dropped like a doe exhausted by the chase. She was pregnant."

Now I knew. Morning Star had been right only in part. She'd never understand the way of things with her brother. "And her father blames you?"

He nodded.

"And for this he hunts you?"

He nodded.

"What can he do?"

His eyes looked hard then, like brittle shards of fired clay. "Imagine what would happen if I took my power and set it loose, without control, without any respect for the wells from which I draw." He made a snatching motion with his hand. "All I desired would be mine."

"But it would come back upon you."

"Yes ... eventually. But for a time I would be invincible. Didn't you feel that when you were in the *jeesekeum*?"

Raw power surging through my marrow. Yes. That's what I'd felt. As if I held on to the very stuff of the land, that huge, wild force that shaped everything I saw, everything I was and could be. "I felt it."

"Then you understand when a person undertakes to tap this power they must be pure, controlled. To fail in this means a backlash. If I hit the water with my body, it would pool away from me. If I hit it hard enough this would still happen, but eventually the water would bounce back with equal energy and that energy consume me. Do you understand?"

I nodded.

"That energy might also consume things that had no part in its creation."

"Like clan members."

"Yes." He shook his head. "This man can be very dangerous. If he meets us I don't want to be around the other villagers. I shouldn't even take you except that he hunts you as well."

Shouldn't even take me. Then he had considered leaving, going, forever abandoning me. I hung my head in an attempt to stop another spate of weeping. "They said you weren't coming back." I looked back up at him, needing to see his face when he answered.

None of the hardness left him. "I'll always come back. When I can't you will know."

"Grandmother says I shouldn't stay with you because you're a man and I'm a woman."

"A very young woman, and I have never denied that I am a man." He gave me a lop-sided smile. "Now pack. We must be gone by dawn."

Part 3
Ningobianong

Chapter 19

For two days we traveled through rain, hop scotching the channel of islands to the mainland. Often I bailed the rain came so hard. Still we paddled. As long as the wind stayed calm our tiny craft would be fine.

By the third day a wind howled from the north, driving wind and waves into our faces. Cold it was. Hard. Like needles of ice. Fighting five foot waves we managed to make landfall at one of the smaller islands without being swamped. How was beyond me. All I knew was that we'd been spared.

We set our wigwam in the lee of white pines. Flight would wait. The next two days we caught up on fletching, sewing, cleaning the gun, checking ammunition, repairing the canoe. We spoke little. I wondered if that weren't for the best. Between the urgency of our flight, my lingering fear from Red Cloud's attempted rape, and the tension that still remained unconfronted between Shadow Song and me, I was sure any misplaced word could erupt into a situation I had no idea how to control. It wasn't so much that we argued. It was more something intangible in the air between us. Something ... I didn't know.

Rain fell in an endless grey curtain that hissed even in my sleep. Sleep was something we snatched in bits and stints. Everything was soaked. The pathetic fire that burned in our wigwam often guttered, filling our shelter with acrid smoke. My eyes burned, watering as though I wept. My lungs were thick with congestion so that it was painful to breathe. All of this and we kept watch as well, resting in shifts. Shadow Song became even more distant after checking our supplies.

By the sixth day the rain stopped, although the overcast sky portended more before long. We raced that day for the mainland, chopping at the water with our paddles, arriving only when the wind created a froth even in sheltered bays. Twice I thought we'd overturn. We didn't. We hadn't even lost anything. Perhaps yet *Nanabush* watched over us, as did our guardian spirits.

For two more days we rested. Even that wasn't enough to heal the sores on my hands that had opened from the abrasion of the paddle. My arms ached as

I slept. I woke once to find Shadow Song applying salve to my wounds. Too weary to protest, I simply let him minister to me.

When done he sat back on his haunches. I felt his need to speak, to sound his thoughts and so I staved off exhaustion and opened my eyes to him, studying him in the gloom of the wigwam. He was worried, that much was plain.

"The powder's wet."

Shadow Song had never been one to rely on his rifle and so his concern over wet powdered alerted me. "Can't we get by without?"

He looked away, back at me, shook his head.

"Why not?"

"We are the hunted now, not the hunters. We will need every advantage."

"Can't we just let it dry out?"

He held up his horn of powder and I saw why it was wet. In our haste the horn cracked and now only a small portion of the black substance remained, and that likely only to last for one or two shots, if he could manage to grind it back into useable form.

I accepted that. I also knew it would mean we'd have to paddle to La Cloche and the Bay post with the hope of trading for a fresh supply of powder. I asked the next logical question, needing to hear Shadow Song's response. "What will you use for trade?"

"I have a few decent pelts from last season. They may do."

"They will have to do." The agents at La Cloche would be interested in little else besides furs, particularly beaver. I questioned the wisdom of such a venture. To trade at La Cloche was to put us directly into the hands of people who could destroy our lives. Surely we could manage without a rifle.

Watching Shadow Song, I knew there would be no arguing this point. He could be painfully stubborn at times. Resigned, I heaved myself up and packed, sure this course would lead us to disaster.

Mercifully, the rain stopped. We headed out by mid-morning, paddling hard to cover as much distance as possible while the weather held. By early afternoon the heavy cover of clouds tore apart, shredding like old sheets. The odd spatter of rain still wet us. It wasn't enough to fuss over. We continued on our way, the north channel flying beneath us. My hands bled but I hid this as best I was able, unwilling to slow our progress.

We made good time despite my difficulty, so that by mid-afternoon the next day we would make landfall at La Cloche, conduct our business and head deep into the forest. I slept easily when we made camp along a rocky shore. I had my doubts Shadow Song slept at all. When he woke me dawn was barely upon us. By the light of the quick fire he'd stirred I could see the fatigue in his face, the way his eyes were rimmed in red. The volume of *Paradise Lost* lay opened near him.

I did not ask if he kept watch all night. His tension was enough to quell any conversation I might have considered. Instead, I ate quickly, packed quickly, and set myself into the bow of the canoe for another day's long paddle.

The sun was just into its afternoon descent when we rounded the point to the trading post. There was no traffic upon the water, it being the off season. I could see a large freight canoe overturned high up the cobble beach, the honey-coloured logs of the Bay's building. A pole ran both the Union Jack and the Bay's colors, the flags flapping listlessly in an errant breeze. My pulse stirred, skipped. I could only hope we wouldn't be recognized.

"You are my wife," Shadow Song said suddenly, the shore coming closer. "Play the part you did in the village."

I was grateful he couldn't see my face. I was sure I blushed. My hands trembled and it wasn't from the stresses of paddling. I nodded, sure he watched me.

We brought the canoe in as far as prudence allowed and then waded it in for fear of taking out the bottom on the rocks. Shadow Song preceded me, four fine beaver pelts over his shoulder. I had planned to use those pelts for a new blanket. My old rabbit fur would have to do until the trap lines filled this winter.

I followed a few steps behind him, head lowered, playing the part of the shy, obedient wife. The door of the post was open. We walked into gloom and the musky smells of fur, gun powder and whiskey. A man bent over a barrel off to my right, poking through coarse salt for some sort of dried flesh, likely pork or fish I assumed. He was of average height, all gone to wiry muscle as seemed to be common among those who made the backwoods their life. He watched us closely, scratching the prodigious beard that hung to his chest. My heart was throbbing. I hovered behind Shadow Song when he slapped down his furs and grunted, "Powder."

The man at the barrel leaned against the wall, pulling a pipe out of his pocket. "Bit late in the season to be trading, Injun."

Shadow Song gestured to the furs and then to a keg that clearly was one filled with gun powder.

"Likely inferior furs. Don't see how these are gonna be worth much."

"Good furs," Shadow Song said. "Trapped early winter."

The man strode over to the counter, casually inspected the glistening beaver pelts that should have been worth a great deal of gun powder. There was not a flaw on them. Another man appeared through a doorway behind the counter, big, bluff, clearly accustomed to heavy work. He wore leathers, fringed across the shoulders and the top of his boots. His hair was dark as was his beard. I turned my face away quickly, longing to flee. I knew this man. A person would think that with all this land and all the possibilities that governed life, the likelihood of just bumping into someone one knew from long ago would be nigh unto impossible. Life, however, was full of impossibilities. Here, before me, stood a ghost from my past, a man who had shown me kindness when I first set out on my journey in Upper Canada. I could only hope that the years had not lessened Paul Rogette's kindness.

From behind Shadow Song I watched recognition cross Paul's face, watched his gaze slide from me to Shadow Song. He said nothing. He looked down at the beaver pelts.

"Two horns," the trader said. "That's all I can give you for these goods."

"Six," said Shadow Song. I wondered how he managed to stay so calm, that he didn't tremble with fear as did I.

The trader shook his head, sliding the furs off the counter to stow in his inventory. "Sorry. Two is generous at that."

"Make it five," Paul said. "There's nothing wrong with those pelts."

"Robbery," the trader sputtered. "Why I've a good mind – "

"To heed my advice and be done with it. You can't cheat every redskin that comes through here. These pelts are top quality. If you want more from this Indian I suggest you deal fairly with him. Give him his five horns of powder."

Red-faced and grumbling, the trader turned away to his stock and prepared Shadow Song's barter. Paul gave him a brief nod, moved to the end of the counter and stood in front of a notice nailed to the logs. Before he covered it completely I saw a rather crude sketch of an Indian man and a young white girl with an official statement beneath it.

The trader passed Shadow Song the horns. The horns were shoved into a bag slung from Shadow Song's shoulder. With a grunt he turned, grabbed my arm and we walked to the door.

"Headed north?" Paul asked behind us. "If so, I'd head for the French River. Lotta people there with some big powerful medicine man, lookin' for blood and revenge. Could be interesting hunting."

My heart lurched. Shadow Song shoved me ahead of him and I heard him grunt an acknowledgment to Paul. I stumbled down the steps and across the cobble beach, frightened and grateful and so scared I wanted to burst into tears right there. We shoved the canoe into the water quickly and paddled at a reasonable pace although I longed to race, to put as much distance between the trading post and me as possible.

Shadow Song steered us in a westerly direction. Not until the trading post was lost in the distance did we speak. It was Shadow Song who broke the silence.

"We will head past the Mississagi River and then north. There are good wintering grounds there."

I heard the catch in his voice and knew he also was frightened. I couldn't bring myself to ask him why Paul had helped us. All I knew was that we were safe for the moment.

For several days we paddled close to the shoreline amid brilliant sun and drenching rain. Fog kept us land-bound for several more and then we were off again. When finally we came upon the river Shadow Song hunted for, we angled upstream, keeping close to the banks to lessen the pull of the flow. What river it was I had no idea. I supposed it mattered little. We had no map but the one in Shadow Song's head and I had never been lost with him as guide.

The river was broad and deeply cut so that even paddling in the shallows gave us good draft. Its bed was granite. Periodically shoals of pink sand cut the channel as the river twisted and turned. Another three days were taken in penetrating the river. Finally we had travelled as far as we could go. We beached. I hauled packs and bundles onto my back, wincing where my shoulders had rubbed raw from our earlier flight. Shadow Song took lead on the trail, he carrying the canoe upon his shoulders and the pack upon his back. Even he bent under the weight of his burden, near to a hundred pounds of pack and eighty of canoe.

We travelled far and long, ill-supplied for the winter, past the headlands of Huron's north shore into a place where the land was old and the spruce bogs began. This was fur-bearing country. Lynx, bear, bobcat, beaver — these were in abundance. Moose flourished in the lakes and bogs. The hunting here would be good, enough to augment our poor store, and the intrusion of whites unlikely.

By now the forest was touched with colour, reds, golds, as if a slow fire burned and flickered on the leaves. One morning, early on the trail, a massive flock of geese flew overhead, a dark V against the pink of dawn. They called, filling my world with their sad song of winter to come. I felt the weight of their song and said a silent prayer to the *manitous* that this year we would be spared. When I heard the ululations of the loons, I was glad for their leaving. If I had to listen to their lonely sound I thought knowing of the desolation to come would have been more than I could bear.

By the time the forest was ablaze with colour, under the advantage of favourable weather, we reached a likely area for winter camp, well into Odawa country. We set our wigwams, one in the shelter of a hemlock stand that would protect us from winds, another at some distance for when my cycle would come, and yet another for our store of goods.

Shadow Song quickly took to the hunt, scouting the area for sign. I traveled through the forest, searching out the banks of the lake we camped near for a stand that might afford us a harvest of wild rice. A few days later I reported my find over morning tea.

"Is it any good?" Shadow Song asked.

"It's not the best, but I'm sure I can salvage enough to stretch our stores."

He nodded gravely at that. He knew all too well if we weren't well supplied, the winter could be deadly enough without threat of capture.

Shadow Song rose, beckoning for me to follow. He righted the canoe and we paddled. It was a sparkling day, the sky a brilliant cobalt, the sun warm as it wouldn't be for long. What few deciduous trees there were had shed their leaves, exposing limbs stark and bare against the deepening pines. There was a bite to the air that forecast a frost tonight, again.

The lake was mirror calm, not a ripple upon its surface but for where we crossed it, our paddles hissing with water as we went. A woodpecker drummed, stopped, drummed again. Chickadees peppered the air with their calls.

We crossed the lake to its source river, followed it, portaged a little and then set into a swamp where the rice grew in a drowned meadow. The water here was inky black, a contrast to the pale yellow of dying grasses.

Most of the rice-heads were still heavy, bowing in an errant breeze. Our canoe rustled against the stalks. I back-paddled, held us anchored while Shadow Song ran his fingers along a head, tapped into the cup of his hand and tasted the long, brown grain. He nodded, took up his paddle while I sat myself in the center of the vessel, two sticks in my hands. It occurred to me at that moment I'd become accustomed to the capricious canoe, confident of how to move and when. Again I thought of Paul, of our time in Hornings Hills and more recently our meeting at the trading post.

Shadow Song gestured irritably, chastising me for my day-dreaming. I set to my duty, bending the stalks over the sides of the canoe and smacking their heads to release a shower of kernels. Bend, smack, move, bend, smack, move – we continued our harvest until well after noon. By the time we were done we had four small sacks filled, had sung four songs of thanksgiving and smoked four pipes of tobacco. It was a sacred number. For that we were grateful. At that moment a cow moose and her calf broke through the forest and waded into the lake, grazing peacefully as we were downwind of them. We watched them reverently. To take this game was to break strict taboos.

While the weather lasted we dried and stored whatever we could, putting aside duck potatoes, Queen Anne's lace, Jack-in-the-pulpit, wild onions, pickerelweed and more, this with a liberal supply of fish and goose we had brought with us. To this Shadow Song added a bull moose he had the good fortune to bring down. We even had a little maple syrup and sugar left from the preceding spring.

By the time the first snows flew we were as prepared as we were going to be. We shared a fire in the wigwam, huddled into furs while Shadow Song told me stories about *Nanabush* and *Mandamin*, of *Pitchi-robin* and of *Kineu*. The one I remembered most clearly that early winter was the story of *Geezhig* and *Wabun-anung*, lovers who had been betrothed. Just before their marriage *Wabun-anung* died, leaving *Geezhig* in grief. So great was his love for her that he set out on a quest to find the Land of the Souls, despite warnings from his elders. After much privation he was granted his wish. His spirit fled his body and he travelled to the mysterious land where all souls dwelled. When at last he reached the shore, *Wabun-anung* was there. That was all he was granted – to see her once again. He woke to find himself back in his body, back in the land of the living.

For days I lingered over the tale. Such sadness. I wondered at this, at the way all of life's sweetness was made just a little painful. There wasn't leisure, however, to moon over this tragic story for long. Chores took my attention quickly enough and before long the story had been relegated to memory.

As the winter progressed, we thought perhaps we had escaped our hunters. Game was good. Our stores looked as though they'd stretch through the winter. We were confident, in our isolation, that our fortune would continue. How could it not? Everywhere the forest was silent, a vast world of pine and hemlock, fir and cedar. Only the tracks of the Elder Brothers marked the snow. Not once in those months did we come across any sign of humans.

It was in the midst of one of these intense solitudes that I thought of England, of a life almost dim in memory, and of a great grey cathedral I often visited with Maman and Papa. I looked up at the towering trees around me, and the splinters of winter sunlight lancing through them. Still the forest reminded me of that solemn cathedral, of pillars rising endlessly into high vaults. When I broke down into tears I was grateful Shadow Song wasn't there to see. My grief would only bruise him.

The winter deepened. A blizzard blasted us and buried our wigwam nearly to the dome. Shadow Song read by dim light from his books. In those tense days

I could only think of the *windigo*, the terrible spirit of a man who, in the desperation of starvation, had consumed a potion and slaughtered his own family for food, thinking them beaver. Shadow Song grew withdrawn. That did nothing to allay my fears. When at last the blizzard abated, he left for the hunt.

It was while Shadow Song was gone a man found me. I was stitching a new tunic and set of leggings for Shadow Song, enjoying the clean fire, the warmth, my sense of well-being. He bent through the opening, silent as death. I glanced up, startled. Odd he seemed, his manner of speech blurred, his face never the same each time I looked at him. All of the signs were there, but I was too amazed by his presence to heed. I offered him food, tobacco, and then we spoke.

"*Waenaesh k'dodaem?*" I asked.

He answered he was one of the *Mukukee* Clan, the frog clan.

"*Waenaesh keen?*"

He was one of the people of the Indian Peninsula, and added, "My woman suckles a child."

I nodded. Was his hair grey? I couldn't decide, my attention wandering over him.

"Her milk doesn't flow. The child will die."

No, not grey, I decided, just flecked. And his face, what of that? ...

"What can I do to save the child?" he asked.

What was I thinking? This was a young man, likely a father for the first time. How could he have any grey hair at all? Just look at his eyes ....

"Perhaps you have something I could use?"

I didn't even think when I offered him the leaves of the milkwort. This would aid his wife, I knew. Had I thought, I would have realized he knew I was *midewequae* and had sought me out. That should have alarmed me. No one knew where Shadow Song and I had gone. I realized none of this at the time. He smiled. I felt it was a rather revealing smile, cold, calculating. He bent his way out of the wigwam. As payment he left me tobacco and a fox pelt.

Such a large gift for such a small cure. I caressed the long guard hairs of the ruddy fur. Surely I could have accepted something smaller. I shrugged and set the lustrous thing to one side of the wigwam, abandoned my sewing and turned away for my snares, slipping my feet into snowshoes. As I went I sank not at all into the wind-driven snow, gold now in the late afternoon sun. The sound of my scrunching seemed very loud to me, my head light, my senses disoriented. Shadows around me were long and blue. I should have checked the lines earlier, I realized. That would have been prudent. Prudence was a luxury I could not afford at the moment. It was important that I check the snares now, right this moment.

Cold, I pulled the fur of my cloak around myself, thankful for the leggings that did much to stave off a chill. I headed east along the lake, up a rise where I had set my first line of snares. The first turned up nothing. That wasn't unusual. I scrunched my way to the next. When I dug it out it also was empty. As was the third, and the fourth, and the next one after that. By now I'd set into a cumbersome run through dense pines, twice stepping on my snowshoes and pitching into the snow. Desperation and anger confused me. The eighth and ninth snares came up empty. I attacked the tenth, stripping off my mittens and driving my fingers into the snow. My skin flamed, burned by cold. It seemed not to matter. I dug furiously. The snare caught, held, bit into my numbing flesh. That pain brought me back to sanity.

I sat back on my haunches, stunned. What was I doing out here?

The pain in my hand called my attention. The snare had gone deeply and I was cut, bleeding. I loosened my hand from the wire and packed snow around it to slow the bleeding. There was nothing I could use to bind it and so I waited until the burning of the cold lessened and I knew the wound had been numbed. Luckily, I had not cut anything major and would be left with a surface scar. Gingerly, I pulled my mittens back on and rose.

Why had I done this? This wasn't at all like me.

Around me the shadows were deepening. I looked out over the lake. The sun had almost dipped beyond the horizon. Night would take the forest quickly. With a growing sense of dread I refastened my snowshoes and set off at a sensible trot to camp. Night did fall quickly. My pace slowed. It was only by instinct and luck that finally I trudged to where our wigwam was set, hours beyond sunset. I was shivering violently now, my feet almost numb in the tall, fur-lined boots.

A light from the wigwam stopped me mid-stride. My mouth dried.

Was Shadow Song back? Cautious, I called out to him softly. Silence. There was only the groan of the trees. I unhooked my toes from the snowshoes, set them upright in the snow and slipped my knife from its sheath. Stealthily, I crept to the wigwam, ducked down inside, my knife before me ready to jab.

What I found in our lodge was worse than a blow. Shadow Song lay sprawled upon his back, his leather tunic shred, blood dark and dried upon his clothes. His skin was pallid in the fading firelight, his breathing shallow and ragged. He didn't even stir when I knelt beside him. There was the look of death to him. I knew that look well. The knife slid from my hand.

Don't let him die! I thought. *Calm. Only stay calm*, I told myself. To panic now would serve neither of us. Even so my hands fluttered when I touched his cheek. Heat. Such heat from him.

I looked over his body, assessing what had happened. None of it made any sense. The open slashes across his chest and belly looked like a bear attack, recent. But the bear would be sleeping. And the fever? The wounds weren't deep enough to cause a fever.

Somehow I managed to keep my hands steady enough to slice away the remainder of his tunic. I boiled water. Bathed his wounds. Prepared a poultice and applied it. I covered him with the best of our blankets and furs, set the lustrous fox pelt beneath his head, fretted over him, desperately trying not to cry, not to fall apart with him so ill.

Don't let him die!

It wasn't until that moment, watching him lie so still, so pale, I realized there would be a huge hole in my life should he die. Survive without him I could. The world, however, would have lost its sparkle.

For three days I watched over him, sleeping only in snatches, slipping a thin broth between his teeth. I kept his wounds clean but still his fever wouldn't break. On the morning of the fourth day his eyes opened, suddenly, as if something had jolted him. Why I flinched I didn't know. It was just there was something odd about his wild stare, something not quite right.

"I'm hungry."

I shuddered. His voice sounded so hoarse, so hollow. I ladled soup into a bowl and fed him as I had the previous days. His hands prevented me. He seized the bowl stiffly and drank it all down, wiping his mouth with the back of his hand. Always his gaze stayed on me, bright, almost feral. My alarm mounted. I could feel the hair on my nape bristle.

"More." He gestured with the empty bowl.

I served him another. Still there was that wildness about him. He emptied that one also. Asked for more. When I served him this one he grabbed my hand, upsetting the bowl. Soup splashed against his chest. He clutched the fox pelt in the other hand, grinning, his lips roving over my hand in a way that said this wasn't a man-thing he did. It was evil. Wrong.

"Beaver," he breathed. "I want beaver."

Still his lips nipped at my hand, his tongue drawing circles. *Windigo!* I snatched back my hand. He lunged. My breath came hard and fast. I dodged, looking to his other hand that still grasped the fox pelt.

Sense crashed over me at that moment – the old man, his gift, his odd way. Hadn't I lost my senses after touching the pelt he'd given me?

Shadow Song twisted, breaking open his wounds, lurched for me again. I slipped my knife from its sheath, let it fly. It caught the pelt cleanly, pinning it to the ground and free of Shadow Song's grasp. He slumped, groaned and lay still. All of the same motion I flicked the pelt onto the fire.

Something unearthly screamed. The sound of it set my teeth on edge. To my horror the pelt writhed on the fire like a living thing. Blue flame shot to the hole in the roof of the wigwam.

"*Numae* help me," I cried, more afraid than I ever thought I could be. What I witnessed, I knew, was the soul of the shaman who hunted us, there in the fire. The pelt sizzled, snapped, bending as fire consumed it. Blue flame contorted around it, forming, forming, now a face bent in agony. From somewhere I found the control to relax, let my spirit stretch to those other benevolent spirits around me. Power from Mother Earth surged through my marrow, hot, white, and in the next moment I felt my soul slip from my body into the blue flame.

It was like drowning in power gone awry. There were no limits. There were no guides. I felt the wantonness of what the shaman had done and forced myself to bring order back into chaos. In that contact the shaman's soul died away with a wail, thinning, thinning, and then was gone. Wherever his body was it would soon follow his soul, I was sure.

Trembling, I gathered my spirit back, forced myself to smoke in thanksgiving to *Numae* and Mother Earth, then turned to Shadow Song. Again I washed his wounds. I bound them. I covered him in furs and kept watch over him. That night his fever broke. I slept fitfully in the meagre furs I left for myself, thankful that the worst was over.

After that, during the days that followed he grew stronger, slowly and slowly. It had been about fourteen of these agonizing days later, after I finished feeding him a thin broth and inspected his wounds that his hand gently caught mine. He pressed my palm to his lips. He smiled, but he did not open his eyes. There was such contentment on his face, such gratitude, weak though he was.

I caught my breath, swallowing tears. My pulse was fluttering raggedly. I patted his cheek and crawled to my side of the wigwam and lay upon the grass mat, pulling my cloak over myself. It was impossible to sleep I shivered so violently. The temperature outside dropped, growing colder, colder, settling into a snap that could kill the unwise very easily. In the end I gave up chasing sleep and huddled into my knees by the fire, watching Shadow Song snoring. Somehow I did manage to nod off for a moment. I awakened with a flinch when he touched my foot. I looked at him. His eyes were open, clear, warm. Yes, he was definitely mending.

"How long have you been without sleep?" he asked gently, his voice still tremulous.

I shrugged, shivering, trying to make light of these past days.

He lifted away the furs. Warmth rose like an ether. I blushed, averting my eyes from his nakedness. "Come under the covers."

I shook my head. "You're still ill."

"And you're cold. Come under the covers."

"It isn't seemly."

He gestured again. "As you said, I'm still ill."

He was. What could happen with an ill man? And I was cold ... and the mound of furs did look inviting .... I slipped into the cocoon of warmth beside him, settling my back to him. He winced when I accidentally brushed against his wounds. I pulled away, saying, "This won't work —"

His arm caught me around the waist as he settled. I relaxed when he pulled me under his chin and nested his knees against the back of mine. So odd this feeling, a man at my back, the luxury of his body's warmth, the way his chest rose and fell with breathing, the smell of his skin ....

Sleep wrapped me quickly in luxury.

Chapter 20

Within two weeks Shadow Song was well enough to walk about our camp, although that's all I would allow him to do. Walk. About our camp. It nearly drove him to distraction. Every time he attempted to lift a kettle of hot water, follow me at my lines, do anything I might construe as work, I'd shoot him one of my dark looks, arching a brow. So he walked, paced, like a caged animal around the boundary I set for him. He nearly shouted at me that he was mending well enough. For a shaman as he to suffer the edicts of his very young apprentice plainly was a matter that chaffed. After all, he'd protested once, exactly who had taken care of whom all these years? My reply was that I had a good teacher. Now he must be a good patient.

Today I was off to my lines. I left him with the usual admonition to do nothing, go nowhere and to rest. Stores, I explained, were getting low and so I hoped some small game had been snared for tonight's pot.

"Just walk," I added, straightening from my snowshoes. "About the camp."

He shot me a surly look.

"Promise me."

"Yes, yes."

"Promise me."

"I'll walk, about the camp."

"And that's all."

"And that's all."

I favoured him with one more measuring look, turned and set off for my lines.

The day had that rare quality to it that comes when spring is teasing. I knew shy young *Zeegwun* of the south was winning back the land from the old shaman *Bebon* of the north. I could feel the blessing of warm sun on my face. This pleased me. I let my senses stretch, pool out and out the way I had learned years ago. Throughout the forest I could hear snow melting, plopping in sudden sheets from pine branches. It scattered under my snowshoes in wet kernels.

Soon it would be time to leave these wintering grounds for the maple stand. Morning Star, Lightfoot and Grandmother would be greeted once more. The three children would be older, perhaps wiser. The eldest boy, Deer-Coming-Down, might even have begun hunting. Regretfully, I acknowledged the fact there would probably be the same endless arguments. I should leave Shadow Song's wigwam for Morning Star's. I would be yet another year older. I would be in need of a husband this year. It wasn't good for a young woman to be too stand-offish with her suitors. The prospect of all this was not one I relished. There would, however, be time. Shadow Song must mend. There were a few weeks yet before the sap would run.

By the time I inspected my lines it was close to noon. Two rabbits, a partridge. Not bad. I smoked in thanksgiving and chanted a prayer. Things could be worse had I not discovered the evil spell upon the fox pelt.

Game in hand, I set my path back to the camp, waddling in the walk of snowshoes. When I approached, I chose stealth, sure I would catch Shadow Song at some task he wasn't to be about. My view was clear enough from behind a screen of junipers.

He stood in the center of the camp, stripped to the waist, a pole in his hands above his head. He bent to and fro, muscles rippling, stretching, pulling the newly healed wounds I was sure almost to the limit. They gleamed an angry red. A frown cut his brow, his jaw clenched clearly in discomfort. Yet still he twisted, turned, lifting a leg in a parry. Every line of him glistened with sweat. He was beautiful, just as he had been that first time I'd seen him. Now, however, his beauty seemed more intense to me, more immediate. Beauty and power and deadliness all there in him. Fire and ice. My fingers tingled with memory of touching his chest, the way his flesh had moved under my hands. Even now I could feel the heat of him at my back as we nested together under the furs.

I have never denied that I am a man. I remembered him saying that. Why should he deny that? Wasn't he everything I wanted in a man?

I swallowed, only too aware of how my heart raced, of how my pulse throbbed in the hollow of my throat, of how something stirred in my loins ....

No. I mustn't do this. He was a man, yes, but not my man.

With a cough and much commotion I shuffled into camp, throwing him more than the usual amount of warning looks. I said nothing. I only tossed down my game, lanced my snowshoes into a drift and set to skinning, plucking and gutting.

He paused in his exercise, measuring me I knew. I looked up at him. He had his hands on his hips, the pole abandoned to the ground. I said nothing, averted my gaze. I could hear him pull on his tunic, throw the cloak of wolf fur around his shoulders and lean upon the pole to observe me.

"It's a good catch," he said. I could tell he was testing my mood. I nodded, working the pelt away from the rabbit's carcass. The fur would be woven into another blanket or robe. Still, he watched me, I knew. Perhaps I should launch into one of my lectures. By now my hands were bloody and I didn't feel up to lectures.

"I'll go hunting tomorrow," he said.

I paused, trembled slightly and continued. "Do you think that wise?"

"It is if we're to eat any better."

I looked up at him sharply, seething with sudden anger. "I've done the best I could."

He smiled, a slow curling of one side of his mouth, that arrogant, mocking twist that could so enrage me at times. He offered not another word. He only watched me, his clay-brown eyes seeing more than I wished, things I desperately needed to keep hidden. There, in the sunlight, he was too masculine, too intense for one inexperienced girl of sixteen.

I looked back down to my work, my cheeks ablaze. Memory of his kiss in the summer camp washed over me, the way his lips had overwhelmed me, the way his tongue had flicked warm and sensuous, the way he had bent to me and whispered, *She's mine*.

I dressed the animals with more zeal than I felt, determined to look upon him as little as possible. For the remainder of the afternoon I remained in a prickly state of silence, feeling him watching no matter where I moved. He, for his part, only sat upon a rock, checking his bow, luxuriating in the first warm day in months.

That evening we ate in silence. There were no stories. He, instead, played his flute, watching as I combed out my long hair by firelight and then plaited it into two braids. Shortly after I lay myself on my side of the fire, beneath my cloak, fully clothed and with my back to him. I heard him return the flute to his bag, and climb into his nest of furs and comfort. He watched me all the while, I was sure.

When I shivered from the cold, as surely he knew I would, he invited me to share his blankets. I declined.

"It's cold," he said.

I turned slowly, trying hard not to look at the way he'd propped himself on one elbow, the way firelight gleamed off his chest. Should I?

"Come." Gently. So gently he said that. There was nothing there to raise alarm. It had been so warm with him at night .... I rose and slid into the furs beside him, my back to him, my pulse racing. As always he draped his arm around my waist and pulled me closely, nesting my head under his chin. I closed my eyes, trying to let sleep rock me away. After a while my senses blurred. I slept. I woke. Something hard was against the small of my back, tapping. I stiffened, all too aware of his erect penis. Pulse hammering, I scrambled from out of the covers. He smiled up at me, shrugging.

"Stop that!" I hissed.

"I am a man, *wahboos*."

And I was a woman. He didn't have to say it. I knew this all too well.

I threw myself under my cloak on my own side of the fire. I wasn't sure if I was angry with him or with myself. For a moment I kept my silence, afraid my voice would tremble if I spoke too soon, and then: "It would be wise of us to head for the sugar bush when you return." Hunters be damned. Uncle be damned. I could hear him snort a laugh.

"As you wish."

Chapter 21

I was glad for the days that followed. Shadow Song's absence not only allowed me to set my thoughts in order, but to prepare our household for a move. It was plain to me what I must do when we joined Morning Star and Lightfoot. I would ask if I could live with them. This was not a decision I made easily. The thought of life without Shadow Song cut, deeply. Yet I couldn't stay. It wasn't seemly. It wasn't done. I was neither his daughter nor his wife nor his sister, and if things continued I would dishonour both of us. I also considered the tension between us. With both of us so distracted, our guards would be down and that could only spell disaster where Uncle was concerned. I harboured no illusions that Uncle might have given up the chase. He had pursued me all these years. Nothing had stopped him thus far. He wouldn't stop with the death of one man.

As I packed I came again upon my copy of Milton's *Paradise Lost*, and I wondered, not for the first time, why both Shadow Song and I were so drawn to this epic. Certainly we both had read it and read it again, periodically reciting the downfall of Lucifer, that most beautiful and pathetic of angels. As I wrapped the book carefully in leathers I wondered if we both didn't feel some kinship with this most loathed of angels, he who had been elevated to high degree and then rejected paradise. There were some, I was sure, who would agree with that comparison.

Four days after he left, Shadow Song returned from a successful hunt. I had not heard rifle shot and so I assumed the deer he dragged home sledge after sledge had been a bow kill. As always, I assisted in the dressing of the animal. My greeting was cool, formal, my attention firmly planted upon my work. I told him nothing of my decision. Several times he attempted to strike up a conversation. I answered in monosyllables. After a while he gave up, although I knew he watched me as I prepared a smoking lodge a prudent distance from our camp and lay the strips of meat out for preserving. Late into the night we ate roasted venison. It was savoury. It was succulent. I ate until I ached.

Full, and tired from the day and my thoughts, I retired. Again he watched me intently as I lay myself upon my side of the fire. This time he offered me none of the extra blankets and none of the warmth he could afford. I woke late the next morning. Shadow Song was outside. I could tell from the sound of his movements. Stiffly, I crawled out, sure I must look a sight. Shadow Song was not completely successful in hiding the smile that touched his lips when he saw me. He motioned me to the fire, the way he used to when I first came under his care. Breakfast was prepared – more deer meat and tea. I moved carefully, sluggishly, lowered myself to the large trunk of a fallen tree we used as our bench. We ate. He offered me only one item of conversation.

"Our way is clear."

I looked over at him briefly. He seemed calm, contained. I realized he'd been soul-travelling in his sleep last night. With a nod I accepted his news and chewed as quickly as I could, knowing we would have to be on our way soon if we were to make good distance this day.

Once more I shrugged into my pack, placing the head strap over my forehead. With a groan I settled its weight. We set off, all our goods upon our backs. Shadow Song paced us carefully. His wounds were still tender. A bout of over-exertion could be damaging, something, I told myself, he should have thought about before going off to chase that deer.

My temper remained sharp as we journeyed. I was grateful we didn't speak. Something in the way Shadow Song surveyed our surroundings told me he had sent his soul on ahead as scout. His lips moved silently – prayers, I assumed, to his guardians. When we camped at night my sleep was fitful and so I did more than my share of watching.

Two days out Shadow Song grew tense. He walked uneasily, fretting with the burden of the canoe upon his shoulders. I realized an ambush on us would be successful now. Shadow Song would have no time to slip either his bow or rifle from his shoulder. One shot was all he'd need. He wouldn't get it. Not the way we were.

We'd been on the trail for several hours this day when he paused, lifted the canoe from his shoulders and rolled it to the snow. I watched him as he looked ahead, down the trail at something out there.

"Stay here," he said.

I knew from the tone of his voice to ask no questions. My skin tightened. I watched him set off ahead, rifle in hand, reaching for powder and shot. I lost sight of him when he slipped around the bend of a large hill ahead. To track him by sound was impossible. He moved lightly, as he always had. There was no knowing where he might be.

The minutes strung out, tightening with tension until I felt I would snap. Just when I was about to go in pursuit of him he came back along the trail, a hard look to his face.

"What is it?" I asked when he came abreast.

He shot a glance over-shoulder. "Come with me."

There would be no discussion for the moment, I knew. I followed at his back, leaving our goods behind. His reticence did nothing to ease my growing alarm.

Some distance along the trail we struck off into the woods. The sense of wrongness within me grew, raking my skin until I felt there was only this evil in the world, this terrible evil that twisted through the air. We passed a cedar blackened and bent, as though it had been molten and cooled, never to be green again. I reached for Shadow Song's hand. His fingers closed around mine, tightly. This thing unnerved him also. I felt it clearly in his skin.

Many more trees were like the cedar now, the snow gone as if terrible heat had been here, heat that wasn't fire but something else. Finally we came upon the remnant of a wigwam. There wasn't much left. The upright poles still stood, some broken at the top as if a thing had exploded from within. Only a few sheets of bark ringed the perimeter. Footsteps marked the ground, etched into the earth not in the way of a melt, but as if they had been incised when this person sketched a staggered course away. A stone pipe lay along this path, feathers scorched. I bent to it, reaching.

"Don't!" Shadow Song snarled.

I jerked around. His face looked like stone, his clay-brown eyes shards.

"It was his. Don't touch it."

I straightened, smoothed my skirt as much to smooth my pulse. "The shaman's?"

He nodded.

I remembered what had happened the last time I touched something of the shaman's. The fox pelt had infected me, luring me away on a fruitless journey so that its evil could work upon Shadow Song. I glanced at the pipe, the lovely carving on the bowl. "But surely it isn't – "

"Evil?" His mouth lifted in something resembling a smile, harsh and mocking. "Anything he's touched is twisted." He gestured to the ring of devastation, the trees blackened and bent, the way the rocks themselves seemed to scream in silent torture. I looked where he indicated, seeing pain upon pain. In my own feeble way I could hear the pleas of Mother Earth.

He bent to his heels, digging for sweet grass in his pouch and set it alight on the ground, keening a prayer for the wounded land. When he rose he looked at me. "He's still alive."

"But, I saw – "

"His spirit die upon the fire?" He shook his head. "This man is old and wise and crafty. I should have realized – "

"But you were ill."

He nodded. "And too willing to believe I might not have to meet this man again."

Meet him? I could find no way to make myself say those words. Meet him? "Why?" I finally managed.

"Think."

Because my uncle had hired him. Gifts had been accepted. A bargain made. An old shaman like this wouldn't let a little thing like death stand in his way.

Imagine what would happen if I took my power and set it loose .... I looked around the circle of death. *All I desired would be mine* .... I looked up at Shadow Song. *For a time I would be invincible* ....

There was an old score to settle, the death of a daughter. This would be fuel enough. I pointed to the footsteps in the ground, traced a line, aimed at the horizon obscured by the trees. "He's headed south, to the lake, to gather strength. Eventually his path will cross ours."

Shadow Song turned on his heel and pursued the trail back to our goods. I followed.

Our journey that day was silent, as was the next and the next. Frightened as I was I still would not share warmth with him at night. I remained on my side of the fire. It wasn't long before my dour mood returned. I avoided looking at him. What, I wondered, were we doing heading back to where danger could find us? Indeed, yes, I needed to resolve my dilemma regarding Shadow Song, but at what cost? Would I put all of his family, and indeed the whole summer village in jeopardy? Council was what I really needed. I was too stubborn to seek the only council I valued.

Still we walked, heading for the maple stand near the shore of Huron where his sister and her family would gather. Travel at this time of year wasn't easy. One day *Bebon* would regain strength and the land chill, snow fly in sopping great clots of white. The rock would be treacherous, slick. Often we slid, fell. The next day *Bebon* tired and *Zeegwun* gained control, throwing warmth into the air. Ice melted. Snow dissolved. The earth became pockets of mud.

This day I felt like arguing. My sleep had been frayed, augmented by the sores on my shoulders and the ache in my neck I wouldn't allow Shadow Song to treat. I had been too tired to treat them myself. Besides, I relished this pain. It kept me sane. It kept me from mooning about like some love-sick cow. It kept me from thinking about our very real danger. Shadow Song had called me stubborn, plain and simple. I was.

We had been traveling for some hours. The trail descended now into a little valley. Shadow Song made his way down, readjusting the weight of the canoe on his shoulders. I followed behind, gingerly. Moccasins were not the easiest footwear in which to navigate slippery terrain. In the next moment my feet shot out from under me. Pain jolted up my back. I slid, skewed sideways, narrowly missing Shadow Song. I could hear the rasp of snow beneath me, carrying me down the hill. I think I screamed as I bounced from tree to tree, screamed until my mouth clogged with snow and mud. The poles for the wigwam snagged, broke, snagged again as I crashed through junipers and came to a halt. I could hear Shadow Song dropping his load and bounding down the slope. By the time he reached me I was in enough pain to chew on tears.

He stood over me, dropped to his heels. "Are you hurt?"

I wobbled on my back, head down-slope, feeling the blood rush to my brain. "Fine." I wanted to scream at him I was so frustrated.

He pressed his lips together, sucking in his cheeks, all the while trying desperately not to laugh. That angered me more. Here was I, covered in mud, overturned like a turtle in the sun. I thrashed for some kind of hold.

"You don't look fine," he said softly.

I stopped my thrashing, stiffened. He extended me a hand. I glared at him. "I'll manage on my own."

He shrugged, rose and turned away for his load. I could see his shoulders shaking as he left. Damn him anyway! I wobbled and tried to roll myself over. I was still wobbling when he came back down the slope, canoe and pack shouldered. "I'll wait for you at camp," he called back to me and left me sputtering in his wake.

Yes, I was being stubborn. Yes, I was looking for an argument. Damn him, did he really have to go off and leave me like this? I fumed and fussed until finally I managed to get enough of a brace against a tree that I was able to right myself. Every limb aching, I trudged along his trail, cursing him and myself as I went. Several more times I plunged to the ground, and several more times I had to right myself.

It was near to nightfall when I stumbled into camp, bruised, almost in tears, covered in filth. Shadow Song dumped an armload of firewood on top of the very large pile already near the entrance to the wigwam. He made no comment about my state, and offered no assistance. I was glad he took my look as a warning.

Wincing, I slid off my pack, rubbed the back of my neck. I studied the wigwam, realized he'd cut new poles and bark, covered it with skins to keep it warm for tonight. Finally, I looked up at where he stood by the entrance. He gestured for me to enter. I dropped my gaze. Already my mouth watered for want of that delicious something I could smell brewing in the wigwam. Without decorum I shoved myself through the opening and slumped to the furs, wincing where fir boughs dug into my bruised rump. I ate everything he gave me. When he pulled out his flute and played it was like a siren's call and I slept where I sat. I stirred when I felt his hands moving over me, helping me from my sodden clothes. Weakly, I protested.

"Hush, *wahboos*. Let your shaman nurse you."

With a sigh I gave myself up to his tender mercies. I felt warm water laving my limbs, salve upon my sores. He piled blankets and furs over me and stoked the fire to keep me warm. The last thing I remember from that night was him rocking me with my head on his lap, and of him humming.

For two days we rested. I did little. Mostly I sat inside the wigwam, pretending to stitch moccasins. He watched me, covertly, I knew. Still, my thoughts were such that I was consumed with little else but my dilemma.

Morning Star's argument played again and again through my head. *What do you think people will say when we go to the summer village?* It was a sound argument I realized now. What would the people of the summer village say this year, now I was older, definitely a marriageable woman? That Shadow Song had raised himself a woman? What would my future prospects be then?

She should stay with us now. Another of Morning Star's arguments. This, also, had the ring of reason to it. If I timed matters right, I could save both of us from gossip, from words that could damage as badly as blows. What was a medicine man without his people? A sorcerer weaving spells in the dark. He'd be like the old shaman who hunted us. Then there was to consider that the shaman might swing all his attention to me if Shadow Song and I parted. He had, after all, been hired to hunt me. Shadow Song would be free, finally, after all these years.

It was then I realized if I stayed with Morning Star and Lightfoot I might very well place them in jeopardy. Uncle probably would use them as he used Shadow Song. The matter of impropriety still would remain. I would still be in a household with a man who wasn't my kin, just as Shadow Song had said. What would people say then? That I was safe? How safe would I be against a strange man and a shaman on the hunt?

I'd been safe all these years with Shadow Song. Now that I could be a wife....

He'd had a wife. He knew what sweaty loins and sharing households and loving a person was all about. What made me think he could possibly want that with me? Why would he want to again share that place where pleasure and pain meet in a man and woman?

Do you wish to leave me? Leave him! It was still an intimate, personal question, one that was no easier to confront now as then. How could I leave him? How could I stay?

I looked up and realized he sat across the fire watching me. How could I stay? How could I leave?

I saw in him the man, not the holy one, not the healer, not the maker of magic. At that moment, sitting across the fire, he was just a man, as real and close and warm as my own breath. Didn't I understand him as intimately as I knew myself? I knew him in every way but that one that would make me his wife. How could I leave? How could I stay?

"Would it help if I made gifts?" he asked then, his voice low, husky, like a deep wind winding through my senses.

I fled through the door and ran out to the day, gulping the chill air. Gifts! He'd make gifts to me? The way Red Cloud had made gifts to me and presented them to Grandmother?

What would he do with me as wife? Continue to run from the men Uncle would send after us? No. It was better to leave. This problem was mine, not his. I'd not hurt him as payment for the years of sanctuary he'd given me.

I returned to the wigwam and bent to my task, knowing even as I did I cut him with my silence. That couldn't be helped. There were other considerations.

The next day we traveled, reaching the river. Paddling was difficult because we had to fight ice, albeit thin, and ice to a birch bark canoe is like a knife; but with the two of us determined to attend only to our journey we managed satisfactory distance and came through with no damage. Throughout the next days we set about our tasks deliberately, speaking only out of necessity, eyeing each other carefully. There were no other signs of the old shaman. That was a relief. Still, we watched, aware we could be caught off guard at anytime, that for us to return to Manitowaning was lunacy at best. Shadow Song made some statement that he would rather be on familiar territory when his hunters came for him. It was one of the few things we agreed upon.

Two weeks later we had navigated the North Channel and struck north to the sugar stand. We found Morning Star's camp without difficulty. As always there was little commotion at our reunion. I set about putting our wigwam for storage in order and set to the chores of sap gathering. Morning Star and Lightfoot had already tapped many trees, letting the buckets fill. I made note of the buckets – tin, plainly traded for furs Lightfoot had gathered over the winter. I hung buckets of bark. They were not as modern as the others, but I took satisfaction in the fact I used little from the white world. That I made this hypocrisy by carrying Milton's epic tale was irrelevant.

That night, as usual, Morning Star and Lightfoot copulated copiously. I wanted to scream with frustration but instead only buried myself in the furs. The following day the men went off hunting, taking the two boys with them. I watched as Shadow Song left, the way the fringes across his shoulders and arms tossed, the way his jet hair streamed behind him.

I looked back at the pot and stirred the sap. Grandmother sat nearby, telling the youngest daughter tales. The old woman's age showed prominently now. Winter had not been kind to her. It occurred to me she might not survive another. Morning Star came near, hauling another bucket of sap and dumped the load into the kettle I stirred. Now was as good a time as any to approach her.

"I wonder, *Od-ahwamaun*," I began, choosing the proper form of *his sister* to address her, "if I could speak with you?"

She looked up at me sharply. "Then speak."

"Well, I was wondering, would it still be all right for me to share your fire?"

She laughed. "Share my fire?"

Grandmother's attention was upon us now. My cheeks burned. "Yes. I was wondering if it would still be all right?"

"Share my fire with another woman?" She laughed again, cruelly. "A woman who isn't even my kin?" She turned her back and sauntered off for the trees.

I looked over at Grandmother, searching for some support. The old woman shook her head and said, "It's not seemly."

"What is seemly? I'm no threat. I'm not interested in her husband. What made living with her so right last year and so wrong this year?"

Implacable as always, the old woman answered, "That you are more a woman this year. This is the difference."

"And is she so unsure of herself as a woman that she'd find me a threat?"

"Virginity is often attractive to a man."

"I'm technically not a virgin, damn you! Red Cloud saw to that, no thanks to you, and as for innocence, I've seen enough of the good and evil that can be between a man and woman." I smashed the large wooden spoon to the ground, whirled and hefted Shadow Song's axe. If there'd be no home for me with Morning Star, then I'd live alone, damn them all!

For most of that day I worked, praying to the trees for their gift of lodge poles, for the bark that would shield me from weather. I was spurred periodically by Morning Star's laughter, the gestures she tossed in my direction when in conversation with Grandmother. By late afternoon I had built myself a wigwam. I bundled my few belongings, taking only a portion of the blankets, a small quantity of our meagre store of food, a few utensils I thought Shadow Song might spare me. What I'd do for an axe and canoe I had no idea. These were skills of which I knew nothing. There was time yet. Sugar making would continue for a few weeks, plenty of opportunity in which I could observe the men at their crafts.

When my household was in order, I returned to my place by the fire, stirring, stirring, endlessly stirring. If it was a little more brisk than what was required I defied anyone to challenge me. Who could deny me a right to my share if I helped in the making?

Again Morning Star came near, provoking me with her smug looks. I would not be provoked.

"It doesn't look too bad," she said, nodding to my wigwam. "I'm sure it will keep you warm."

I kept stirring.

"I'd be glad to see what I've got to spare."

"Thank you, no."

"You can't possibly expect to take care of yourself using those old fashioned things – "

"I can, have and will."

Morning Star made a derisive sound. "You realize you can't come back to the village."

I said nothing, wishing the woman away.

"Another scouting party will be waiting there for you. I heard it myself at La Cloche. Seems your white uncle has been talking to white powers." After some tense moments she finally gave up goading me and set to chores of her own.

I ate nothing that night with the hope I might purify myself enough to seek a dream. No dream came. At dawn I stirred stiffly, threw water on my face and returned to my place at the pot. I stood there stirring when Morning Star and the children emerged. I was still there stirring when Shadow Song and Lightfoot returned in the afternoon with cuts from a bear. There would be a feast tonight. My heart was in none of it.

This was Shadow Song's kill. I knew even before I saw the hide. Evidence of it lay on Lightfoot's face, the way he glowered, plainly angry that a man with a bow could out-hunt a man with a rifle. Something else showed on Shadow Song's face. I knew too well what that was. He kept looking from my wigwam to me, back and forth and finally came to rest on me. Question there. Hurt. I looked down to the frothing liquid in the pot.

I listened to him speaking with his family, heard him disengage himself quickly. He gestured to me to assist him dressing the meat. Without a word I joined him and we set to our task. I took the skull and adorned it in paint and ribbons, hanging it from a tree to set the spirit free. He carved the meat into large slabs when finally he spoke.

"You've built yourself a wigwam."

I swallowed, feeling fear and remorse. "Yes."

"Not the usual kind of wigwam a woman builds."

"No."

The motion of his hand stopped. He looked up at me, his eyes soft, showing his wounds, the things he would not say. "Then you're leaving."

If this was so right for me to do, why did it hurt so much? "Yes."

"You took enough to keep you?"

"Enough."

"Is there anything you need?"

"An axe and a canoe – "

"I'll show you how to make them tomorrow." He straightened. "Are you sure this is what you want?"

"It's what's right."

He nodded, but I wasn't sure if it was in acceptance or whether it was more in understanding. "And after sugar-making?"

I shrugged. "Find a place that would be suitable for summer and winter – "

"Live alone."

I nodded.

"What will you do when your uncle's men come looking for you?"

"Fight them as best I'm able. Run. Whatever is needed." I glanced away. "They should leave you alone now."

"Is that what you think?" He shook his head. He said nothing further, bent and again put his knife to the meat.

Somehow I found the courage to work beside him for the remainder of the day, avoiding his look, avoiding his touch, sure this pain would suffocate me before nightfall. In a way I hoped it would. It would be just payment for the way I hurt him.

Out of respect for Shadow Song I cleaned myself for the feast, putting on my best doeskin dress, tying a headband round my head. I wore a new pair of winter moccasins, my softest leggings. We all ate of the bear. Grandmother told stories, to which I only half-listened. Lightfoot boasted about his winter hunting. Shadow Song slipped away for a moment, returned in a deer hide, a rack upon his head.

Lightfoot let out a whoop, ducked out for his drum and began a rhythm for the medicine man who danced the Deer Dance. There in the firelight, beneath a clear night sky, Shadow Song moved, graceful, elegant, mimicking the movements of the deer so well I almost believed him a deer – the way he stamped a foot, trotting, his head twisting from side to side as though listening. Entranced, I followed his every movement. When the dance ended my heart was racing, my face flushed and my eyes stinging with tears.

Wolf-cry went up at a distance. My skin tightened.

"Our clan-brother," he murmured, turning slowly toward the trees. He slipped the hide and horns from his body. Everything seemed to hush. Even the children were wide-eyed and wondrous. The only sound now was the snap of the fire. At the perimeter of the camp gleamed a pair of eyes. Wolf.

    Shadow Song sank to his knees, fished sweet grass from his pouch and set it alight. The wolf emerged into the firelight, padded slowly, slowly toward him, its grey back rolling with power, head low, eyes intent. It stopped across from the sweet grass.

    Wolf and man, they stared at one another. The wolf dipped its head, swung round and disappeared into the trees and the cries of his pack. At that moment I wondered how I could ever live without him, ever isolate myself from the wonder that wove through Shadow Song's life.

Chapter 22

As he promised, Shadow Song taught me the art of weapon making, how to search for wood, stone, how to sing to them, how to strike the stone just so to make it chip. If done properly a stone axe was as effective as metal. A stone arrow tip as deadly. One just needed to know how to do it.

Bow making was another matter. There was the selection of just the right wood, of carving it to the right length and thickness, of laminating hide on its out-face. Hunting with it proved trying. I was sure if I were not to starve I'd have to rely on my traps, although a person could starve from a diet of rabbits. Pray, he told me, that other animals offer themselves.

Canoe-making was something Shadow Song offered to teach me when we reached the lake. There was no point carrying more than was necessary. That much we agreed upon, that, and the fact we'd travel together to the shore. If I still chose a life of isolation afterward, so be it.

Morning Star and Lightfoot bothered me little after the night the wolf visited. I slept in my own lodge and kept my own counsel. Shadow Song followed my lead, which surprised me. In all our years together I'd never known him to separate himself during sugar making.

When finally camp disassembled it did so as it had assembled, in groups, without fanfare. Morning Star and Lightfoot left first. We followed a few days later, uncertain of our final destination.

The weather held fine although a few times clouds scudded across the sky, scattering showers. By now there were signs of growth. In sunny clearings early flowers had thrust up yellow-green leaves. Grass sprouted. Everywhere there was bird song and the honk of geese flying in long vees northward. Even the hawks had returned. Their cries sliced through me. I wondered if I'd ever hear their scream again and not think of Shadow Song.

Our first camp was to see the return of an argument. It was over wigwams.

"You've always been safe with me," Shadow Song protested when I maintained it was wiser I remain apart.

"It's not seemly."

"Who's here to worry about?"

"I am. You are."

"I really don't care what's seemly. I do care that our friendship might die, that this thing you insist you must do not interfere with what's between us."

I shook my head, looked away.

He threw the lodge poles to the ground. "Stubbornness. Plain and simple. Look, you'll have your own side of the wigwam, as always, your own blankets, as always, your own bowl, your own spoon, your own blessed privacy, as blessedly always it's been!"

I turned my head from side to side in refusal, bent and gathered the poles and set to work. He groaned in exasperation, turned his back to me and sat upon a rock while I took care of the camp.

After that day we ate separately, slept separately, did everything separately but travel to the falls at the Bay of Islands. That much we agreed upon – to travel to the falls. By the time we reached that special place where water rushed over the white cliffs we barely spoke. I set our wigwams at the head of the falls, in the lee of an arc of pines. As soon as camp was made Shadow Song seized his medicine bag and set off. There was no need for him to say he went to fast. I knew this. It was probably best that he did so.

While he was gone my cycle came and I was glad he wasn't there. When I was done, he was still gone and worry took my senses. Perhaps he just left, I reasoned, the way the women of the summer village had said last year. But without his canoe? Without supplies? Yes, I could see him doing that, leaving me the things I'd need in my solitary life.

Five more days, I decided. What would it hurt to wait out five more days?

I fished while he was gone, gathered the few early herbs that grew around the first of spring, and worried. Day by day the air warmed. I found myself sweating while I worked. One afternoon winter grime and the itch of fleas pushed me to hazard a chill and attempt my first bath of the season. There was still a little soapwort in my pouch. I took it, a robe of deer hide and a change of clothes to the foot of the falls. Here the walls of white stone curved around a clear pool. Pockets of cedar grew like tufts of green from niches scattered willy nilly. The air was still. I felt as if this bowl of rock filled with liquid light, warming my body, touching me with brilliance. A ledge dipped behind the falls, carved from long years of wave action and sapping. There, I decided, would make the best place to bathe. It was sheltered. It was concealed. I stripped at the shore and crept along the slick rock until I was behind the veil of water.

Despite the brilliance of the bowl the water was deceptively cold and I gasped when I immersed myself in the thin falls. Shivering, I scrubbed with the herbs and braced myself for a long, long showering. I heard a hawk scream. Alarmed, I withdrew and tried to look through the water. The world was a blur of grays and pinks, blues and greens. Nothing distinguishable was there until I detected human movement. There. At the shore. A motion like silk.

I wanted to run. It was possible we'd been tracked. It was possible I'd be ambushed here, naked and vulnerable. What resistance could I offer? A wild thought occurred to me as I watched this, or these, intruders approach. Perhaps Shadow Song had been ambushed, killed. Why else would he have been gone so long?

I bent and reached for a rock, watching the movement out there for signs of numbers. I could make out only one body, one man. In a moment he would be upon the ledge. I would see him. I raised my arm to hurl my rock as hard and as far as I could.

The man stepped up to the ledge. Shadow Song. I didn't know whether to laugh or cry. The rock slipped from my hand. I stood there shivering, thinking I should cover myself, my hands too limp to do anything. He was as naked as I, glistening and wet, a look on his face I knew nothing about. I tried desperately not to examine every part of him, not to look upon his belly, his thighs, his penis. I was aware of the stillness in the bowl. Not a breeze stirred. All I could hear was rushing water. Sunlight penetrated the falls intensely. He walked fluidly. My pulse skipped.

He stood not a breath from me now, the look on his face warm, demanding, yet there was nothing of demand in anything he did. With one arm he reached around me and set his palm upon the small of my back, gently, so gently, like a sigh his touch was so light, his other hand brushing my cheek. He said nothing. There was only the endless sound of rushing water. He bent to me, pulling me closer so that I felt my breasts touch his chest, my belly against his. As if in a dream I felt his lips brush mine. No more than a feather touch. Again, lingering, again, a little longer, until his mouth was upon mine, soft, soft so soft and his tongue quick upon my lips. I opened my mouth to him. I leaned into him, wanting this, wanting to love him, wanting him to love me. I felt his fingers slide down my throat, over my shoulder and trace a line of pleasure around my breast.

In one movement he lifted me into his arms. I sank into what he offered, nested my head against his shoulder as he carried me to the deerskin robe I'd left on the shore. He took his time. Slowly, he set me upon the robe, settled himself behind me. There, in the nest of his arms I watched his large, long-fingered hands move, over my breasts, over my belly, down to that throbbing place between my legs, his lips on my neck, my ears, his breath warm and urgent. I longed to turn, to touch him but he kept himself firmly at my back, giving me pleasure. When finally I begged him to let me know what it was like to touch a man he laughed, gently, turning me so that I could take my fill of him. He lay back, murmuring instruction, satisfaction so that I controlled all he felt, as he did with me. When finally we joined we did so at my invitation. With hands and motions he guided me over his hips. It was a strange yet assuring sensation to feel him inside me, to feel the way our flesh conformed. All the while he watched me with those clay-brown eyes, those eyes that saw exactly what I felt, knew exactly what I thought, and I found myself hurtling toward a knowledge I craved with all my being until finally, at last, as the hawk screamed overhead I shuddered, felt him tense and I collapsed against him sweaty and relieved and engulfed with tears I could not explain.

So the brilliance of the bowl remained. The afternoon waned. I lay there in the cradle of his arms and knew, without any discussion, there would be no separate wigwams, no separate lives, no separate anything from now on.

That night we once again slept together under the robes, flesh to flesh, man and woman. I felt as though this was the way things had always been and always should have been. There was no home for me but the one I found with Shadow Song.

At dawn, it was I who approached him.

Chapter 23

We remained by the falls for all of that summer, fishing, hunting, making our camp apart from the rest of the world. I had long since packed away our marriage garment, a tunic from each of us stitched together at the sleeves to symbolize our union. It was only to be sundered when one of us died, or when one of us wished to divorce. I chose not to think of either prospect.

Often we discussed whether or not to join the village at Manitowaning. The discussion always ended without conclusion and we slept or coupled in the warm sunlight, listening to the falls rushing like the sound of blood in our ears. It was a time of inactivity, as if all of the tumult and running had paused. To refrain from decision was like a drug quickly consumed and quickly addictive.

Without thought we prepared for another winter even as the summer seemed endless. We dried fish and flesh. We gathered berries and roots. No travelers came near and we went searching for none.

By the time the grasses in clearings had dried to rustling, golden feathers, nausea overcame me daily. Shadow Song laughed and soothed me, rubbing my belly where soon it would swell, he assured me. Just the thought of having a life within me gave me pleasure. This child would never face the terrors I had. This I vowed. Even as I thought these things I prayed to whatever spirits would listen that this child would not be a girl, that this life would never have to know those special torments only a woman endures.

It was around then a young hunter carried his son into our camp, the boy suffering from fever and a cough that racked his frail body. Shadow Song shooed me off, warning me to brew quantities of slippery elm tea and drink it. Four days later, when the boy recovered and the father and boy returned to Manitowaning, I learned of an influenza epidemic that was plaguing the island, caused, so Shadow Song told me, by association with whites. Fearing for my child and myself, I made slippery elm tea my beverage of choice.

In ones and twos the people of the island found us, for it wasn't long before news of the location of their shaman and his *midewequae* spread. We did nothing about our discovery. Perhaps it was ignorance. Perhaps it was delusion. It didn't matter then. All we wanted was for this peace to continue.

When the hardwoods among the pines lit with colour we still remained near the falls. By then my belly had rounded into a little pot. We made no move to head farther into the forest for winter. Game was bountiful. A harvest of herbs, roots and berries was ours for the taking. It was quiet. It was serene. Why move?

Winter snow flew, soft and enveloping. I couldn't ever remember noticing, as I did that winter, the peculiar muffling effect the snow had on the sounds of the world. It seemed to me everything spoke in whispers, hushed, sleepy.

We spent the hours reading to one another. Often I thought of Lucifer's plight as we read from *Paradise Lost*, realizing now how it must have felt to forever seek the approval of so supreme a being, and in realizing, at last recognized what drove Shadow Song. He had been taken from his people young, raised in paradise and elevated to high degree. Esteemed, charismatic, he lived a model life only to find he forever begged mercy at the hands of his creators. Unable to live in paradise, he returned to what he had been taught was hell. Unlike Lucifer, however, the world he came to rule was not one of endless torment. The forest was indifferent. It could nurture and it could destroy. There was no malice in it. Neither was their benevolence. No lies governed the forest. Truth, raw and powerful was the legacy Shadow Song reclaimed.

It was in the deep of winter that I endured the rigours of childbirth and pushed our son into the world. He was large, ruddy and howling. I thought he would tear my body in two as I grunted to deliver myself of him. Shadow Song laughed as he took our son from between my legs where I squatted, and named him. It was a fitting name. Noise-in-the-Night learned quickly to scream in my sleep so that I would roll over and nurse him as we three huddled under the furs for warmth. Silently, I thanked the spirits for hearing my prayers.

Soon our world was absorbed with the wonders of our child. Shadow Song fed me concoctions to ensure a healthy flow of milk. He laughed a great deal that winter. There were moments, watching him with our son, I wondered if Papa had held me thus, cooed in that fashion. He looked up at me during one of these moments and watched me intently, everything about him relaxed and warm.

"Thank you, *wahboos*," he whispered.

Tears sprang to my eyes. I swallowed hard and smiled. This was the child he'd been denied all those years ago. This was the child that had died unborn. Afraid, I sought the protection of the *manitous*. Surely our world would be safe. Surely we would at last be at peace. I woke that night from a dream, whispering, "S'excuse moi," into the darkness. I had asked one too many favours.

Spring brought a *midewenini* to our camp. We smoked. We ate.

He said, "*Kekinoamaged, Wahtanuhgumoowin*, the *Midewewin* meets and we seek your council."

Very powerful that address. Not only had the messenger invoked the title of teacher, but the power of Shadow Song's name. This was not a man who could now be ignored. Shadow Song looked over to me where I sat cross-legged by the fire, Noise-in-the-Night suckling loudly at my breast. With all my heart I wished him to stay. I could not ask this of him. He had responsibilities to the *Midewewin*. To have expected him to shirk his duty would be to rob him of something essential. Neither did I give any outward sign of my acceptance of this summons. To do so would indicate to this messenger that Shadow Song was incapable of making his own decisions and I would not dishonour him in his people's eyes.

"Ten days," he answered.

Clearly the delay did not satisfy the messenger. He did not, however, argue. Shadow Song was a shaman of such high degree that to have argued would have been an affront. It had been bold enough to have summoned him.

With a nod, the messenger rose from the fire and strode off into the forest for the easy path around the falls.

"It has been a year," Shadow Song said when we were at last alone. I knew what he meant by that: perhaps it would be safe for us to return. Perhaps the hunt had at long last been abandoned.

We packed without haste the remainder of the day and the following set off upon the trail that would take us around the falls and down to the river where our canoe had been hidden. Noise-in-the-Night rode upon my back in a cradle board, not unlike a larger version of the clay doll I carried among my possessions. In clear weather and fair winds, we paddled back toward the island of the *manitous*. I observed every rock and tree as if it would be the last time I saw them, wondering that I had not noticed in all these years that particular pine, broken and bent upon that particular rock that looked like a rabbit, the way the current pulled in this particular channel, the way any number of small things had grown or formed.

Eight days later we reached Manitowaning. Much had changed in our absence. The pines and maples that had been profuse were now felled, stumps smouldering in the ground. Stakes and ropes clearly marked where a village of buildings would rise. The bark of saws penetrated the peace of what had once been our summer home as lumber was cut for homes for the Anishnabeg. We were being civilized. We were being boxed. I felt panic stir and I looked up to where Shadow Song stood upon the shore, pulling the bow of the canoe to land.

"We will not stay long," he said quietly. From the look on his face it was clear he was as unsettled as I about all this industry.

We set our wigwam a healthy distance from the mass of lodges that made up the native village. Pottawatomi and Odawa had joined the Ojibwa, evidence of the activity of both the Anglican and Catholic churches. All of them watched us covertly as we worked, displaying the same awe and deference of our own people. We three caused quite a stir. Quickly, I was the topic of gossip among our own people: the woman in Shadow Song's wigwam was his wife. She had borne him a fine son. Nothing was unseemly anymore.

Later in the day I hefted Noise-in-the-Night to my hip and went to pay my respects to Grandmother. To my astonishment the old woman approved. My visit wasn't to last long. A young woman approached me with tobacco. I knew the way of this. A year's absence made little difference in my role as *midewequae*. I nodded in the direction of my wigwam. The girl retired there to await me. I made sure Grandmother was comfortable before I left. I turned for my wigwam, bent through, settled Noise-in-the-Night and made the proper supplications with tobacco and chants. The girl and I drank tea and then I asked her what service I could offer.

"There is a hunter in our village," the girl said, "whom I love, but – "

"You're not sure he loves you and you want a potion."

The girl's eyes widened. She nodded. It occurred to me this girl was probably about my age and yet she regarded me as an Elder.

"And your parents?" I asked. "How do they feel about this?"

"Everyone admires him."

"That tells me nothing of how your parents feel."

She hung her head.

"You haven't discussed this with them."

She indicated she hadn't.

"Discuss this with them first. If you still wish a potion after that we will talk about it."

Disappointed, the girl back out of the wigwam.

To my surprise, most of my day passed in much the same manner. Advice. Medicaments. Gifts for our son. It was plain the villagers were going out of their way to display their deference, because most of their difficulties were simple and could have been dealt with without my assistance.

Shadow Song left quickly for the convening of the *Midewewin*. I did not participate as I had our son to consider. When Shadow Song returned late in the evening he was greatly disturbed. He sank to his heels next to me.

"They have asked my opinion regarding a baptismal ceremony Elliot wants to hold through the *Midewewin*."

"And?"

He shrugged. "Of course I didn't agree."

"And how many others agreed with you?"

"Two. We've spent the day trying to dissuade the other four from their course."

"You weren't successful."

"I don't know. I lost my temper. I walked out."

That surprised me. Shadow Song was not one to loose his temper, not the sort to give way to emotion and exasperation. The arguments among the members must have been hot for him to have reached this point. "What will you do now?"

"I don't know. If they go through with the baptisms then I can't see how I'll fit into their view of what a *midewenini* should be."

They will have accepted paradise and you rejected it, I thought. They will see you as evil incarnate. I hated Elliot at that moment, hated him for having brought this shame upon a man so undeserving of shame.

We waited that night for some word from the *Midewewin*. None came. I slept although I suspected Shadow Song did not at all for when I stirred in the dark I could see flickers of light from outside the lodge and hear the snap of twigs as they were fed into the fire. Shadow Song did not lie at my back. Tired, I fell asleep. By dawn it was clear Shadow Song had not been with me all night.

Carefully, I shifted and ducked out into the pink light. Shadow Song sat hunched by the embers. He did not move nor acknowledge me. I left to pee and returned, setting about making tea for my husband and not the shaman.

I put the bowl into his hands. "Drink," I said and settled beside him, turning bannock on a stick over the fire. He drank. When the bannock was golden I took the bowl from him and placed the bannock in his hands. "Eat." He chewed without thought, still staring into the fire. I waited until he was ready to speak. Finally, when the morning light touched his face, he looked over at me sharply, frowning. "Isn't this the day the preacher is to hold services?"

"It is."

He laughed, his attention turning to the village that was growing with activity. Children were already at play, boisterous, like jays calling raucously. A group of six men spread out a moose skin, yawning and scratching, picking up their gambling where they'd stopped the day before. Morning-Star and two other women were pounding something in a large wooden bowl. I could hear their song as they worked. None of them seemed at all occupied with preparing for church.

Shadow Song slipped his fingers through mine. "Perhaps the preacher will lecture the trees today."

"Or perhaps you," I added and nodded to Elliot who strode purposefully from between the buildings that were growing in the distance like a pile of bones. Shadow Song groaned and bent into the wigwam, emerging with his pipe and sweet grass. By the time Elliot stopped in front of us he was sweating, his face like a puffing plum. He ran a finger around his white, starched collar, lifted his hat to me. The gesture seemed utterly absurd.

"I'd like to know," Elliot said, glaring at Shadow Song, "why you've kept your people from coming to receive the Word of God."

No preamble. Not a very good orator, this one. And not a very mannerly person. No food, no drink, nothing to display his good intentions. Moreover, he spoke in English, as if every person in the world understood English.

Shadow Song smiled. I knew the meaning of that smile – arrogant, cold. He had a right to feel the way he did. He lit his pipe, offered it to sky, earth and the cardinal points, then passed it to the preacher.

"Just answer my question," Elliot growled.

"We smoke first. Then we talk." He gestured with the pipe.

"No smoke. Talk."

Shadow Song shook his head in dismay, letting smoke drift through the air. "They aren't my people. I don't own them."

"But you are their leader."

"I am *midewenini*."

"A pagan doctor. Witchcraft and demons."

Shadow Song let his teeth show, white and sparkling against his ruddy face. "If you like."

"You're denying them their right to salvation. Do you want them to burn in hell?"

"I deny them nothing."

"But they're here!" the preacher exploded, gesticulating wildly behind him, "engaged in who knows what?"

"They are in their own village, following the ways of the Anishnabeg."

"But I can save them! Don't you understand that?"

"Save them from what?"

"From damnation!"

"How?"

"By making them civilized men of God."

"Tell me, Sir," Shadow Song said, slipping into meticulous Cambridge English, "do you consider it civilized to subjugate a people?" Elliot's face darkened. "Do you consider it civilized to destroy knowledge older than anything you understand?" Now Elliot shook. I thought he would throw up his fists in anger. "And do you consider it civilized to hear nothing of the pain of the land you rape?"

"The Lord said, *Be fruitful and multiply, and fill the earth and subdue it; and have dominion over the fish of the sea and over the birds of the air and over every living thing that moves upon the earth.*"

"He also said, *A fool takes no pleasure in understanding, but only in expressing his opinion.*" Elliot sputtered. Shadow Song was relentless. "And as for damnation, we, the Anishnabeg, have lived with Mother Earth for time beyond your reckoning, and survived, and prospered. If this is damnation, then leave us to it. The village will be engaged this day in holy work. If you wish to learn you may stay."

Elliot whirled and stalked away. I could almost see his anger rising in his wake. Shadow Song continued to blow rings of smoke into the sunlight, clearly pleased with himself and the result of the convening of the *Midewewin*. It was plain there were to be no baptisms on this day of festivities. All was as it should be in the village.

He turned to me and kissed me lightly on the cheek. "Today I will play for you."

I looked up at him, proud of him, pleased he was settled. He would play in my honour today in the lacrosse match, part of the feast for *Oshki-Nitawagaewin*, a celebration of the first hunt of Lightfoot's eldest son. Already players assembled upon the field, challenging one another. That Shadow Song would join them was a matter of great import and speculation for it was not often their *midewenini* participated in such sport. I watched the commotion around a group of men wagering. Once or twice I heard Shadow Song's name rise above the general grumble of their arguing. They were wagering on him.

"I must prepare," he said and rose from my side, striding to the bay where he would bathe and then join the other players. I bundled Noise-in-the-Night onto my back and walked to the bay to bathe our son and myself in my favorite cove. Other women were there also and we made great fun of our bath, splashing and laughing. There were hands enough to care for Noise-in-the-Night. To my surprise, Morning Star and a few other women assisted me in dressing. I chose to wear a fine summer garment of thin doeskin I had bleached until it was pale and white. It hung loosely from my shoulders, an elaborate scatter of shell-beaded fringe across the bodice that tinkled when I moved. My hair they combed with goose grease until it shone and then braided it into one long tail that hung to my hips, woven with a ribbon of blue. Morning Star shouldered the cradle board with my son, waving off my protests.

"Be his wife today, not some nursemaid."

I smiled and thanked her. Together we climbed the hill to the playing field. Shadow Song stood there naked but for a loincloth. He watched me approach, grinning, and then leapt, whooping with the other men as they charged onto the field. In moments the rough-housing antics of the game were in action. The ball whizzed back and forth at dizzying speeds, caught, thrown, caught, passed again, the men glistening with sweat as they ran. A goal. A cheer burst from the crowd. Children around us set into a frenetic parody of the game, bashing each other with their long sticks.

"He seems very happy," Morning Star said, leaning toward me.

I nodded. It was reply enough. Of course he was happy. He had wived again. He had a healthy son. His people had rejected the white ways and were involved this day in the work of the Anishnabeg.

The ball swung toward Lightfoot now, who ran on the opposing team. Morning Star beside me yelled encouragement. Shadow Song ran behind Lightfoot, Deer-Coming-Down flanking him for a pass. In a blink of movement Shadow Song knocked Lightfoot's stick. The ball sped down, caught in the small net at the end of Shadow Song's stick and in the next breath passed to Lightfoot's son. Another goal shot home.

Around me the cheers were deafening. Deer-Coming-Down grinned. Again the ball passed to him. Again he drove it home. Whoops burst through the crowd, men dancing at the perimeter. Even I found myself shouting, laughing, caught up in the joy of the game. I was sure the young man would be a hero by the end of the evening, especially as his first hunt had brought down a moose. No brace of geese, no beaver for this young man. He had brought down a moose. This was a matter of much honour and much pride.

I looked to where Shadow Song ran to harass his opponent. I was sure there was no man as beautiful as he that day, even though it was Deer-Coming-Down who drove the winning ball into the goal.

When Shadow Song retired from the field I offered him water. He doused his head, drank the second cup and then shook water over me like a dog shaking water from his coat. I shrieked, backed away and he caught me in his arms, laughing, laughing again when Morning Star looked at him, her face expressing surprise.

"Be careful with my son, *nemissa*," he said. "He will be a great hunter and a great shaman one day." With a final squeeze he released me and strode away into the crowd.

Morning Star and I left with the women to attend to the moose for the feast tonight. Clearly she was proud of her son, as she had every right to be. She chattered inexhaustibly to the other women who had come to help. It was banter harmless enough. I listened while I adorned the bell with ribbons and sweet grass and then sat near them nursing.

Not long afterward meat was set to roasting, early duck potatoes gathered with strawberries and thimbleberries. All of the villagers ate throughout the long afternoon and into the night. We smoked the pipe. We sang. We played games and we laughed till we thought we would suffocate with laughter. Hunters each in their turn pledged to assist Deer-coming-Down whenever it was required, a custom passed from generation to generation.

By dusk dances had begun so that the forest rang with voices, drums and the sound of stamping feet. To my surprise there was no whiskey throughout any of it. I watched Shadow Song. That lack of alcohol sat well with him, it was clear. He sat cross-legged on the ground in a place of honour near the fire, arrayed in feathers that hung from his headband, beaded collar and fine leather. He watched all that occurred. He watched me.

Night grew and Noise-in-the-Night slept despite the commotion, passed from hand to hand among the women who took turns watching the infants of the village.

It was while Deer-Coming-Down enacted the Snowshoe Dance that things went awry. He bent and twisted, mimicking the hardship of a winter hunt. Others of us danced at the edges, I among them. Morning Star danced near me, Noise-in-the-Night upon her back. My attention was upon Morning Star. I heard a shot. For a moment her face twisted with surprise. Screams overlapped the receding blast. I watched Morning Star sink, sink, her hands out before her, a bloody bloom on her breast. When all sound silenced she lay at my feet, her blood and flesh on my face, a gory mass on her back where once my son had been. I felt the wail rise from my throat, the hole open in my body where once Noise-in-the-Night had filled it.

A voice reached us from the edge of the trees. "That's a warning to your medicine man." An English voice speaking English words. I lunged for a rifle, almost reached it before Shadow Song grabbed it from my hands, his face hard, looking into the darkness for the murderer who had stolen his son.

"Who are you?" I heard him say, his voice gone to gravel and emotion.

"You know who we are, why we're here."

A hiss ran through the crowd. The keening of the women rose and ran on like a raw nerve. On my hands and knees I reached for Shadow Song's thigh, brought his attention down to me. When he looked at me I could see his grief, see the apology he longed to give me in this moment of jeopardy.

"Leave the village out of this," he answered the voice in the darkness.

"They'll be fine if you meet with us across the bay in the morning."

"And if I don't?"

"Remember a winter two years ago."

I felt every person turn to Shadow Song, each asking the same unsaid question: What of the winter? I remembered the winter. I remembered a fox pelt. I remembered Shadow Song close to death.

I turned to my son who lay dead upon Morning Star's back, unable to stop my trembling, unable to stop crying. My fault. My fault. All my fault. "It's me you want," I screamed, turning back and looking at Shadow Song.

"Both of you," the voice answered. "Tomorrow. At the bay."

In the silence that followed I felt my sobbing was like a roar. Lightfoot grabbed for Shadow Song then, a knife in his hand, his face contorted in rage and grief. Blood spurted on Shadow Song's shoulder. I screamed again, now afraid I would loose all my loves this night. Shadow Song twisted, seized Lightfoot's wrist and smashed Lightfoot's hand to his knee. The knife burst free. Lightfoot snarled. Shadow Song caught him by the shoulders, yanked him up to face him. "Listen to me!"

Lightfoot spat in his face.

Shadow Song didn't even wince. "By all that I am, by all that is sacred upon Mother Earth, I swear to you the death of *ningwis* and *nemissa* shall not go unavenged."

My heart stilled. I was aware, distantly, of the fear that settled over the crowd. Their shaman had spoken. He had spoken the intimate titles for *my son* and *my sister*. He had spoken the words of revenge. I could hear him speaking other words, from another time: *Imagine what would happen if I took my power and set it loose .... All I desired would be mine.* I felt fear now.

He turned away from all of us then, rigidly, as if he relaxed his world would unravel around him, past me to our wigwam where he hefted his axe and chanted to the trees for a gift. Blindly, I joined him, my voice raw with tears.

Late into the night, amid whispers and the keen of women, we set our son and Morning Star upon their funeral biers, their feet to the west so that their spirits would leave for the Land of the Souls. Shadow Song stood beside me like a spectre of darkness, his jaw bulging with unvented emotion.

"In four days," he said to the villagers, "I will return."

In four days we would inter the bodies. I followed him back to our wigwam, walking the path the villagers parted for us, hearing their whispers, hearing our grief. Shadow Song ducked through the flap. I followed. He grabbed me almost as I entered, threw me to the furs and made love to me, violently, desperately, and when at last he spilled his seed into me he collapsed and wept on my breast in great, shuddering sobs. I couldn't tell the difference between his tears and my own.

Chapter 24

Shadow Song asked me to come with him, no questions asked, no opposition voiced. Although I knew I should stop him from this path I didn't. If we could unleash enough power to cripple my uncle forever, then whatever happened was worth it. He had killed our son.

The night was moonless, the sky a deep indigo where stars were scattered like rock salt. To paddle through this darkness was treacherous, but we sent our spirits ahead, feeling out the water, the rocks, guiding our canoe by what Mother Earth told us.

When we reached the shore it was as Shadow Song had said it would be – deserted. Our hunters would have camped in a more protected area, a place where their prey wouldn't look. Here the rock sloped gently to the water. A series of canoes was overturned at one end of the crescent, beneath a stand of gnarled pines. At the other end the rock rose sharply into a wall that thrust out to the lake, now dark and foreboding. I shivered despite the night's heat. Shadow Song touched my arm, gesturing. I nodded and set off to gather firewood, a task done more by instinct than by eyesight. This I heaped into a pile on the open space of the rock. Crickets scratched in waves of song, first before me, then to the west, to the east, and then stilled altogether when Shadow Song set his fire-bow into action.

A spark flared, caught the tow of cedar bark. He blew gently, his face harsh in the small glow and then it burst into flame. He set this in the pine cones and they in turn ignited brilliantly, flames licking the smaller brush we wove through larger dead wood. From branch to branch it sped until the pile exploded into flaming leaves of amber, sparks shooting high toward the stars.

We sat, cross-legged on the rock. Shadow Song mixed a pigment of white. He chanted, a sharp, nasal whine that tightened my skin. I couldn't stop trembling when he leaned toward me and touched my face with paint. I shook so badly when it was my turn to paint his face that he caught my wrist in his hand, held me tightly – firm, firm, be firm – and guided me, all the while watching with those eyes like shards of clay.

We said nothing. Only the snapping fire and cricket song broke the silence of the night as we smoked to the spirits, praying for guidance, praying for forgiveness for the way we would twist our power. Wind swept through the cove, hot, drying. Another blew coldly. Yet another and another howled as the spirits of the cardinal points joined us here at this terrible task.

Shadow Song set his pipe aside and took a piece of newly cut birch into his hands, chanted over that while he sliced and whittled. I watched him with a feeling there wasn't enough air to breathe, rattling my tea tin to invoke power. Under his hands an arrow shaft formed, long, elegant, slender, as if Birch yielded to his touch. Now I joined the chant, swaying, giving Shadow Song the power of my spirit.

He turned to the stone now. His palms pressed the rock before him, guiding our song to Mother Earth. The ground quivered. Still we chanted. It quivered again. Under his hands the stone split, spitting out a chunk of quartz, clean, white, an aberrant mineral released from its limestone bed. It was an unlikely choice for an arrow head unless it was one with power in mind, a gift from Mother Earth.

Our chant shifted now until the stone in his hand resonated. Only with his fingers did he strike, shards flying like brittle snowflakes around him until the sharp, pointed thing within the stone lay exposed. He held it aloft between thumb and forefinger, turning it this way and that. To me his face looked as hard as the thing in his fingers.

He attached the head to the white shaft of birch with a pale strip of tendon from a moose. Still we chanted, differently now, more like wind in trees. Although Brother Gull didn't fly at night, one pencilled a gyre on the starlit sky, riding the winds that swirled around us, down, down, down until he settled on the rock. We centered our attention completely on the bird. It cocked its head one way, another, lifted its wings and shook them. With a shriek it climbed into the air, three feathers spiralling down to my outstretched hands. With these white feathers Shadow Song fletched the arrow.

By now it was painful to use my voice. I shivered so badly I thought I'd bite my tongue. Power ran through me from Mother Earth so that my body felt like flame, fed from the marrow that burned. I could only watch as Shadow Song drew power from me, his eyes constantly flicking from me to the arrow and back and again. He rubbed the entire arrow with the juice of the death camas, scarlet pimpernel, bittersweet nightshade and others I knew were deadly and dire. He pinched the wound on his shoulder till it bled freely again and used it to paint the symbols of our guardians upon the shaft. In the next motion he grabbed my hand, sliced open my finger and with a gesture indicated for me to trace the symbols with my own blood. That done, he leapt to his feet and threw the thing into the fire.

White flame exploded through the russet, paling, paling until the fire burned like snow, without heat. Ice. A fire of ice. He turned his face skyward, crying a chant that terrified me as he moved in a rhythm around the white flames. I could do nothing but join him, caught in the flow, moving across the stone. The wind caught my hair and whipped it out beside me on a long arc of darkness.

I looked deep into the bowels of the flames where an arrow hung suspended, bloody hued. Without thought I danced into the fire, felt the flames licking around me. I closed my fist around the glowing arrow. Shadow Song was there with me in the midst of the conflagration.

Nothing seemed real. Distance distorted. My heart hammered a rhythm of its own in my ears. All I could see was his face, the hardness of his face as the flames danced eerily around us. He bent to me, his hand also around the arrow. His mouth was on mine, demanding in a way that had nothing to do with sexuality. This was power. For me everything became fluid, as if there was no substance to anything in the world. At that moment I watched his hand descend to me, the arrow pierce my breast. I felt none of it but his mouth on mine. He drove the arrow home to my heart with the palm of his hand and caught it as it passed through my back.

His lips still bruised mine when I felt the shaft in my own hand. Without knowing why, only knowing that I must do this, I plunged the arrow through him as he had plunged it through me.

He let me go then, in his hand the shaft that was clean, white. With a leap he left the flames. Disoriented, I backed away. The fire was before me now, not around me, burning golden instead of white, heat where there had been ice. Through the flames I could see him dance.

For a moment reality overlapped a vision from my past – a man who held an arrow aloft like bone burned clean, chanting a high, nasal whine; a woman whose hair streamed out on the wind like a dark scarf.

Everything blurred then. Whether I danced or not I didn't know. All I knew was that an arrow had been created this night whose purpose was first to torture and kill a man who had scattered torture and death, and to second forge peace and leadership for the Anishnabeg who would be left behind. Wild power had been created this night. Its effects even now would come crashing down upon us.

Chapter 25

It was the cry of *Kaikaik* the hawk that woke me. I groaned, stiff and cold and aching from more than my uncomfortable bed. In a moment of panic I did not know where I was or what had caused me so much pain. I tried to open my eyes but found them crusty and sealed shut. When I rubbed at them I flinched, rolling lumps of dried tears between my fingers until I had unglued my eyes enough that I could open them. Blinking, I could make out the ashes of a large fire that had burned on this flat shelf of rock. I remembered dreaming. Or had it been a dream? I shifted, pulling my knees under myself to kneel upon the white stone.

There was a numb place over my left breast. It made me feel as though I were short of breath, as if I had been left with a hollow place. Absently, still wondering where I was, I rubbed at this numbness, frowned at what my fingers found. Truly frightened now, I unlaced my bodice and yanked open the front. To my horror I found a wound there, white, puckered, as if something had plunged through me. I could feel that hollowness right through my body. Afraid now that my dreams had been real, I reached to my shoulder blade in an attempt at denial. Under my fingertips I could feel another wound.

In that moment I remembered it all: Morning Star falling at my feet, the look of surprise and pain on her face, my son a bloody pulp upon her back, not even recognizable they had mutilated him so. I remembered Shadow Song making love to me desperately, achingly, as though in coupling he might recreate the child that had been taken from us. I remembered wailing, a long, tortured sound that started somewhere deep inside and wouldn't stop. If I opened my mouth that wail would haunt this shore.

Gasping back tears, I turned, found Shadow Song. He lay upon his belly, in his hand an arrow so white it was unearthly, as if it were made all of one substance hard and perfect. The head was a notched, brutal looking thing. He frowned deeply in his sleep. It looked like a cut. Around his face his black hair splayed, three hawk feathers touching his cheek where they hung from his headband.

Again *Kaikaik* cried. I looked up to the paling sky. Clouds were underlit in crimson and gold. Across them the hawk carved perfect circles.

Shadow Song

It had all been real. All of it. I wished for it all to have been a dream.

Afraid, I reached out and nudged Shadow Song's arm. He stirred. I nudged him again, saying, "They'll be here soon."

I looked over to the grey ash from last night's fire. The wood had burned so completely that not even charred bits remained. There was only this fine silt. It looked the way I felt. Grey. Without substance. A remnant of something that had once been vibrant and alive.

I turned my attention back to Shadow Song as he hauled himself to his knees, watching him shake his head as if trying to clear his senses. All I could do was stare at the scar over his heart. I knew there would be one like it on his back. I had done that to him. Wild power. Now it would come back upon us.

They had killed our son.

Shadow Song looked where I pointed out across the bay. A canoe approached. Three men were there, a steersman, bowman and another who rode shotgun. White men. They were close enough for me to recognize them from the summer two years ago, the three scruffies who had come looking for us.

I reached out and touched Shadow Song's fingers. He glanced down at me, his face pallid, the look of the hunted and haunted about him. He picked up his bow, nocked the arrow of white, drew and let it sing out. *Kaikaik* cried. I heard the men laugh, clearly in jest that he should shoot from such a distance. They laughed until the one who rode shotgun fell over the gunwales and the weapon splooshed into the mirror-calm water.

When the arrow appeared in Shadow Song's hand I sucked in air. The bowman sighted his rifle upon Shadow Song.

"Put down your weapon!" he yelled.

Slowly, Shadow Song set the bow and arrow aside.

"Stand away!"

Shadow Song took my hand in his, drew me to my feet and we moved a few paces away, enough to make our hunters comfortable. By now they were within two lengths of the shore. I gripped his hand tightly. Kaikaik cried. I looked up, drawn by the shift in the bird's call. Where the hawk had spread its wings to cup the thermals, it now fell to the men in the canoe. They were oblivious of their peril as they came nearer, nearer, now less than a length from the shore. I watched as the bird tilted its wings, braking, its talons extending out and out and caught at the steersman's ear, all as he turned in astonishment. He was close enough for me to see his astonishment shift to terror when his ear drooped and blood gushed. He flailed uselessly at the air, screaming, "Get off! Get off!"

The bowman turned. The gunwales dipped to the water. Still the hawk attacked. For a moment the oarsman lined a bead on the bird, dropped his aim, the rifle and back-paddled quickly.

"Grab your paddle!" he barked at his partner.

He had turned the canoe and was heading back out to the bay before the other man managed to fend off the hawk and take up his paddle, stabbing at the water.

It wasn't until they disappeared around the point that Shadow Song spoke. "They won't be back for a few days. We must fast now."

Without question, I walked with him to the shore, righted the canoe and set off with him for Dreamer's Rock. It was guidance more than anything I wanted now. I wondered if the spirits would visit me at all after what I'd done last night.

We made landfall quickly. Shadow Song had set us to a gruelling pace. We separated as soon as we beached, each to our own place where hunger and privation might grant us a dream. I chose the same place I had every time I came here, an alcove of rock that looked out over the thousand islands of the lake. I made a small fire, smoked, chanted, and prepared myself. By nightfall the second day lack of sleep, hunger and grief quickened my visions. I felt as though I spun through the spirit world, shoved from one moment of prescience to another. At the end of it I found a core of calmness that was neither pleasing nor terrifying. It just was.

Weak, I descended the rock and found Shadow Song waiting by the canoe for me, his face drawn, his demeanour closed as if what he had seen was more than he could bear. We exchanged no greetings, no small gesture of affection. He righted the canoe and together we set off across the water.

It was cloaked in this eerie silence that we entered the village and began the burial for Noise-in-the-Night and Morning Star. Elliot and Anderson watched from a prudent distance. I was relieved they didn't interfere. All the while Lightfoot wept, the women wailed. When at last we covered Noise-in-the-Night and Morning Star with earth I felt prepared to do what we had begun.

Before noon we had packed what few provisions we would need for our journey. I waited by the shore for Shadow Song while he lingered behind to speak with his mother. It was a scene I preferred not to witness. After all these years, good-byes were still something I found difficult. I knew we would never see this village again. This trip south would be my last.

It was of good-byes I thought when he joined me and we set our course for the Indian Peninsula.

Chapter 26

From Manedoomini to the Indian Peninsula we traveled under clear skies and on calm water, favourable conditions for an unfavourable journey. It occurred to me it had been from terror I fled with Shadow Song those many years ago. It was to terror I returned along an old and familiar path. It was all I could do to staunch my tears, to stop myself from pleading with Shadow Song to flee away north, north, where we might find some peace and perhaps make another child. My breasts demanded a child. They were filling with milk, in need of Noise-in-the-Night to drain them.

Even as I thought these things I realized there would be no peace, not as long as Uncle lived. If it wasn't the shaman he hired to hunt us, it would be someone else. He'd not rest until he had me back in his control, until he had silenced the truth that I knew. He had reached across an ocean to destroy his own brother. What would stop him from reaching across a province?

Shortly after we made landfall on the mainland it became clear we were being stalked. It wasn't so much that there were physical signs, more a sensation. Both of us were strung so tightly we vibrated to the slightest ripple in our environment. At Cypress Lake Shadow Song halted, looking at the ground, the sky, cocking his head as though listening. He built a small fire, lit sweet grass and inhaled the smoke. I watched him with his eyes half-lidded, sinking into that place of spirits. Abruptly he rose, kicked out the fire and we backtracked along the trail, stealthily. A few hours hiking through hardwoods and cedars we found sign, three sets of barely discernible footprints.

Shadow Song looked up at me where he squatted, tracing the outlines in the damp duff. "Two white men, one red. Two young, one old." He didn't need to say our hunters were the two from the canoe and the old shaman. I longed to ask him the shaman's name, to have a face for this evil we had fought for so long. It was fruitless to even think this. To have spoken the shaman's name was to invoke his power and he was powerful enough.

Shadow Song rose and signalled for us to return to the canoe. We went carefully, knowing our hunters were now before us, not behind.

Three days later we must have passed them for Shadow Song had us backtrack again. He watched from a prominence as the two white men stumped through the forest. We could catch glimpses of sunlight reflecting on them as they went. The old shaman was concealed. Shadow Song knew he was there, guarding his way, doing everything to hide himself.

"They'll try for an ambush," he said after a moment.

I shuddered.

"We'll set a watch tonight." He looked down at me, hard, unreadable. He frightened me as I never thought he could. I'd never seen the hunter in him, this cold, lethal manner. He must have seen my fear because the look on his face softened, his fingers touching the part of my hair. "I know you're afraid." This thing must be done. That unspoken phrase hung between us.

There would be no reassurance from him. Nothing but truth. I expected nothing less. After we had created that dire arrow what else was there to say? That I knew its purpose and was loathe to assume responsibility? That I'd rather run and hide than risk everything – our happiness, our chance to find some peace in our lives?

I reached up and touched the puckered flesh over his heart, remembering the way that arrow sank into his body and slid through, easily. I wondered if his wound felt as hollow to him as mine did to me.

I withdrew my hand, trembling, spun on heel and descended toward our gear. The taste of blood sat bitterly in my mouth I'd bitten my lip so hard in an attempt not to let the howling start. They had killed our son!

We paddled and portaged throughout the day, covering ground quickly, stealthily. At night we camped without a fire, not daring to risk discovery. Dinner consisted of dried rations. I curled under my robes quickly, lying near Shadow Song for some sense of security. When he woke me for my watch a drizzle had set in. I hunkered under the robe and listened to the endless sound of rain on leaves and the constant creaks of the forest. My breasts ached. I rubbed them periodically, feeling the milk dribble from my nipples. In silence I wept. By dawn the rain stopped and left the forest damp and banded in mist. My breasts still ached.

Again we traveled, into and out of water, climbing the rocky hills and picking our way down gingerly. Always we were careful to make as little impression upon the forest as possible.

During my years away I realized the land had changed. More and more clearings were evident the farther south we traveled, evidence of settlers. I wondered for how long the forest had remained untouched, growing in its silent, wondrous way. Now it seemed that in a very short time it had been stripped, moulded into something to serve its masters. Even the forest animals that had once approached me without fear now scurried for cover. The place of worship had gone. They'd desecrated the cathedral.

Wherever possible we avoided the clearings, skirting along the edges like wary coyotes. We spoke little. Perhaps that was best. I watched him with a growing sense of foreboding, as if what I would have to pay for the happiness I'd known with him would be greater than I could bear.

Our greatest shock came when we paddled into the Beaver Valley. What had been a lush expanse of forest and swamp was now denuded. Only stumps pocked the land like great warts, ditches draining the remnants of beaver meadows.

I watched Shadow Song as we beached the canoe. He straightened on the shore, looking over the valley, the barren ridges, the barren bowl, back to the river that was shallower than it had been the last time we'd traveled this way. I watched tears rise brightly in his eyes, saw the anger on his face when he looked away. In an attempt to console him I reached for him, found myself trembling and let my hand drop back to my side. There would be no comforting him, I knew. I bent and helped him to conceal the canoe amid deadfall.

He tarried over detail at the shore, covering our tracks with a fussy hand. With him fretting about our trail, it took most of the day for us to climb the rocky prominence that overlooked all this desolate expanse. The only thing that hadn't changed in all these years was that bluff. Rough, craggy, it remained tufted with cedars like a defiant old man. Turkey vultures rode the air effortlessly, sweeping wide arcs against the pale curls of clouds.

Our climb was long and laboured, but worth the effort for when at the summit we had an excellent vantage. Surely no ambush could overpower us here.

We risked a small fire, only for the purpose of making tea to slake our thirst. I palmed the sweat from my brow and sipped, trying to relax, knowing I shouldn't. To relax was to let down my guard. We could still be ambushed. I remembered that winter. With a groan I rubbed at my breasts that were now hard and warm to the touch.

Shadow Song sank down beside me, his back to a bent birch, his attention somewhere out in the valley below.

"Sleep," he said softly.

I shook my head. "I'm fine."

He smiled, ghostly and wan, closed his eyes a moment. I could see the tremendous fatigue on his face, the lines around his eyes, the sunken cheeks. He looked over to me, suddenly warm and attentive and patted his lap. "Sleep. I'll watch."

I watched him carefully, longing to accept his offer. "You're sure?"

He nodded. I watched the hawk feathers drift at his cheek. He reached out and touched my shoulder, pressing me down. I acquiesced, pillowing my head on his lap as he circled my ear with his fingertip.

"Do you remember the story of *Geezhig* and *Wabun-anung*?" he asked, his voice barely above a whisper. I nodded, wondering at the emotion I detected in his words. "How she died and he went in search of her to the Land of the Souls?" Again I nodded, watching his face, the sharp planes of his cheekbones, the long nose and flared nostrils, his mouth so wide and sensual. I reached up and traced the outline of his mouth, slowly, carefully, wanting always to remember what he looked like. He kissed my fingertips. I smiled. His lips parted and his tongue touched my fingers, his hands reaching for the lacing of my bodice. I winced when he touched my breasts. With a groan he lifted me into his arms and kissed me, his fingers kneading my painful and swollen breasts. I felt his tears salty and urgent on my tongue, and then his lips upon my cheeks, my throat, and then hot and demanding upon the nipple of my breast. The pain lessened as he drank, replaced by another pain just as urgent.

"Please," I whispered, my lips brushing his ear. "Please, *nedegamahgun*," my husband I said, and reached down to his loincloth to take him into my hands. He shifted and lay over me, sucking now upon my other breast. Oh the pleasure of that, to feel his mouth hot and wet, to feel my milk flow freely. He shoved my skirt above my waist. A breeze stirred coolly against my exposed bottom. I squirmed beneath him, wanting to wrap my legs around his back, to take him inside my body, whatever orifice didn't matter only that I should have him inside me. "*Ahpagish*," please I again begged him, "*ne-owewedegamahn*." Make love to me.

His lips left my breasts that felt empty now. He knelt over me, watching me carefully. He bent and licked my lips, whispering, "You fed our son well," and kissed me deeply. I could taste my milk on his tongue, sweet and rich. He nibbled at my throat now, down and down over my breasts where sunlight spattered warmly, across my belly and down to where I felt my pulse thrum. His tongue was quick and hot. I bit my lip so as not to moan for I knew we should not choose now to couple. We could be ambushed. I didn't care. My husband shared with me these tender indecencies and I longed to drown in what he offered. My eyes closed to the sunlight sparking through the leaves. With pressure from my hands I indicated for him to turn so that I could pleasure him as he pleasured me. I burst into sensation all of a sudden, feeling the waves of ecstasy roll over me as I teased him with my mouth. In a moment I felt him also shudder and I swallowed.

This was not enough for him. He turned abruptly, his tongue in my mouth and we joined traditionally. I lost track of time. All that was real was the rhythm of our bodies, of our breathing, of the quickening of our hearts and the sweat that ran down our thighs, all the while sunlight showering us with motes of scattered brilliance. I yearned for that bright spot of release that would come because of what we did. When I felt my muscles tighten and then twitch around him he hissed through his teeth. Beneath my palms the skin of his back goose-fleshed. Dizzy, I collected him into my arms. My world filled with the sound of his breathing, the soughing of the trees and bird song. When I slept I didn't know. I woke to the sound of Shadow Song's groan.

I jolted upright, found him sitting against the birch. His face twisted with pain, then relaxed.

"What is it?" I asked, alarmed both by his discomfort and the length of the afternoon shadows.

"He is here," he whispered. He looked over to me, his eyes clearer than they'd been in days. "Whatever happens now you must not interfere."

"But – "

"Promise me."

"We should go – "

"No more running now. Promise me, *wahboos*, you won't interfere."

I winced.

"Promise me."

"I promise."

He rose, smiled, bent down to me and touched his lips to mine gently, turned and retrieved his bow and the white arrow. His attention was upon the cedars when he said, "Remember that the arrow returns to the user."

"I remember."

"Good. Wait there."

I wanted to drag him back, to flee down the cliff to the river and paddle north to safety, but I only sat there, dumb, mute, unable to deny my *kekinoamaged* anything he would ask of me.

He slipped among the cedars like wind, fleet, silent, no mark upon the earth where he had gone. Despite his warning I followed, sending my spirit ahead to guide me. I could feel something ahead, a trembling, as if a hole had opened in the spirit world. Sweat slid between my breasts. I ducked a branch, stepping carefully. The hole ahead seemed to widen, strengthen. A cry tore through the trees, gurgled and went silent. My heart jumped. Death. I could smell it.

Afraid, I stepped another few paces, and another, and another. One of the hunters lay across my path, a wound in his back where something had exited cleanly. He bled prodigiously from that wound. For a moment he scrabbled in the duff. I watched him with indifference. His rifle lay smashed at the foot of a birch.

I stood there a few moments, testing the air, listening for some clue. My heart thudded so hard I could barely breathe. Then I felt it again, that opening in the air. Another man screamed, followed by the sound of someone crashing through the trees in my direction. I pressed myself against a cedar and watched as the remaining hunter ran past me in a blur of red and blue, clutching his heart as he raced over the edge of the cliff. His screams receded as he descended and then the screams stopped.

Both hunters dead. Only the shaman remained. Again I thought of that winter, of the fox pelt, of fighting the shaman's spirit in the fire. I remembered the camp we had found, the twisted trees and scorched earth. How could Shadow Song fight something like that?

At a distance I heard a low cough, one I had heard on only one previous occasion and that had been enough to frighten me. A cougar coughed just that way when cornered, low, menacing, a warning to go no farther. I heard a twig snap. My hands trembled as I touched the trunk of the cedar, looking around me wildly for some sign of the cat or Shadow Song.

All was stillness. There was not even bird song to bless my ears. For how long I stood there I had no idea, waiting, waiting for something to happen. I heard the crashing of branches before I saw Shadow Song. He sprang through the trees, dark hair a stream behind him. Not a bowshot away the cat bounded in pursuit. Both of them headed straight for the cliff. My fears galvanized. I ran after them, snapping tree limbs, only distantly aware that my face and arms were scratched and bleeding because of my race. Desperation replaced all caution. It was imperative I reach the cliff before them. What I would do when I got there I had no idea. I only knew I had to stop them.

When I broke upon the bare rock of the cliff face all I could do was stare, all my protests dead as horror developed before me. The bobcat crouched, snarling in front of Shadow Song who stood balanced on the edge of the white rock, that cool, arrogant twist upon his mouth. The bow lay at his feet. I longed to rail at him to seize it, to shoot this beast. Instead I watched him, in his hand the arrow clutched like a dagger. Overhead *Kaikaik* cried.

He looked over to me then, his face filled with such longing and the things he would never speak. He said only one thing to me, "Watch for the turtle. Listen for the hawk. I'll always be there," and all of the same moment the cat leapt. As if embracing his death he closed his arms around the beast and plunged the arrow into the back of its skull. He tipped over, over, his feet sliding away from the edge, his attention never leaving me as he fell and I scrambled to stop him, fell as I reached the precipice, fell as I stretched out my arms to save him. As if watching some distant dream I watched him descend and smash upon the rocks below.

Kaikaik cried once more, circled down and down until it settled on an overhanging branch just out of arm's reach, studying me with its bright eyes. I disregarded it. My attention was centered upon the broken body of my husband far below, my breath coming too rapidly and harshly.

I turned and ran, not looking where I went, only ran to reach the bottom, scrambled over the scree until finally I squeezed my way through to where he lay. I blinked furiously, trying to focus on him, bent and rolled away the body of a man and not a bobcat that lay over Shadow Song. The arrow stuck out of the old man, unbroken even after the fall. I had no eyes for this. I knelt beside Shadow Song who stared blindly to the sky. I brushed the dark hair from his brow, quivering. If I felt anything I was too numb to realize. In a void I managed to lift his body onto my back and climbed my way out of there, back up to the prominence where I built a bier and lay him upon it with his feet to the west where his spirit must now go.

Sunset came and I watched. Night followed as did dawn as did day. For four days I watched, screaming at the vultures, my eyes dry of tears. I felt nothing. I ate nothing. I did nothing but stare at his body, at the headband of white and black, the feathers in his hair, the loincloth and medicine bag. On the fourth day I scraped a hole with my hands until my fingers bled, resorted to using a flat rock, and then I lay his body in the ground surrounded by the few things he had carried with him – his bow, his medicine bag, his books. It wasn't until I scattered earth over him and piled a mound of rocks that I felt myself giving way. In a flash of white light the arrow appeared on his grave. I sank to my knees and let the wail pent inside free, mumbling over and over again, "S'excuse moi...s'excuse moi...."

Chapter 27

My days all flowed one into the other, without meaning or direction, day into night, night into day. Moon and sun made little difference to how I gauged my actions. To go on was beyond me. To go back was impossible. I considered neither and remained upon that white ridge of rock wishing for my world to end.

It occurred to me one day that I hadn't eaten for some time. This I knew only because my belly ached. I ate dried fish from our packs, finishing my meal by wandering through thimbleberry canes. When done I stared bleakly at the scratches on my arms, wondering how I came by them, not even realizing I had grazed in a prickly patch. Bewildered, I stumbled to the cairn and slumped upon it, resting my cheek against its cool, hard cushion. Still the arrow lay there, white, powerful, like a demand to do something I could no longer remember.

"Will you teach me, *Kekinoamaged?*" I asked, but the rocks beneath my cheek remained silent as they had for as long as I could remember. A vision came to me then, another and another. I wanted none of them, but they came nonetheless. Soon the spirits gave up on visions and simply visited me throughout my waking hours let alone my sleeping. I argued with them, questioned them, always questing for the thing that had left this hollowness inside me. The spirits filled me with knowledge. They did nothing to fill the place Shadow Song and Noise-in-the-Night had left.

I wandered in this between-world, ever reminded of a task left unfinished both by the spirits and the arrow that would not go away. My fasts were frequent, not out of desire for a dream, rather out of lack of desire to live. Often I curled myself into a knot on top of Shadow Song's grave, rocking to and fro, knowing both *Kaikaik* and *Makinauk* watched.

The nights were terrifying. Often I woke, reaching for Shadow Song's hand that would cup my breast as he lay at my back, only to find I was alone on his grave and the moonlight or the rain touched me. Often I forfeited sleep to forget what had been, but in wakefulness that empty, screaming thing inside would not rest. There could be no peace.

My last vision convinced me of that. Dry eyed, bleak, I saw my surroundings clearly for the first time in weeks. By now the leaves were turning colour. It was time to head north for the wintering grounds, to harvest *waubuhnoomin*, the wild rice that grew in watery meadows.

Again I walked to the precipice, watching as memory recreated that day when Shadow Song had fallen, carrying the old shaman with him.

Listen for the hawk. Watch for the turtle. I'll always be there.

So it was that I abandoned Shadow Song's grave and set off with a lighter pack than before, taking with me those few trinkets that were dear to me, my medicine bag and the arrow that burned like ice in my hand. From here I decided to head south, not north, to walk my way to Hornings Mills rather than paddle. It was a sense of grim determination more than caution about shallow streams that made me choose my path by foot.

I skirted the villages and farms. These pockets of white civilization wounded me as I had not thought possible. I, like Shadow Song, had rejected their world. I was damned. Overhead *Kaikaik* flew along my path, or rather guided my path, as did *Makinauk* guide me through the trees.

By the time the leaves were falling I knew I was on the trail to what I had once called home. The lane should have soothed the hollow place within me. That was what home was supposed to do. The world around me was wrought of yellows, like gold from the crucible, leaves whispering one upon the other in a benediction. I closed myself to their blessing. I would not acknowledge the rich smell of decaying leaves, the coolness of the breeze upon my fevered cheek. I stared, blinkered, at my path. Leaves chattered beneath my feet like the voices of those who had gone on before me, calling, calling, a seductive summons I would soon accept. There was only for me the purpose of the arrow. All else was unimportant as I knew it would be the night we had created this hated thing.

I paused. I knew that around the bend the log cabin would appear. The loft window would glare at me, a window out of which I had once stared while captive. I shivered. How many years ago had I spent those eleven days in that garret?

I looked over-shoulder, seeing now the leaves, the rocks white like weathered bones among the interminable trees. I knew now home would be forever at my back, behind me, lost along this endless road I had walked, back where Shadow Song and Noise-in-the-Night had left their bodies for the Land of the Souls. Ahead of me would only ever be desolation.

The arrow burned coldly in my hand. It demanded of me a task. Only after that could I rest and think of things that might have been.

Turning back, I rounded the bend. The maples were larger, a ring of russet around the dark cabin that was now undergoing expansion – clapboard, a full story. I wondered what caused this spurt of activity. What optimism had seized Uncle Edgar?

I stepped into the cabin. For me it was like walking into the past. The harvest table still stood before the fire, a bunk to one side, the work table, the fireplace – all unkempt, stinking, the way it had been the first time I walked in with Paul Rogette. I almost expected to see the burly guide here. He wasn't. He wouldn't be. He was lost to me like so many others. I looked at the chairs and realized it had been a very long time since I had sat on one. I chose the floor instead for my vigil. *Kaikaik* flew in with me, settling on the table. *Makinauk* chose a dark corner.

By sunset Edgar Fleming shuffled in, banging dust from his dungarees with his straw hat. He stopped. He looked up. When he saw me through his one glacial eye and horrifying scars I didn't tremble at all. He had lost his hold upon me. I knew the demons he could summon. They were paltry by comparison to what I'd experienced.

It was then I realized he didn't recognize me. How could he? I had grown from child to woman, my skin dark from years in the sun and wind, my hair plaited in the way of the Anishnabeg women. Even my clothes revealed nothing of the white world. Why would he think me the same person who had fled from this cabin all those years ago?

"You've been hunting for me," I said at length. I watched shock cross his face, a flicker of fear, his attention shifting to the hawk. Yes, he remembered that day. He touched the ugly scars on his face. "So I've relieved you of the effort of having to hunt. The prey returns." Wary still. I could see it in the way he rolled his weight onto the balls of his feet – fight or flight. "Now that you have me, what do you want?"

The lump of his throat bobbed. "Where's the medicine man?"

"Gone where you can't reach him."

"So you're alone?"

I smiled, let my attention flick to *Kaikaik*. "As alone as I ever am." I watched him absorb that. "I'll relieve you of saying it. You want me dead because you know I saw you rape and murder Jane Vanmear. More, you want me dead because I escaped with a man you hate more than you love life." I watched that old anger return to his face. "Isn't that right?"

It was the moment for which I'd waited. He lunged. I leapt to my feet, twisted and stabbed, missed my mark when he slipped sideways. The head of the arrow bit into his biceps, deeply, spouting blood. I snarled and drove it in with the palm of my hand, laughed when it punctured the other side. His eyes were wide with unbelief. Trembling, he pulled the shaft through as to yank it back the way it had entered would be the more grim alternative. He hissed, threw the bloody shaft away. In the next moment it burst into flame and disappeared. It gave me satisfaction that he shook. I knew he shook from fear not from anger.

"What have you done?" he snarled.

"I think that's obvious."

He charged. I didn't move. There was no point. This was what I'd been yearning for since Shadow Song died. The back of his hand detonated on my face. I reeled. My ears rang. Small points of light flowered before my eyes. I did not cry out. I stared at him, defiant, proud. He growled and hit me again. Still I would not whimper as he wanted. He wasn't the only one who craved revenge. Again he hit me, now with his fists, again and again and again until I lost count and was beyond caring about any of it. A task had been fulfilled. Now I could rest.

Once only *Kaikaik* fluttered.

"Be still, Brother," I gasped. The hawk took flight out of the door. Dimly, I was aware of *Makinauk* following, unseen by Edgar.

I woke in a pool of pain, feeling wood planks beneath my back. Somehow I elbowed my way up, blinking. The room was very little the way I remembered, although after a few moments I realized it was indeed the loft because a hatch in the floor was closed. I dragged myself to it, clutching at my ribs where I was sure they were broken. Breathing was tortuous. Carefully, I tried the handle. It was locked. I hadn't expected anything else.

I looked around, in no hurry. I had lots of time. There was no commode, no tray of food, no bunk. There was, however, clear evidence of renovations going on as was apparent in the lathe and plaster that covered the logs. He had begun to frame in a door, leaving a dark hole in the wall that revealed the old logs. I didn't need to be told this was meant as my grave. He'd starve me up here, bury my body in the wall and forever hide his sins of a lifetime.

A few moments later I heard the shuffle of footsteps below, erratic footsteps followed by a lighter tread. A groan. A woman uttering soothing sounds only to be silenced by his sharp retort. So, he thought he'd take a bride. That could be the only explanation for all this industry. It was show, a mating dance to attract a suitable bird to his stinking nest.

No matter. The poison of the arrow would work soon enough, but probably not quickly enough to set me free in the land of the living. Besides, it was not the land of the living I sought now. Shadow Song waited for me in the Land of the Souls. I knew this because he'd asked me if I remembered the story of

Geezhig and *Wabun-anung*. Maybe there we would know some peace and again set about raising our son.

When the noise below me receded, I unbelted my medicine bag and took out the few trinkets I kept there with tobacco, paper, quill and ink. I set to writing a note, a task that felt odd after so long. I dropped this with the empty lavender bottle, the tea tin, the clay doll and tobacco into the hole in the wall. Perhaps someone might find them one day and realize what had happened in the village of Hornings Mills was not the fault of the Anishnabeg but of a man demented with hatred.

Outside *Kaikaik* cried. Carefully, I moved to the window. The leaves were still clinging to the maples, red as the blood that seeped from my broken lips. I remembered the first time I had seen those maples. They had been green. That had been the summer I met Shadow Song and the forest had been so green it hurt my eyes.

Afterword

The research that went into the writing of this book spanned several years and created a journey of fascination. Some of the characters in the book are based upon actual historical characters, others leap from my imagination.

The story of the tragedy in Hornings Mills is based upon a true account. In 1830, Lewis Horning, a hardy 60 year old Pennsylvania Dutchman left his prosperous holdings in the Hamilton/Ancaster area of Upper Canada to pursue a dream in the Queen's Bush. Horning, with the assistance of Henry Bates, William Silk, the Vanmear family and ten others, was to establish a settlement far from the active trading centers to the south. The land was rich, peopled by the Ojibwa and Chippewa who called themselves the Anishnabeg. To the north hardwood forest grew. Eastward flowed the Pine River and the valley that had been carved by glaciers, while to the south there were numerous small lakes ideal for mill ponds. In the west were vast beaver meadows, swales and cedar swamps, the latter two the result of poor drainage caused by the Niagara Escarpment. It was here, in the west, that the infamous Melancthon Swamps lay, swamps that were ancient, slow, moving in ways that were to shape the future of Horning's dream.

So it was that by 1831, despite age and hardships, this hardy group had built grist and saw mills. Indeed it seemed the village would prosper. News of Horning's success reached Hamilton and Ancaster, and the entire project lauded.

And then the summer of 1832 happened. Relatives of Horning had come to assist with the raising of buildings, and, perhaps preoccupied with this, and a cow that was to calf, Lewis Horning turned away two natives who had come to the mill to trade venison for flour.

Shortly after it became apparent the cow had wandered, he suspected into Melancthon Swamp. A conversation between Horning and his hired man was overheard by Jane, Susan and Oliver Vanmear, ages sixteen, fourteen and nine, as well as Lewis Horning Jr., also aged nine. It seemed the entrepreneur offered his man a dollar if he would search for the missing cow.

The children, seized with the idea of earning the dollar for themselves, set off to the west. They disappeared. The other Horning brothers – Peter and Robert – searched while the adults were still involved in building. They found a native trail that led directly into the heart of Melancthon Swamp, apparently where the four children had gone.

The alarm went out. For days the village people scoured the countryside. Nothing of the children or the cow was ever found. The Anishnabeg, of course, were blamed.

Six years later, disheartened, Lewis Horning packed up what remained of his family and returned to Ancaster. The other families soon followed, and the village of Hornings Mills quietly slipped back into the Queen's Bush. There were to be other adventurers, men bent on stripping the land and shaping it for their own good, so that the village was not to disappear altogether. But, always, that day hung in the background.

Only Oliver Vanmear was to ever surface, found in the Marigold Tavern in Oakville many years later, still simple-minded and erratic. His story was that all four children had been taken captive by the Ojibwa, the girls married off, Lewis Horning Jr. rumoured to be a strong hunter. Was his story true? To this day no one knows. Perhaps he told people what they wanted to hear. Perhaps he told the truth.

The *Baltic*, which Danielle takes from England to Quebec is real, as is her commander, Earbage. Conditions aboard ship, the outbreak of cholera at Quebec and the opening of Grosse Isle as an immigration point are all lifted from historical documents, although I have played with the actual timing and dates to suit my purposes. Fares, ferries and stages are based upon real costs, ships and companies, as are the details of *Midewewin* and Ojibwa society based upon historical records and books of the era.

Captain Anderson, Superintendent of Indian Affairs, Reverend Adam Elliot and the teacher Mr. Orr were all present on Manitoulin Island around the time of the novel.

Trading posts mentioned throughout the novel are all based upon historical accounts of Hudson Bay posts.

I found the name of Fleming in a graveyard near to Hornings Mills, and purloined it for the purpose of giving Danielle some historical background, albeit fictional. Shadow Song sprang directly from imagination, although for me he became incarnate and dogged my days for a full year while setting down the first draft of this novel.

The Anishnabeg language references I have taken from an original copy of an English/Ojibwa dictionary from the 19th century. It, among other rare books, came into my possession through the kindness of a bookseller, Darwin, in Toronto, now long dead from an AIDS related illness; Darwin had one of the largest collections of native books in North America. I am forever indebted to his love of the native peoples and his passion for collecting knowledge for them.

I would be remiss in my acknowledgements if I failed to recognize the support and effort offered me by Kelly Stephens, my daughter, and Grant Hallman, fellow scribbler, both of whom were indefatigable in their proof-reading and comments of the novel.

Other Books by Lorina Stephens

Touring the Giant's Rib: A Guide to the Niagara Escarpment, Boston Mills Press (tour guide)

Credit River Valley, Boston Mills Press (tour guide)

Recipes of a Dumb Housewife, Published by Lulu (cookbook)

And the Angels Sang, Published by Five Rivers (anthology)

Available through

Lulu http://stores.lulu.com/fiverivers

Five Rivers Chapmanry http://www.5rivers.org

And online retailers everywhere